SEVEN  DAYS IN SEATTLE

"For without words, in friendship, all thoughts, all desires,

all expectations are born and shared,

with joy that is unacclaimed."

— KHALIL GIBRAN, *The Prophet*

SEVEN DAYS IN SEATTLE

A Novel

RITA A. GORDON

12:56 a.m.

California

CONTENTS

Seven Days In Seattle is a story about a woman coming to terms with who she is amidst complex relationships with family, friends, exes, and a man who was supposed to be a one-night stand. This story takes place mid-journey to her becoming the woman she wants to be.

With that said, please be aware that this story discusses a condition that is similar to Hyperthymesia, a memory condition wherein people can recall details of past experiences with extreme accuracy. It is a condition that has many unknowns and is still being researched. The situations referenced in the work are not considered accurate representatives of this condition. Additionally, this work describes cases of dissociation, a disconnection between a person's thoughts, memories, feelings, actions, or sense of who they are. With that in mind, I advise you to consider your health and well-being before diving into Raven and Noah's story.

Lastly, I want to take a moment to share that this is only an introduction to Raven, Parker, and Noah's story. There are no conclusions or happy endings in this book. There will be some happy endings in the future and some happy-for-now scenarios. However, for now, join me as the story unfolds, and let's journey there…together.

CHAPTER I

The Way We Were

Raven

SOMETIMES, THERE ARE MOMENTS WHEN YOU HAVE TO LAUGH HYS-terically just to keep from crying. Then, there are moments when you just want to scream.

"Parker Page, I swear I'll kill you if you don't give that back to me," I yell across the kitchen counter, then dash to the other side where my soon-to-be ex-best friend Parker clutches my phone, scrolling through the contacts. When I'm directly behind him, he lifts his arm and holds my phone above his head. He's a six-foot-four-inch-tall wall of muscles. I'm a five-foot-six piece of brown paper and have to jump in my bare feet to try and reach it. "What are we, twelve? Give. Me. My. Phone." I jump up again and miss. When he extends his arm over the counter, I do the only thing I can in a moment of desperation. I jump on his back.

"Woman, if you don't get off my back. Let me handle this situation." He leans over the counter and turns to the side to get me off his back. Gravity takes over and I swing to his front, and like a koala, I cling to him, bringing him down to the counter, hovering over me. My shoulder shoves a fruit bowl that tips over. Oranges, apples, and lemons roll the length of the counter, and one after another, I hear them collide with the delivery bags containing our dinner. A wave of uncontrollable laughter washes over me when I think how ridiculous we must look. And it feels good to laugh after sulking the last two days. I pull Parker's arm forward until he's forced to lean over me on the counter. Still straddling him, I lick his face to distract him and manage to grab the phone from his hands.

"Got it," I say triumphantly, but it comes out more like a pant. Parker is still leaning over me, arms on either side of my head. "Now you back off *me*." I reach up and muss his curly dirty blond hair. Our faces are so close that I get a whiff of him. It's deep, woodsy, and sweet, and I'm tempted to dip my nose in his neck, but I don't dare. "This is sexy, but you really need a haircut. Now get off," I tell him.

The look Parker gives me is a mix of surprise and seduction. He touches his wet cheek. "What was that?" He straightens, grabs me by the waist, lifts me like I weigh nothing, and gently stands me back on the floor. I walk across the kitchen and sit on the opposite side of the counter.

"What?" My lips spread into a sly smile.

Parker retrieves a bottle of wine from his wine fridge, opens it, and fills two glasses. He hands me a drink across the marble counter. I lift it to my lips and sip. Parker always has the best wine. He must have been a sommelier in another life.

"The woman with perfect recall is asking me *what*."

He has a point. I don't forget anything. It's both a blessing and a curse that I can recall in detail what I've seen and heard. It helped in my profession as a lawyer, but unfortunately I could never utter the phrase, "I forgot." Only my closest family and friends and my boss, Alejandro, know about it. It's not something you talk about. People either pick up on its existence or don't. Parker picked up on it when he became my best friend at Stanford University. We had almost every class together since we both studied law. Parker knew everything about me and vice versa, so there was no pulling the wool over his eyes.

"That's me, using my feminine wiles to get what I want," I tell him.

"Be careful," he growls. "I may be your best friend, but I am all man."

"Yeah. That part I remember."

It's etched like glass in my memory because, for five years, Parker Page was my man in every biblical sense of the word. And he's right. He is all man. Just not mine. Well, not that way anymore. We're very much alike. Both stubborn. Both opinionated. Both passionate. And if I'm honest, we're both a little wild, which is how I ended up on his back on a Sunday night at the age of thirty.

As I watch Parker move seamlessly through the kitchen, I reflect on that time of our lives. In all appearances, we were the perfect match. Young, beautiful, intelligent, determined...unstoppable. And for a while, we were, in essence, perfect...for a while. We tried to make it work as a couple. We really did. But in life, there are obstacles you can't move on from. Well, mainly one I couldn't move on from. However, we found our rhythm as friends; it just works better this way—we're inseparable. And right now, my best friend, my confidant, my protector, has latched on to a bone named Blake Wallace, my ex. The man I discovered was cheating on me.

Parker opens the food delivery bags and plates our pasta. Then he carries both plates to my side of the counter and sits beside me.

"That's what I thought," he says and hands me a fork. "But seriously, let me deal with Blake."

"That's not necessary. I've already dealt with Blake." I twist the fork into my pasta until a large roll of noodles forms, and then lean in and eat the entire thing. "Hmm," I moan. "I swear pasta and wine are my love language."

"I know," Parker says, then picks up his napkin, puts a finger under my chin, and turns my head toward him. He wipes the corner of my lips. "You're such a mess."

"I know." It's the story of my life.

"So, tell me. Did you confront him before or after dinner?"

This is not a conversation I want to have. To stir up bad memories that lay rancid in my mind like the stench of sauce that's gone sour in Tupperware. It's a lid that's best left unopened. But I always tell Parker everything, so I prepare myself and down the rest of my wine in one gulp. I think about that moment in the restaurant as Parker refills my glass.

"Mr. Wallace, it's good to see you again so soon. I trust you and your lady friend had a good meal last night?"

"Yes. Everything was great. The ribeye was perfection."

"Will you be having the same this evening? I can go over the specialties if you like."

"Let's wait for my girlfriend to return. She's in the restroom," he said. I waited for the manager to leave before returning to the table. I don't know if I waited out of embarrassment or whether I was trying to help him save face. I should have outed him in front of the manager, but that's not how I operate.

When the manager left, I returned to the table.

After I was seated, Blake reached across the table to touch my hand. I pulled my hand away like his touch had burned me.

"Is everything okay?" he asked, and my blood began to boil. My mind started racing, and every disappointing interaction I'd had with Blake flashed through my head. I felt dizzy as the scenes played on repeat in my mind.

"Rae, is everything okay?" he repeated, pulling me out of the dumpster fire he'd started.

I took a deep breath. "Did I hear the manager correctly? Oh wait," I snapped my fingers. "We both know I can't misunderstand something I can recall verbatim. You lied."

"I—."

"I'm talking. You need to listen. You said you were with 'the boys' at the gym last night. Mr. Manager here says you were with a woman that wasn't me. So, I can assume three weeks ago, when I asked you to go with me after work to have drinks with Parker and our friend Josh, and you said you had to work late—you didn't really have to work. Two weeks ago, Thursday when you couldn't break away for lunch, when you, and I quote, 'never miss a lunch,' you really didn't miss lunch. You just didn't want to go with me."

"Rae, let me—."

"Explain? No, let me explain. Your actions speak louder than words, Blake. So, I'd say you've said enough. I'm not that woman. I don't need to settle for less. You should have said something four months ago at the charity event if you didn't know what you wanted. But you didn't. You know why, Blake? Because you are a pathetic excuse for a man and a colossal waste of my time. When I walk out of here, don't call me, don't text me, and as a matter of fact, lose my number. When you see me in public, pretend you don't know me because that's what I'm going to do. I don't have any more room in my brain for trash, Blake. Goodbye." I grabbed my purse and left the restaurant. I wandered into the bar next door, ordered a drink, and called Parker.

"Rain. Hey, babe."

"Parker, come get me."

Once again, Parker came to my rescue and I'm here walking him through another one of my failed relationships.

"I couldn't stomach the thought of sitting through dinner with him after overhearing his conversation with the manager. The fact that he didn't have the guts to tell me to my face that he didn't feel our relationship was working makes me feel cheap and unimportant."

"You're right. He should have been man enough to talk to you. He should have apologized."

"He should have, but he didn't. So, I confronted him before he could order, then left him sitting there. You know me, there is no retort once I lay out all the facts."

I eat more pasta. When I notice Parker isn't eating, I raise my chin toward his plate. He twirls his pasta and takes a bite. I scrunch my nose. He rolls his eyes. I put my fingers to my lips and blow him a kiss. It's silly, but we have a way of speaking without words. We've had that ever since we met in our contract law course at Stanford. One day, our professor was upset because some students did poorly on the test, and he admonished the entire class. His German accent was so heavy that he was almost unintelligible as he ranted, *"You're not going to get this by divine inspiration. If only I were a brain surgeon."* Our professor's voice boomed in the lecture hall. I had an urge to turn to my left, and Parker turned at that exact moment. Our eyes locked and I pursed my lips. He raised his eyebrows and he shook his head. We held a whole conversation without saying a word, using only body language, as our professor continued ranting in the background. Once we were out of the class, we huddled outside the door and laughed like old friends.

"I'm Parker." He held his hand out to me between laughs.

"I'm Raven. People call me Rae."

"What's your full name, Raven?"

"Raven Rain Nichols."

"Rain. I love the sound of that. I'm reminded how essential it is to all life. Can I call you Rain?"

"Yeah. You can call me Rain."

That was twelve years ago, and although we're no longer a couple, we've been inseparable ever since. And now, the way Parker looks at me tells me how deeply he still cares. We've been through too much together. Whatever *this* is between us, it's good, it's precious, and I'll do everything within my power to protect it. Sometimes, I think that's why it was better that we stopped being a couple, to hold on to what we have—to conserve *us*.

"It wasn't your fault," Parker tells me. "I can't believe the audacity of that man. I hate that this happened to you, but I'm glad you weren't with him long."

He's right. One second is too long to be with anyone who doesn't treat you as you deserve. I was with Blake for four months. Early in the relationship, he was attentive and seemed interested in my work as a real estate attorney. But over the past few months, he became preoccupied. Thinking back, I feel so stupid. I should have read the signs. I've been focused on proving myself at work, and rightfully so, but it sucks how this went down. I never would have learned about him cheating if I hadn't stepped away to freshen up in the restroom before dinner. I was stunned to hear the restaurant manager mention seeing Blake the previous night with a woman. He had told me he was at the gym. That wasn't the truth. He was having dinner with another woman at that restaurant.

"I get it wasn't my fault, but you can't just call him up and give him a piece of your mind. I understand you're only protecting me, but you and I are attorneys. We have reputations to uphold. This could go sideways."

"You may as well hand over your phone because I'm calling him whether you like it or not. I can guarantee that he'll rethink doing this to anyone again."

"I'm not giving you my phone. If you want to call Blake, do it on your own." I shake my head, resigned that my best friend won't take no for an answer regarding something like this. Because even though we're no longer lovers, Parker is still protective of me. I get it. We're both invested in each other.

If I'm being honest, it goes much deeper than that for Parker. In the past, when my relationships went sideways, I ended them first. If I didn't, once Parker found out that they were heading downhill, he'd take matters into his own hands. He's not a mean guy, and he'd never hurt anyone unless they hurt me, but they undoubtedly wished they'd never met me when he was done. Parker Page is powerful, privileged, and used to getting his way. He comes from one of the most elite families in California. His family is part of a group you'll never hear about in the media—they're that rich. So, if he tells Blake to do something, then Blake would be wise to proceed with caution.

"Okay. I'll handle this. But not like I did the others. I'll talk to him. At a minimum, like you said, he owes you an apology, Rain."

"Fine. I'm done with this conversation, and I'm done with men. Anyway, I need to focus on my career. This meeting in Seattle could be my ticket to becoming a partner."

Being an ambitious overachiever has done wonders for my career, but it hasn't afforded me time to nurture relationships with men. That is, except for Parker. But I needed to break free of him to prove I don't need a powerful man in the room to validate or protect me. That despite everything, I can stand on my own merit. I've been so focused on this that I haven't put the time into getting to know the men I've dated. I would have noticed signs that Blake wasn't all in sooner if I had.

"You will, Rain. You have one of the most brilliant minds in real estate law. And don't be so jaded regarding men. I wasn't so bad, was I?"

"Oh my god, Parker. I didn't mean—." I don't finish. Instead, I hop off my stool, throw my arms around Parker's neck, and hug him dramatically. I kiss him on the cheek and muss his hair again. "The fact that you are still in my life says everything, and don't you forget that."

Parker untangles me from his body and glares at me, reading my face. After a second, his brows unfurrow, his expression softens, and he seems satisfied with what he sees. "You have everything you need for the week?" he asks. The mood lifts and I return to my seat.

"Yes. Thank you for volunteering to drop me off at SFO tomorrow. Car service is so impersonal—there's no one for me to hug before I leave. I think that could be awkward for the driver," I whine, and my admission gets a chuckle.

"Depends on the driver. Well, at least you get to see your sister. It's been a while. Tell her hi for me."

"Yeah. Let's see how Robin is. You know she can be finicky at times." Rather, all the time, I should have said. We're so different that sometimes I wonder whether we're even from the same parents.

"It'll be fine, Rain."

"It would have been better if you had some time off to go with me. This is my first break in a year."

A year ago, Parker saw that the demands that I was putting on myself were taking their toll and suggested we drive down the coast for a three-day weekend in Carmel. He was right; I needed the break. It allowed me to momentarily clear my head of men, my memories, my work—it was the best weekend ever. I should have listened to him when he suggested I take a break from dating. If I had, I never would have given Blake a second look. I wouldn't be in this position: scrubbing the recesses of my mind, remembering the time wasted on him. Ugh, stupid Blake Wallace.

I don't need this mess in my head. I need to focus. Focus. Focus, Rain. I direct my eyes to Parker's mouth as he speaks. I trace the curve of his lips with my gaze.

"My calendar is set for the next month, or I would fly out for a few days. And my parents need me to review some contracts for them."

"They have people for that."

"That's what I told them. Anyway, I'm sorry I can't be there. Hopefully you get time to see some sights before you dive in with your client meetings."

"I have a list of things to see and do. Let's see how far I get. It's not all fun and games, in any case. I still plan to work a few hours after I arrive tomorrow. And of course, I have to check email throughout the week to stay on top of things. Also, Alejandro wants to brief me before I get into vacation mode. He says this could be the biggest deal of my career."

My boss, Alejandro Rodriguez, is the founding partner in the law firm. A top international attorney, he is outside counsel for some of the most prestigious corporations in the world, Ross Enterprises being one. A year and a half ago, he poached me from my firm to focus on building out his real estate division. Our client, Ross Enterprises, is expanding their company to more locations and needs an attorney who specializes in real estate development to review real estate contracts and advise their legal counsel. That's where I come in. Structuring real estate contracts to protect Ross Enterprises is right up my alley. If I nail my next few projects, I could potentially make partner, which makes next Monday's meeting a big deal.

Parker begins clearing the counter and putting away the food containers. I return the spilled fruit to the bowl, then wet a towel and wash down all the marble counter surfaces. That's another thing we share—we're both neat freaks. When the kitchen is clean, Parker goes to the sink to wash his hands. I stand beside him and wash mine, too. When I'm done, I hold them out with my palms up. Parker gives me the "you're something else" look, shakes his head, and dries my hands. I bump him with my hip.

"Thanks, Parker."

He pulls me to his side and kisses the top of my head. "I have to prepare for a brief. I'll be in my office for a while. You want to watch TV or something?"

"No, I'm good. I'll plop on the sofa in your office and catch up on my reading. But first, I'm changing into my PJs."

It doesn't take long for me to shower and change. I wander through the house, taking in the space that's become my second home. Parker and I share the same taste in modern design. His grey-toned walls, mahogany furnishings, and brass fixtures reflect our shared aesthetic. As I walk toward the office through the narrow hallway from the main bedroom suite, a photo on the wall catches my eye. It's a picture of me and Parker throwing our caps in the air on graduation day. Seeing the image brings back fond memories of our time together in college.

We were two people figuring out what it was like to be adults living on our own. First as classmates and friends, then as lovers. Even back then, we were inseparable. Like an addiction, the need to be near one another was all-consuming—we loved each other that much. Whenever

Parker was near me it was as if the world fell away. I don't know if I was prepared for that kind of love, having come from a broken family. It scared me. It still does.

It wasn't until our third year of undergrad that we formally started dating. We continued dating while working on our juris doctorates, even though we went to separate schools. However, something shifted during our time away from each other. I used to think it was the stress of school, the distance, or the fact that we were getting older and growing into our own. But that was me playing tricks with my mind. Truth is, Parker and I were speeding down a path to becoming…more. Then, one night, our relationship took a terrible turn that threw us off track—if I'm being honest, me more so than Parker. I think I used the situation as a catalyst to refocus. To try and become my own person. By the time we received our JDs, we were no longer a couple, yet despite pushing past the passion and the pain, our friendship was preserved.

When people ask why we're so close that we seem like more than friends, we have a standard response. We say we've talked about it numerous times but can't explain our connection. We don't try anymore. We just know this is the way we are. At least that's what we say. But it's a lie. I know exactly why. I made a promise to Parker a long time ago. A commitment that became the ultimate tie that binds us, one I don't know if I can ever satisfy. When we broke up, I said the thing you say to someone who can't stop loving you no matter how bad you are for them. We all have our secrets, and the promise I made to Parker is mine. So yeah, if anyone asks, that's the way we are—inexplicably tied together.

When I reach the study, I find Parker on a call. I lean against the door frame, watch his beautiful face be all business-like, and pause before entering.

"Yes, I need that case cited. Don't forget all the corresponding notations. Right. Are you ready? Great, I'll see you tomorrow," Parker says to someone in an authoritative voice I seldom encounter.

After he ends the call, I walk into his study and stand beside him at his desk. He pulls me to his side. "Rain." My name slides off his tongue like silk, and I smile.

"Why haven't we created our own firm?" I ask. My hand instinctively slides up his neck and into his hair. It's soft. Silky.

Parker takes my wrist and flips it to check the time on my watch. I remember the day he brought it for my birthday, the year we started dating. He told me to wear it always as a reminder that our time together is precious. I thought walking around with a gold Rolex every day was silly, but I got used to it. He kisses my fingers and then releases me. He reaches across his desk, picks up my iPad, and hands it to me.

"Honestly, babe, I don't know. Don't we already spend so much of our lives together?"

He's right. Although we don't live together, we share meals at least four times a week, whether we meet for coffee before work, have lunch together, or have dinner. And when we don't see each other, we communicate by phone, typically via FaceTime. We even use our friendship as a litmus test for people we date. If they can't accept that Parker and I are best friends, they're out.

Catching his hint, I take my iPad and move to the sofa facing his desk. I prop pillows on one end, lay back on them, and open my email. My eyes automatically shift to Parker when I feel him watching me, waiting for a response.

"I suppose you're right. Don't forget to set the alarm for six, and don't you dare leave me lying on this couch if I fall asleep. I swear I'll kill you if I wake up here."

I hear the crunch of a paper before I feel it bounce off my head. Then, as if on cue, we laugh.

CHAPTER 2

Too Good at Saying Goodbye

Raven

Peace is the feeling of tranquility when I'm genuinely at ease with myself and free to just…breathe.

I open my eyes to a sliver of light slicing through the curtain, signifying a new day. I inhale—slow and deep, in and out, allowing each breath to replenish me. I'm in bed. I don't know when I fell asleep or how long I've been here. But I know how I arrived. I know because I'm wrapped in the protection of Parker's powerful arms. And at this moment, I feel safe. I am at peace.

It's so quiet that I hear the clock's second-hand ticking on the nightstand. I told Parker to get rid of that antique years ago. It's so annoying. I'm in a catch-22, anticipating the alarm will sound off soon and needing to circumvent it, but I hate to wake my sleeping giant. His breaths come slow yet heavy as he sleeps. One. Two. Three. Four. I count, then listen for a few beats before slowly turning to face Parker. He's such a beautiful man. Behind those closed eyelids is a set of the purest aquamarine-colored eyes. There was a time when I couldn't keep my hands off him. In a way, we both can't help but cling to one another even now. After twelve years, it's all we know. But I think about him differently now.

I look over his shoulder at the clock. It's almost time. If this were the weekend, I'd watch him while he slept in, or in a fit of mischief, I'd jump on the bed and wake him up in a start, but it's Monday. He has to take me to the airport, and then, like the true professional he is, he'll go to work and present his brief and be all brilliant.

"Parker," I say softly. I kiss his cheek and roll over him as I get out of bed and shut off the alarm before it starts. Nobody wants to wake up to that god-awful sound. A small groan comes from my sleeping giant, and my not-so-subtle maneuver did the trick. He's awake. Before I get far, I feel his hand on my wrist. He pulls me back to the bed, and I land on his chest. He sits up, pulling me with him. He pushes the hair out of my face and studies me momentarily, searching for clues in my eyes, and I know what he's looking for. I'm here, Parker.

"Good morning, Rain."

"Good morning, Parker. I need to take my shower."

"How do you feel?"

"Good. I was watching you while you slept. Listening to your breaths, counting them."

"Did that help?" he asks, moving his thumb along my cheek.

"Yeah, it did, because you're so cute." I can't help but smile at my admission, which earns me a playful spank on my butt.

"Next time, wake me up. Now go have your shower." I roll my eyes. He pushes me off of him and rolls back over in the bed. He will sneak in five more minutes of sleep since he knows I'm okay.

When I'm showered and dressed, Parker walks into the room, towel-drying his hair.

"You know you're the only one I give up my shower for," he tells me.

"Give me a break. This place has, like, what, five full baths?"

"My point being—."

"Your point, Parker Page Esquire, is that I'm your favorite person in the whole wide world. Now put on that sexy black suit, white shirt, and red tie I love, and let's go."

While Parker finishes getting ready, I make our coffee, toast, and a fruit parfait. It isn't long before we are on the road and at the airport. Living in the heart of San Francisco makes for a fast drive to the terminal. When we arrive, Parker gets out, opens my door, and helps me with my luggage.

"Listen, Rain." He pulls me into him. "I understand this thing with Blake sucks, but forget about him. He's nobody. Trust me, people like him will eventually get what's coming to them. Got it?" I nod in response. "Now, have a good time with your sister, live your best life, and kill it at your meeting next Monday. I'll be here to pick you up when you return." Parker brushes the long, natural brown curls on either side of my face over my shoulders. He dips his head to catch my gaze. "You good?"

"I'm good." After I reassure him, he lifts my chin and gives me a chaste kiss.

"Good. Now have a great time. I'll see you next week. Love you." He releases me and goes to his car. I wave to him before he drives off.

My flight to Seattle is only two hours and fifteen minutes long. My car service, which is every bit as reserved as I expect, meets me upon arrival, and forty minutes later, we arrive in the inner city in front of my building. Typically, I would have booked the Four Seasons, but I opted for the corporate apartments offered by my client instead.

The driver gets my luggage, and before I head in, a woman passing by hands me a flyer. She's nicely dressed in blue ankle jeans and a pink lipstick-colored shirt.

"We just opened a new restaurant around the corner." Her words come out rushed. I take the flyer, and she chases the next person.

It doesn't take long for me to get settled in the apartment. I check my watch. Good, I have time to clean out the rest of my email before logging on to my video call with my boss, Alejandro.

"Raven." Alejandro's voice is positive but professional. "It's good to see you've arrived in Seattle safely. How was your flight?"

"Good. I hope you're well."

"I am," he assures.

I don't wait for Alejandro to make small talk. Efficiency is my strong suit. Keeping things moving means no extra clutter in my head. Instead, I immediately dive in and discuss the legal language in the real estate development contract between my client, Ross Enterprises, and their client, the commercial real estate developer.

I'm working directly with Ross' in-house counsel to modify the agreement, redlining the sections, and adding contingencies that protect them should something go wrong in the construction process. I also restructured the payment timelines to ensure my client didn't cut a final check unless they were satisfied with the work delivered. In my experience, most commercial developers are trying to negotiate the best deal in their favor—my job is to ensure the risk is balanced. I wouldn't want my client to end up like a lot of companies did when the pandemic hit and construction stopped mid-stream, leaving business owners paying for work that had yet to be completed or buildings they couldn't occupy.

"Great. Let's get to it. I received the changes to the contract last week, incorporated my edits, and resubmitted it to Ross Enterprises. There are issues around disclosures and security we'll want their client's attorneys to review and approve," I say.

"How do you anticipate Monday's meeting will go?"

"Although the agenda is straightforward, I anticipate both parties will wait until Monday's meeting to discuss their last-minute changes."

Alejandro nods. "And you're comfortable with handling that off-the-cuff?"

"I can cite you every line and every change on this deal by heart. Yes. I feel good about this. However, three things that could potentially stall contract negotiations could likely arise."

"Which are?"

"Concerns around ethical behavior. I noted this because the real estate developer made significant edits to this contract section. I also foresee concerns arising around construction logistics since Ross Enterprises plans to use the development firm globally. Negotiating leases out of the country is complicated. The only other thing that could derail the deal is a stalemate regarding any new contract changes requested. Both parties want this deal to happen, so I suspect in a stalemate they'll compromise, but that could take time."

"What's the likelihood of any of these issues coming up between now and Monday?" he probes.

Alejandro is testing me as I respond. I watch him closely on the monitor. He's known for his megawatt smile, but his smile hasn't graced me with its presence since he got on this call. He's all business. His brow is raised. He's waiting for me to prove I know what I'm doing. That I can handle this without him.

"You know the infinite number of variables at play here." We both do. Ross Enterprises is one of the largest technology companies in the world and a leader in artificial intelligence. They're targeting a twenty-thousand-person expansion in multiple cities across several countries.

"You've got your work cut out for you. But I'm here for you. Are you ready for this? I'm handing you my biggest client, Raven. Real estate is your specialty. This is your path to making partner." I suck in a deep breath at hearing the words I've been dying to hear. This is my path to becoming a partner. I can do this.

"Yes, you know I'm ready. Have I ever let you down? You hired me for my brain. June came to us because she knows my work from when I helped her at Soala Technologies. This is the chance I've been waiting for." I can do this. I have to…for me.

"They're expanding fast, Raven. This is the first of many deals we expect to handle for them. If this goes well, five more are potentially waiting in the wing."

"I'm committed to this."

"Then keep me posted and let me know if anything comes up that you feel you can't handle."

"I've gone through all the files already. June's out of the country, so a few questions came in overnight. I responded to everything during my flight this morning. I have everything reviewed and committed to memory. The meeting is at nine o'clock next Monday morning. I'm only gone for a week. I promise I'll let you know if anything comes up."

"Sounds like you've got things covered."

"I do. And Alejandro, thank you for bringing me on board." We say our goodbyes and I end the call.

❦

THE RESTAURANT MY SISTER PICKED TO MEET AT IS ON THE OTHER side of town. My sister Robin is four years older than me and lives with her husband in a suburb of Seattle. Although we're close in age, we're nothing alike. In fact, we're total opposites. I'm ambitious, opinionated, and passionate, yet wild. She goes with the flow like a wave washing across the shore. At times, like our mom, she's unreliable, which has caused problems for us in the past. She didn't make it to my graduation, making me feel like I wasn't important to her. She's the type that will cancel on you at the last minute and not understand why you're upset about it. This is why I find it peculiar that she suggested I come to Seattle before my client meeting to spend time with her.

As usual, I'm the first to arrive. I check in at the front desk and am escorted to our table. The restaurant is bright and airy. It has a minimalist café vibe with chrome chairs, square white tables, and muted sage green walls with abstract art. Music plays over the speaker system, but it's easily drowned out by the chatter of people and the clatter of dishes.

When my sister finally arrives, I hear her before I see her. "Yeah, yeah. Got it. Don't worry. Tell them I'll be there. Sure. Listen, I have to go. Yes. Bye," Robin says and ends her call.

She pulls out a chair and takes a seat. In typical fashion, we don't hug. I'm the hugger. She's not. Over the years, I've learned not to try. When I did, I found myself disappointed by the experience. She would hold me at arm's length and tap her fingertips on my shoulder like you see on those housewives' shows. No, thank you.

"Hey, Robin. Sounds like you're still caught up in meetings."

"Yeah. There's always something else to do. It's good to see you. How was your flight? Hopefully no delays."

"It was fine. I got in a few hours ago. How's the house remodeling going?"

"Slow. You know contractor delays due short supply issues since Covid."

"Yeah, it's impacted almost everything, even how I structure contracts."

Robin moved to Seattle right after college to take a job. We both have demanding jobs that consume our time and don't allow us to get together that often. Despite our lack of closeness, I'm usually the one making an effort to get together. Maybe it's silly, but I think that families should be close. I believe that when you're together, no matter where you are, you should feel at home and be yourself. I haven't felt that way with my family since I was eight. So here I am trying to bond with my *maybe she will, maybe she won't show* sister Robin.

Despite her rolling-with-the-flow standard of living, she is a brilliant marketer. It comes easy to her, which has allowed her to climb the corporate ladder despite what I perceive to be her faults. On the other hand, I had to work hard to prove myself. Even in grade school, I was head-down and focused on my studies. Sometimes, I look back and think maybe that's why my sister and I aren't as close as most siblings, because I was too head-down. But I had to be. Having a mom who was just as aloof as my sister left me where? Alone. The age difference with my sister also meant we had a separate group of friends, adding another barrier between us.

Despite the success I've had so far, I can't stop. I'm determined to prove myself. So, when Alejandro asked me to join his firm, I did not hesitate to say yes. Landing a spot at one of the top international legal firms is the direct result of my drive and discipline.

The server comes to take our order. We both order shrimp Caesar salads and iced tea, which is one of the few things we have in common. Throughout the meal, we catch up on what's been going on in each other's lives since we last spoke. I gather she's doing well from the conversation. However, Robin's body language, the way she's fidgeting and keeps looking at her phone, tells me that she has more to share.

"Listen, Robin, while I'm in Seattle, there are a few things I want to make sure to see, so we'll have to coordinate on dinner." I pull out my list to review with her. "Oh, you mentioned Bram had a few recommendations for me. How is he, by the way?" I ask enthusiastically, even though I don't spend enough time around the man to know him better.

"He's good. Speaking of Bram, he's going to go on a last-minute business trip to New Orleans."

"Oh, so I won't get a chance to see him while I'm here? Tell him I'm sorry I missed him."

"Actually, I'm going with him. I've never been to New Orleans, so when he asked if I wanted to go, I said yes."

"Wait, what? You asked me to come here. Did that little fact enter the conversation between you and Bram?"

"I didn't think it would be that big of a deal."

"Oh my god. Are you kidding me? I swear, Robin, you do this every time. Wow, you couldn't have told me sooner? This is just great." I don't even try to conceal my frustration. This is why I came prepared with a list of things to do. If I'd known, I would have never come to Seattle so early. This is bullshit. I should have stayed in San Francisco. Ugh.

"The opportunity just came up. It's a three-day event. I'll be back before the end of the week," she says, like she's handing me a consolation prize. I don't want it. I saw this coming and should have followed my instinct.

The server arrives to collect our plates and I hand him my credit card. "Would you like dessert?" he asks.

"No. Thank you." I've lost my patience and appetite and don't want to hang around her any longer than I have to. I direct my attention back to my sister, trying to rein in my frustration. "So, when are you leaving?"

"In the morning. After I leave here, I'm heading home to pack."

And there it is—bloody hell. Robin could have told me this at the start of the conversation. But no, I have to pull it out of her like a witness on the stand.

While I wait for my receipt, I text my driver. In the time it takes the server to return, my sister has her purse and jacket in hand, ready to leave. We stand up and I start to hug her, but don't. We say our goodbyes and part ways. She heads to the restroom and I walk outside to the car.

The day feels unsettled and sullen. I didn't want to leave Parker this morning. Despite how tenacious people think I am, beneath the face is a woman trying to heal, trying to forget. Parker helps me do just that. So, leaving him to head to Seattle on the heels of a horrible breakup to run my most important meeting was hard. He'd move mountains to be here if I asked him, which is why I didn't. Because despite my desire to have him here, I need to navigate the next chapter of my life alone.

Today's conversations with Alejandro and Robin were equally difficult for different reasons. Alejandro needs confirmation that I can deliver on the deal with Ross Enterprises. Unfortunately, despite my previous successes, I have to constantly prove myself as a woman. This is my chance to be seen as the lead counsel and confirm that I can do this on my own. That I have what it takes.

My sister, well...I don't know what she needs. Whatever we have going on between us has gone on way too long, and I feel like I'm grasping at straws trying to find a solution. Although part of pulling myself together involves improving my family relations, I can't force Robin to spend time with me. She needs to meet me halfway. It's dramatic, but in a city full of people, I feel completely alone and don't know why. It seems I'm getting too good at saying goodbye.

CHAPTER 3

Power

Noah

OUR FATHER ONCE TOLD US THAT POWER ISN'T EVERYTHING; IT'S THE only thing. It's a motto I've taken to heart, so when my brothers come into my office congratulating me on closing our largest deal, I feel every ounce of power. My brothers and I run the Knight Development Corporation. Headquartered in Seattle, it's one of the most prominent commercial real estate development firms in the United States.

"You outdid yourself on this one, Nik," my younger brother, Mak, announces. He walks over to my credenza and pours us each a glass of whiskey. "Time to celebrate."

Mak is the President of Investment Management and the last of us to join the firm full-time. Despite being our baby brother and a confessed Casanova, he's Katherine Johnson brilliant. I'm good with numbers, but his skills run laps around my brain. He hands me a glass.

"More like crushed it. With over one point five million square feet, this was our largest building yet," my older brother Rok chimes in. Mak hands him a drink then takes a seat near me. Rok leans back on the leather sofa, one arm stretched across the back, the other supporting a raised glass. "Cheers."

Those are my brothers, always looking for a reason to celebrate. I lift my glass, take a sip, and nod to them. My brother, Roman "Rok" Knight, is the Chairman, CEO, and President. He took over the firm when our dad retired early and left the business to the three of us. By then, Rok had already worked through every department in the company. Now, he's the face of the firm, and it's a position that's well deserved. When he stepped into the role, he became the second richest black developer in the United States. The first was my father, Elijah Knight.

In the business world, I'm known as Noah Knight, President of Capital Markets. The growth of Knight Development Corporation sits on my shoulders. Brokering large commercial real-estate development deals is my strength. I drive the company's international business relations with investors, including responsibility for equity sales, debt and structured finance, and global real estate investment banking. In addition to company-wide capital markets and finance, I'm responsible for portfolio management. I serve as Rok's right-hand man, and on his left is our baby brother Mark Knight, whom we call Mak in keeping with our childhood nicknames.

Before retiring, our dad spent more than enough time preparing us to run the family business. I spent my summers in high school working for the company. While I was in college, that increased to at least thirty hours a week. The Knight Development Corporation is not only my business; it's in my blood.

"Cheers," I tell them and take a sip. The whiskey goes down smoothly, and I reflect on how good we have it.

Every celebration has meaning. We weren't born into this type of money. We built it through hard work, sacrifice, and determination. Early in my father's career, his job relocated him to London. That's where I was born and spent the first twelve years of my life. Eventually, my father returned to the States, determined to build a legacy to leave to us. At the time, I didn't fully understand what was happening. It felt like I was needlessly being ripped from my home, culture, and friends, but over time, I came to terms with it. I still had my parents and my brothers. I began focusing on the things I could control, like how I reacted to the world around me and helping my family build a legacy in Seattle so we never had to be uprooted again. Looking across the room at my brothers as we toast, I'm certain it was all worth it. The luxury, the lifestyle, it's all good. But there's one thing I've learned: that as good as this all feels, it comes at a price. There are sacrifices to be made if you want this type of power. Sacrifices I know all too well.

"I've been tracking the shift in the market since the pandemic. Real estate in California is taking a hit. We should discuss the opportunity there. I have some ideas that would make it worth our time. Mak, look at what I sent you, and let's sync on it tomorrow," I say and take another sip of my drink.

"Why not today?"

"I need to head out early."

"Man, you're hitting this hard. Take a second and celebrate. The firm is doing well. Thanks to you and Mak, we have over sixty-five million square feet under construction. Take the week. You earned more than an afternoon break after the work you put in on this. When was the last time you took time off?"

"Yeah, Nik. Take the jet, go somewhere warm without mosquitoes where the drinks are cold, the women are pretty, and get laid," Mak says. I shake my head.

Business advice I'll take. But advice on women is not something I need from Mak. There's a reason we refer to Mak as Casanova. My brother goes through women like water. He's the love 'em and leave 'em type. He waltzes in with his swoon-worthy ways and gets these women hooked, and when they want more, he's out. Honestly, I think he's allergic to commitment. I've also had my share of women. But right now, I'm not looking for that. Managing multi-million-dollar development deals is my life. Everything else comes second, including women.

"Relax, I'm working on some things," I say. There's a quick knock on my door before it opens. It's Jewel, our executive assistant. She's small in stature at around five-two, but she spent time in the military, which makes her great at handling a handful like us. She walks to my desk and hands me a set of keys.

"All set. You can use those or key codes on the door. If you need to stock the fridge, say the word, and I'll handle that for you," Jewel says, and her words earn me curious glances from my brothers.

"Mak, you have a meeting in ten. Don't be late. Rok, your lunch is on your desk," she tells them, then leaves and closes the door behind her. That's Jewel. Fast. Efficient. My brothers and I may run things at our firm, but Jewel Lake, our executive assistant extraordinaire, runs us.

"Who are we meeting in ten?" I ask.

"You're not meeting anyone. Remember you're taking off. And by the looks of those keys, someplace new. So, you did purchase that place on the water," Mak says.

"Congratulations are in order again," Rok adds, lifting his glass.

"Thanks. Yeah, I closed a few weeks ago. The furnishings were completed yesterday. I plan to spend my first night there tomorrow. For now, I'm at the Four Seasons while the movers are doing their thing," I say, feeling a sense of pride.

Although I have personal property in several cities, this is my first standalone house. All my other homes are penthouses in buildings we own across the globe. Of course, we have multiple sprawling family residential homes in and out of the country, but this one is mine. I bought it from a woman whose family and friends spent a lifetime living in it and loving it. Walking into the place felt like a beautiful spot to gather with family and friends, like a place I never wanted to leave. It feels good to have a home in a neighborhood away from the hustle and bustle of downtown. A home that feels like a home.

Mak fiddles with his tie and stands. "You know what's next, man? A wife and two kids."

"It's a house, Mak, not a minivan. Calm down," I deadpan. He walks to the door and opens it.

"Right. I have a meeting. As Rok said, take the week and do your thing. I'll have Jewel clear your calendar. We'll see you at work next week. We got this."

"We're still on for dinner tomorrow," I tell him before he walks out.

I look across my desk at Rok. "Did he seem a little nervous when he said the word wife?" I chuckle because we both know hell will freeze over before Mak marries.

"A tad. Give him a few years to work it out of his system. You were the same way once."

"I was never out of control like him."

"As long as he shows up at work and delivers, I'll leave him to it. Speaking of which, I read what you sent Mak. The plan makes sense. Let's get his take. He'll run the numbers. If he says it's worth the investment, we'll bite. In the meantime, we'll keep you posted if we need anything before Monday. Mak's right about one thing: you really need to take time to decompress. I see you're committed, but find some balance, man. Despite what's happening in the economy, our company is strong. We're in the top five. We got this," he says. I hate to admit that he's right. I've been so focused on work and positioning our company in the market that I haven't had time to slow down and savor what I have.

I steeple my fingers and say, "Okay. Why don't I plan a barbecue at my new house in a few weeks after I've had time to settle?"

"Deal."

CHAPTER 4

Caesar Salad

Raven

Robert Burns wrote in a poem that "the best laid plans of mice and men often go awry," and no truer words have ever been spoken. Two days ago, I found out my now ex-boyfriend was cheating on me. Yesterday felt like a crapshoot. Today comes a close second since I was supposed to spend the day with my sister until I learned that she decided to tag along on a business trip with her husband at the last minute. So, instead of being with her, I spent most of my morning working during my vacation.

As disappointed as I was with my sister's situation, the day wasn't a complete loss. I managed to check some things off of my Seattle sightseeing list. Luckily, the sky was clear today, so I took advantage of the weather and went to Kerry Park to view the Seattle skyline. The view was breathtaking, and seeing the Space Needle standing tall in the distance made me want to go there even more.

After an afternoon at Kerry Park, I wandered through the never-ending shops at the Farmer's Market, sampling the various products like when my dad took us to the ones in San Francisco. That was a long time ago. A time when my dad, mom, sister, and I…well, it was a while ago when things were good. I blink, willing myself to swallow the memories.

Now, I'm hanging out at a sleek modern bar with a view of Elliot Bay and the Seattle Great Wheel, drinking wine, and planning my next move. I have no idea why I'm here other than I have nothing better to do. If Parker were here, I'm sure we'd find all kinds of things to get into. One thing is for sure: I'm hungry and need to get out of here to find some comfort food before returning to my apartment.

I take the last sip of my wine, letting it slide over my tongue, savoring the flavor. After placing the glass on the stone bar counter, I slide it forward. "One more, then you can close my tab," I tell the bartender. He nods in response.

Buzz, buzz. My phone rings on the bar top. A smile crosses my face when I see Parker's picture. I don't hesitate to answer.

"Hey, Parker. Are you checking up on me again? How are your parents? Did you tell them I said hi?"

"About that…" His voice deepens, carrying a weight of gravity that instantly grabs my attention.

"Oh shoot. What now? You sound serious. Parker?"

"It is," Parker lets out an exasperated breath. "I guess you can say they're more than just fine."

The sound of his footsteps tells me he's heading somewhere. The latch of a door clicks, and then it goes quiet. I listen for a beat before responding.

"That's nothing out of the ordinary. Where are you going?"

"Home." I hear the clang of his keys hitting the console table in his foyer. My mind is immediately transported to his house and I visualize every move he makes like I'm there because I've seen it all and lived the moment a thousand times before. "Just wait until you hear this."

"I'm here." The waiter takes my empty glass and replaces it with a fresh drink. I take a sip and wait for Parker to continue.

"No one answered the door, but I knew they were home because one of their cars was in the driveway."

"Your parents were probably busy. You do realize that you're not the only one with a life. Right?"

"I figured that out. Anyway. I let myself in and found Mom spread eagle on the counter with Dad tossing her."

"Oh. Okay, I wasn't expecting that." Shocked, I press my lips together and swallow to stifle a laugh at the visual of Parker catching his socialite parents doing the deed on their kitchen counter. I'm so glad I have a fresh drink. "So, you caught your parents tossing salad. Did they see you? What did they say?" A smile creeps across my face. It's funny, but it's not. Oh god, what if I had been with him? I would have been mortified. There are just some things you can't unsee. For me, that's everything.

"They didn't see me."

"Of course not. Like you said, they were shaking it up hard, like I did those salad containers I used to take for lunch. It was probably Caesar salad," I deadpan.

"Oh my god, Rain." He punctuates each word. "Mom's eyes were closed. I think she was…oh god, Rain, I think I saw my mom having the big O." There's a strange noise at the other end of the line. I hear Parker; he's making gagging sounds, and I cover my mouth when I feel like I'm about to gag.

"Stop making that sound. You know it's contagious. I'm at a bar having a drink, for Christ's sake. Don't make me puke in public." He makes the noise again. "If you don't stop that, Parker," I whisper-shout.

"I can't help it. My mom and Dad were…climaxing." The cringe in his tone is evident and I sense he's about to gag again.

"Yeah, that tends to happen when you have good sex. I mean salad. So now you know what it was like the moment you were conceived." The lawyer in me asserts the obscure fact. The gasp from Parker on the other end of the phone is enough to send me into full-on laughter. Breathing, I try to pull myself together. "Can I have some water?" I mouth to the bartender when he returns with my receipt. I return my attention to Parker, who's audibly faux-barfing. "Did she scream out his name?" I close my eyes and wince, not wanting to know the answer but trying to lighten the mood. A chuckle inadvertently escapes.

"I'm glad you find this funny, Rain," Parker admonishes me.

In a futile attempt to suppress more laughter, I purse my lips, take a deep breath, then sip my drink. This would have been the perfect discussion over FaceTime so I could witness his reaction to all of this. Unreal. I need this after the day I had.

"Seriously, Parker. Did she?"

"I don't know. It was all a blur. I left before I saw anything else. What am I going to do, Rain? I'm supposed to have dinner with them this weekend, and there's no way I'm ever sitting at the kitchen counter again. Jesus, I can't believe what I saw."

"It was salad, Parker. And from what you describe—good salad with meat and tangy dressing." I pucker my lips, press my fingertips to them, and make the chef kiss sound, mwah, while opening my hand. "There's nothing wrong with that. Now, go. Have a drink with your buddy Josh if he's in town. You two can commiserate. Or, pretend you never saw it. When you go to your parent's house this weekend, make a point to have dinner at the dining room table."

"Raven Rain Nichols," He snaps.

"Don't be mad at me! I'm just stating the facts."

"You know I love you to death, but I can't continue this conversation with you right now." Parker huffs. "I gotta go. I'll call you tomorrow." Parker ends the call. I close my eyes and smile to myself. You can't make this stuff up.

"Well. Did she?" I hear a deep, sexy, British-accented voice say beside me.

Swiveling on my bar stool, I turn towards the voice and see this sexy, muscular, caramel-colored, burr-cut-haired man. I'm stunned, silent momentarily as he stares back at me with the most soul-penetrating green eyes, awaiting an answer.

"Excuse me?" I gather my wits, trying to feign annoyance at the intrusion yet lost in his glorious green gaze. This man looks like every Pinterest pinup partner goal picture I've ever seen. But I know from experience that there is no such thing. Four failed relationships in five years have taught me better. After the fiasco with Blake, I need to take five and find myself before jumping into something new.

"Your friend," he continues, bringing my attention back to him. Mister Sexy Green Eyes gets up from his seat, walks over, bringing a lovely scent of amber, musk, and spice I can't identify, and sits on the stool beside me. "Did your friend's mum scream out their dad's name?" A sly, sexy smile forms on his face.

"He didn't say," I respond, getting lost in his eyes.

CHAPTER 5

Nik, Without a C

Noah

WHEN I WOKE UP THIS MORNING, I DIDN'T INTEND TO FOLLOW through with taking time off from the office, but I did. I certainly didn't expect to end up in a bar, sitting across from this gorgeous creature with perfect lips, watching her sip wine. But here I am. My eyes were drawn to her as soon as I walked in. She's wearing a lavender cold shoulder sweater, which stands out against her beautiful honey-brown skin. Her sun-streaked brown hair flows in natural waves over her bare shoulders—that I want to lean down and kiss.

I've never been so captivated by a woman before. Transfixed, I watched as she talked on the phone. When she tossed her head back and laughed, something came over me, and I felt jealous because I wanted to make her laugh like that.

It's not a feeling I'm used to. There was a time before the pandemic when I had a different woman every week. My brother Mak woos them long enough to make them fall in love before moving on to the next, but I don't do that. I have rules. One night, that's all they get—then it's done. Lately, even that's tapered off. It's been a while.

This woman sitting across from me seems different. If this had been any other woman, she'd already have a drink in hand, compliments of me. We'd be negotiating whether we're going to her place or mine. My place being a room at the Four Seasons because I never take my one-night stands to my home. That's too familiar—too personal. I'm not ready for that, or sure I ever will be, because I don't know anything different.

For the longest time, women have been a fleeting pleasure and nothing more. It's not that they weren't important, because they are. I like women. I wouldn't be here without my mom. I watched her work hard to provide her sons with a sense of normalcy following our move to the States. She had to leave her family behind, yet she did everything within her power to help us build a new community of friends despite starting over herself. As a kid, it's hard to see the sadness under the smile that wasn't there before. She pushed me to join social clubs, sports clubs, whatever she thought might pull me out of the slump I was in, missing my friends. Between her effort and Dad's—it worked. Focus and consistency were what I needed. It didn't matter what it was. The routine of it all made me feel stable.

So, no, I don't get attached to women. I need to focus on building a legacy so that when the time comes to start a family, I'm ready. I won't have to worry about uprooting anyone. That's why I spent the past decade focused on building something that can't be taken away…the Knight Development Corporation—our legacy.

Tonight's the first night I've been here in weeks. And now I find myself holding the attention of the most beautiful woman. I can't take my eyes off of her.

"So, does that happen often?" I ask. She gives me another cute look, this one marred with confusion.

"I'll avoid the land mine you're laying for me and ask, does what happen often?"

"You're on your toes. I like that."

"Hmm. The sexy stranger is not used to being around smart women. I'm disappointed." She uses her finger to trace the rim of her glass.

Ouch, she assumes I'm only interested in superficial women. I just met this woman, and she's already struck a nerve I didn't know existed. She's right, however. The women I'm usually with are there for pleasure. Whether they are smart enough to cite the Pledge of Allegiance or talented enough to sing the "Star-Spangled Banner" on key, I never cared. I wasn't with them long enough to hold a meaningful conversation. The only thing I wanted coming out of their mouths, besides me, was, *"Yes, oh god, please, more."*

"You think I'm sexy," I say around a grin, throwing her words back at her. It's not a question. I don't need a response, but the confirmation comes in her smile.

"Seems we're at an impasse."

"I'll give. This BFF of yours…." Her eyebrow arches and I pause.

"I haven't heard that phrase in a while, but go on." I can't help but chuckle at her response.

"Does that happen often? The part where your male friends confide in you about intimate details of their life."

"Yes, my close friends do confide in me. I'm that kind of person. Trustworthy."

She takes a sip of her drink, and I watch, mesmerized, as her luscious lips linger on the rim of the glass. She's wearing shimmering deep purple lipstick that pops against her honey-colored skin. Entranced, I envision those lips wrapped around me, and my dick twitches.

"*He* is lucky to have you."

"Just how long were you eavesdropping on me?"

Something about this woman has me off my game. I hope she doesn't think I'm a creep. Usually, I could care less what a woman thought of me. I would have ended the conversation by saying the only thing that matters is how loudly she'll scream my name when I take her to bed. But I can't bring myself to utter those words to *this* woman. Not now.

"You weren't on the phone when I first noticed you. I have to say the salad analogy was…creative."

"So, you were spying on me."

"Admiring. I gave it a moment to see if you were waiting for a friend. I also noticed you weren't wearing a ring. I was about to approach, then your call came through."

"I could still be waiting for someone."

"Doesn't matter. I'm here now. I'm sure you'll find me more interesting than anything else coming your way."

"Wow," she says, and I can hear the irritation in her voice.

She tosses back the last of her drink. She reaches into her purse, pulls out a platinum card, slides it across the counter, then flags the bartender. He comes over to collect her card, but I pick it up before he can and hand it back to her. I give the bartender my Black Card.

"I got this."

She writes something on the receipt and then leaves it on the bar. "Thanks for the drinks…" She pauses, waiting for me to fill in the blank and tell her my name.

"Nik, without a C."

She stands and throws her purse strap over her shoulder. "Thanks, Nik, without a C." She studies my face for a second. "Although you don't look like a Nik."

This is the first time I get a full view of her. I scan the length of her body. She's in strappy black heels. Her toes are painted a deep purple, the color of midnight, like her fingernails, which I imagine digging into my back as I hover over her. I can tell by how her black ankle pants fit that she has long, lean legs—the kind you get by doing Pilates.

"And you are?"

"Leaving."

This woman has a way of checking me that's new. Usually, women don't say no to me. I tell them what I want and get it. I don't ask twice. I don't know what spell she's placed on me, but despite her walking away, I have to have her.

"Stay." I hear the word come out of my mouth before I realize what I'm saying. I've never had to ask a woman to stay. But here I am—asking. "Let me buy you another drink." I grab the receipt to see what she's been drinking and see her handwritten note that says "thanks" alongside a heart drawing. Cute. I pocket the receipt.

She turns. "Listen…Nik," she says, struggling to suppress her sarcasm. I smirk, which earns me a tentative smile from her. She's reading into my nonverbal cues like she knows me—it's a thing I've only experienced with my brothers. This woman has my interest piqued.

"Just one." I clarify.

She checks the time on her watch. "I'm done drinking, and I'm sure you didn't come here for me. I certainly didn't come here looking for you."

"Yet here we are. Wait. Give me a moment." I pull out my phone and type a message in the group text with my brothers. We are supposed to meet for dinner, but I text them to cancel. I finish the message, put my phone back in my pocket, and look up. "Done." I can hear the pinging coming from my phone with my brothers' responses to my message. I ignore them.

"Canceling on your woman?"

"I would never cancel on you." The pinging stops, and my phone rings. I take it out to silence it and realize my older brother, Rok, is FaceTiming me. Fuck, this could be business-related. We have a lucrative property development deal with a high-tech firm looking to expand their operation coming up next week worth millions of dollars. "Don't go. This'll be short, I promise," I tell her. I take her by the hand, then answer the call. "Rok. Was that you blowing up my phone? This better be good." Before he can answer, my younger brother Mak's face appears on the screen.

"We told you to take time away from work, not from us. What's the deal, man?" I pull the woman's hand to my side, then angle my phone so we're both on the screen. Mak positions the phone so he and Rok are on the screen together.

"Well, shit," Mak exclaims. Rok takes the phone from Mak.

"Hey, I'm Rok, with a K, Nik's older brother. And this one," he points his thumb at my younger brother. "The one with a potty mouth is our baby brother, Mak." Mak holds up his fingers, forming the sign letter for K. Rok elbows him in the side. "I see now why our brother canceled dinner plans with us," he says.

I turn and smile at the woman who's still watching the phone screen. She turns to look at me briefly, then back at the screen. Damn right, she's stunning.

"Hi, Rok, with a K, and Mak." She holds up her fingers, signing the letter k when she says Mak's name. "I'm Rae with an e. It's nice to meet you. Is Baby Mak potty trained?"

My brothers go silent for a second. I'm unsure what's happening until they cover their mouths with their fists and get lost in a fit of laughter. Rok is the first to gain his composure. "Oh, I like this one. Rae, you are definitely a keeper. Nice to meet you. Sorry to bother you two. Nik, we'll let you get back to Rae. I'll check in later this week. Have a good time off, man." Rok ends the call.

Rae pulls away from me. I look down at her and frown.

"Rae? Is that a nickname? It sounds like I'm cheering at a game."

"You're one to talk."

She has a point that I don't dare challenge. I hadn't realized the absurdity of our nicknames, which are our initials, until she articulated it during the call. Rae starts walking toward the lobby, and I follow her. At this point, I don't even recognize myself, going after this woman.

"Come on. Ra…" An image of her lying beneath me in bed flashes, and I hesitate to say her name. "No. There is no way I'm coming inside you while calling out the name Rae." The words tumble out of my mouth raw. It's blunt, but true. Because calling someone as beautiful as this woman, "Rae," is morally wrong.

Rae doesn't even pause. She quickens her pace, and before I realize what's happening, she walks out the door and out of my life. Wait. What the actual fuck?

CHAPTER 6

Ten

Raven

I'M ALMOST AT THE CORNER WHEN I SENSE NIK FOLLOWING ME, and I catch a whiff of his scent before he appears alongside me. I hadn't realized how tall he was until he stood beside me. In my estimation, he's about the same height as Parker. And his brothers, wow, from what I saw on FaceTime, they each look like beautiful, slightly different variations of each other. These guys hit the jackpot when it comes to the gene pool. This leads me to question why Mister Sexy Green Eyes is still following me. He's stunning in a bad-boy billionaire kind of way. He could probably have any woman he wants. He's turning the heads of men and women at this very moment. Blake is handsome, too, and I'm beginning to think I have a type…the wrong type.

"Wait, Rae. Let me apologize."

"Not interested," I say and keep walking, hoping, in vain, that he'll give up.

This man dares to assume I will be under him tonight. That he'll be coming in me calling my name. Hell, I don't even know him. What I sense so far is that Nik is a player, and as fine as he is, rocking a cute British accent, muscular body, perfectly shaped lips, and piercing green eyes—I'm not interested. I keep walking.

"Rae, don't make me beg." The irritation in his voice is evident and I envision his fine face frowning.

"You're way ahead of yourself. That was number five."

"What?"

I stop in response. Nik stops next to me. Just as I envisioned, his eyebrows are furrowed. But the way his perfectly-shaped lickable lips abandon their pout and curve at one side, I sense he's relieved he has my attention.

"You said don't make you beg. That was number five. You're on your fifth time begging me. Stay." I repeat his words, then hold up my pinky finger after I say the word stay. "Just one." I hold up the next finger. "Come on, Ra...there's no way...," I say, stressing his words, and hold up a third finger. "Wait, Rae. Let me apologize. Rae, don't make me *beg*." I hold up my last two fingers and emphasize the word beg when sticking my thumb out. Nik stares at me, mouth open like he's about to say something—stunned. Turning away, I continue walking down the street.

"Stop. Don't make me sing."

"Six," I call over my shoulder.

When I hear a soulful rendition of the song *The Most Beautiful Girl*, I smile to myself. I swear this man is trying too hard.

"Hey...," he calls to me before he starts crooning lyrics about some girl walking out on him.

"What happened to your British accent?" I call out, but continue walking, which only makes him sing louder.

"Tell Rae I'm sorry, tell Rae—."

I stop and turn around. Okay, he has a bit of charm, but this is embarrassing. I need to put an end to these shenanigans. The street is bustling with people witnessing his antics. Nik's about three car lengths away from me, looking like a snack in a button-down white shirt with the cuffs flipped up, black pants, and one hand in his pocket. His eyebrows are arched in a *what did you expect me to do* look. God, this man makes me hungry for more than a meal.

"Don't you dare call me baby," I say, knowing what he's about to sing next.

A smug smile spreads across his face, and he knows he's got me. Why does he have to be so damn tall and sexy?

He extends his hand and waits for me to come to him, and despite my hesitation, I do. Standing before Nik, I recall Parker's words at the airport. "*Live your best life. Have a good time.*" I smile, but beneath the smile, I silently curse myself for what I'm about to do as I place my hand in his.

"Have dinner with me," he says. "Please."

Here we go again. "Seven."

"I see what's happening. Let me try a different tactic. Rae, we're going into that building right there. We'll have a nice dinner, drink, talk, and see what happens afterward."

Nik lifts his hand with mine in it and points to a modern multi-storied glass and steel building across the street. I've seen the building in passing but have never been there before. From the design, it appears to be a multi-use building that serves retail clients and is a mix of business and residential spaces. He's right to change his tactic. I like his commanding nature better. I bite the corner of my lip. My stomach growls.

"Okay. I'll agree to dinner since I was on my way to eat anyway."

"Thank you."

I start walking again, but he doesn't move, so I stop. He pulls me close so that I'm facing him.

"Please tell me you go by something other than Rae." His eyes are pleading with me. What is it with this man? He can't seem to let this go. My name wasn't an issue with Blake or any of the other failed relationships I've had since Parker, which gets me thinking. Nik and Parker are the only men with an issue with calling me Rae.

I sigh. "People call me Rae. But my closest friends call me Rain." I don't add that only Parker calls me Rain. He doesn't need to know that.

He cups my cheek and then brushes his thumb across my bottom lip, stirring something in me. "That's much better. Rain." He says my name in a way that makes me think of water rolling down the window during a storm. It's sullen and seductive at the same time.

We cross the street and enter the sleek, black, wood-clad entrance to the restaurant. A line of people are waiting to get in, but Nik takes me past everyone straight to the front desk like he owns the place. I've already ascertained by his Black Card that Nik is wealthy. I'm not poor, but I don't spend enough to justify a Black Card. However, Parker's been flashing his Centurion since I met him in college, and his family practically owns San Francisco. With that kind of status comes confidence, which Parker has in spades. Whenever Parker walks into a room, his presence commands attention. After twelve years of being with him, I know what it feels like to have all eyes on me. I feel that way now walking in with Nik. I'm smart enough to know that Nik is doing more than well for himself.

"Nik." A man, whom I assume is the restaurant manager, speaks to Nik in a familiar way. Nik places a hand on his back.

"James. Good to see you. This is Rain," he says, and I hear a sense of pride and relief in his tone because he just crossed a hurdle getting me here.

I nod to James. We follow him to a private table in a room partially obscured from the rest of the patrons. The restaurant is dark with black walls, high glossed trim, and an eclectic mix of rich jewel-tone blue tufted seating and mahogany tables. We sit next to each other on a high-tufted banquette. Aaliyah's *One In A Million* plays over the sound system in the background.

"Can we start you with your usual?" James asks.

Nik directs his attention to me. "Would you prefer champagne, red wine, or a cocktail? I noticed you drinking wine earlier."

"Red wine is fine."

"Any particular variety of red?"

I shake my head. It doesn't matter. A restaurant of this caliber will have a quality selection. Years ago, I learned not to read wine labels because it's just another piece of information that gets stuck in my head, and if I drink something I like, I ask for it repeatedly. It's why I like going out and having drinks with Parker at our favorite book wine lounge, Book Society. Like this place, it feels like a luxe secret hideaway. Parker always orders for me, and I don't have to memorize anything. His selections have never disappointed me, and in addition to experiencing new varieties of wine, I get to hang out in a cool atmosphere.

"Vintage Hermitage La Chapelle for the lady, and I'll have my usual. Thank you."

"They're making a comeback," I tell Nik.

"You know your wines."

"No." I know that one. But I don't say I do because it's unnecessary to say when I first had it or who I was with.

James leaves, and a series of wait staff proceed to buzz around us, placing an assortment of food items on the table: bread, dips, nuts, cheese, and sparkling water. Purposely, I tune it out and focus on Nik, who's been staring at me since we arrived.

"Did I say thank you for having dinner with me?"

"On the street, after seven."

"Right. What was that back there?"

"I think you know by now. I have perfect recall."

"Should I watch what I say?"

"That depends. I don't think we came here to discuss my memory."

"You're right. We didn't."

James returns to the table with our drinks. Nik and I agree upon a few seafood options for dinner and some sides to share, and I notice we have similar tastes. Blake and I didn't have similar tastes. He was a meat-and-potatoes kind of guy. I prefer seafood and pasta, something I have in common with Parker. Nik instructs James to bring all the food out together and that he will signal the staff if he needs anything before then.

"I hope you don't mind. Sometimes all the attention is a bit..."

"Much?" I finish.

"Exactly," he says, picking up his drink. "Let's toast." I copy him and lift my glass.

"To a beautiful night in Seattle."

"To my night with the lovely Rain by my side. Cheers." He clinks his glass with mine.

"Cheers."

He takes a sip of his drink, and I do the same. I hear *If You Love Me* by Brownstone through the speaker, and I move my shoulders up and down and groove to the beat. Nik stands and holds a hand to me.

"Dance with me."

I stand, we step a few feet away from the table, and as if we were at a club, we dance. It's carefree and fun, and I shake my hips and pop my fingers in time with the beat close to Nik. He's so sexy as he moves in sync with the song. I'm lost in the music, the look of him, the smell of him. It's all too perfect.

"You're beautiful, Rain. And your moves are…" He puts his fingers to his lips, making a chef kiss gesture. "Perfection."

I move closer to him and do a few body rolls, showing off my moves as Nik lustfully looks on. The song ends, and when D'Angelo's *Brown Sugar* comes on, he places a hand around my waist and dances toward me, leaving just enough space to watch as I roll my hips in time with his. As the song plays, we step apart and back together in rhythm. His hand never leaves me as I twirl around in front of him. Moving closer, I drape my arms over his shoulder, crossing them at my wrist behind him. I can feel his heat radiating between us, and feel his desire rise against me. I look up at him, and he holds my gaze as electricity crackles wherever my body touches his. I want this man.

I'm lost in everything that's him. When the song changes and *Pony* by Ginuwine starts to play, at the first beat, I step away. I take Nik by the hand and lead him back to the table because dancing to that song with a man like Nik, without a C, is the definition of dangerous.

He looks at me, sporting a smug smile. "What?"

"I think you have some secret button you pressed to have this song come on."

"The universe is sending us signals."

"Something else is sending you signals." I laugh and shake my head because he's so fucking fine, and this seductive song about getting into his saddle plays right into his hand. And other unmentionable places on me, if I'm being honest.

"I can't help being attracted to you."

I reach for my glass and take a sip of my wine. As I drink, I notice Nik watching me. Turning to him, I smile, and his eyes drop to my lips. I place my glass on the table, and before I can ask him what he's thinking, he reaches over and cups my chin with his hand. His hands are strong, and I imagine them wandering my body.

"Hey," I whisper.

"Hey." He says, then leans in and dusts his lips against mine. It's soft, subtle, and sensual—everything a first kiss should be. My heart flutters, but before it goes further, he pulls back. "I've wanted to do that since I saw you at the bar."

He dips his head and repeats the gesture, licking the crease where my lips meet. I pull back, surprised by my desire for more…more of his lips, more of his tongue, more of… Nik. He holds my gaze. He's reading me, convincing me with his stare to make the next move. Licking my lips, I taste the sweet traces he left behind. His body calls to mine, and I need to decide soon whether to give in to the feeling or walk away. Because I'm at the doorstep to Nik's house, and right now, he's offering me the proverbial key. There's no turning back if I take it and unlock the door. If I don't take it, I go back to…what?

Nik rubs a thumb across my bottom lip. My body buzzes, I blink, and a slow smile forces its way from my lips. The subtle lift of his eyebrows shows he's questioning me. Waiting for my consent.

"Kiss me," I tell him; instantly, his lips are on mine again. The kiss is soft at first like he's tasting something for the first time. Then greed takes over, and his tongue pushes past my lips and finds mine. He deepens the kiss. A hunger erupts within me, and I lean in for more. We suck and lick until I feel dizzy with desire and can't breathe. My hands creep up his chest and press him to create distance between us. Oh, my god. This man.

"Nik." His name comes out rushed as air escapes my lungs.

"I'm hungrier than I thought." He smirks.

Shaking my head, I can't help but laugh because this man is beautiful, bold, and utterly ridiculous, and if I don't watch out, Nik could be my downfall.

"What am I going to do with you? No. Don't answer that," I tell him, because I already know the answer.

On cue, my stomach growls, and I'm sure he can hear it. I reach across the table, break off a piece of bread, spread some soft cheese, and top it with a sliver of fruit. Nik has some roasted almonds and washes it down with whiskey.

"Are you ready for them to serve dinner?"

I nod, and he lifts his hand. James magically appears across the room, nods, then disappears. When he's gone, Nik pulls me into a kiss that feels so intense and urgent that I'm sure I'll see stars. "Now that I've tasted you, I can't get enough. Tell me I can have you tonight. I swear I'll sing every Begging My Baby song that's ever been written until you say yes."

"Eight."

"Don't."

"I can't help it, Nik. I don't know how to shut it off. It's who I am."

"I know how."

So do I. Shutting it off was always an option. All I have to do is say yes. Then Nik will stop asking, and I'll stop counting. As attracted as I am to Nik, getting involved with him is risky. I can tell already that he's the kind of guy I won't be able to get out of my head. Commanding, confident, powerful. All the things I see in Parker. And all the reasons to walk away.

I came here to escape and prepare for the biggest project of my career. This is my opportunity to prove myself at work; I can't let anything hinder my success. I didn't come here to get involved with someone new. This could be a big mistake.

"Rain." The sound of my name pulls me out of my head. "I'll lay number nine on the table by saying give me one night. I'm not asking for more because one night is all I can give." He doesn't have to tell me what I already know.

"I haven't asked for anything."

"I'm aware. I find myself for the first time in that precarious position. Begging for anything is new to me."

The weight of his words isn't lost on me, and I press my lips into a tight smile. It takes a lot for a man like Nik to admit he's doing something out of character. The way he walked into this building tonight, like he owned it, reveals everything I need to know about him. He can have anything he wants. Any woman he wants. Nik didn't have to ask, but despite that, he did. When I left the bar earlier, he could have ended our charade. Yet he's still here, knowing there's the potential for me to leave at any second, taking with me what he wants—what we both want. Because right now, Nik, without a C, has me feeling ways I haven't felt in a long time. Not since…well, not since Parker.

I close my eyes and then reopen them. I need this man to walk away now. Despite having done it before, having learned from a man who provided the perfect example, I can't bring myself to do it.

Walk away, Nik. Please. Walk away.

"What else have you never done before?" I probe.

"Dated a woman."

"Not ever?"

He shakes his head.

"So, this." I gesture at the table with my hands. "You don't take women out to get to know them over dinner." He shakes his head again. "These people here hovering. They know you well by the looks of things. You mean to say they've never seen you with a woman here."

"Women in my family and business associates. That's it. Dating is not my thing, Rain. I never wanted anything…more. Not for a long time. Listen, Rain, in my position—."

"Don't." I stop him. "Let's not talk about work. Or what you gave up. That's what people discuss on a date or when they are in a relationship. That's not us. I'm just a woman named Rain who met a guy named Nik, without a C, at a bar on a Tuesday afternoon in Seattle. After tonight, you'll never see me again."

"Does that mean you'll…"

"Ten."

CHAPTER 7

The Deal

Noah

When Rain says "ten," I pull her into me, and I cover her mouth with mine and kiss her hard. She groans into my mouth, and my dick twitches. I need to have her beneath me tonight. I break the kiss.

"I'm serious, Rain. Stay with me tonight."

Before she can respond James and his team return with our meal. They arrange all the plates on the table and then leave. I give Rain some time to fix her plate with the items she wants. I do the same. It's quiet except for music playing in the background. She eats a few morsels of food, and I watch every delicate move she makes as she washes it down with wine. I can't take my eyes off her. Then she turns to me.

"How does this work, Nik?"

I hold her gaze. "It's simple. When we leave here, we can go to my place at the Four Seasons or—."

"Four Seasons is fine."

"Okay, when we leave here, we'll go to the Four Seasons. We spend the night together entangled in sex, doing all the things that feel good to us. And you allow me to help you forget everything except for how our bodies feel together."

"So, just sex."

"Just sex. Nothing personal."

"No feelings."

"Only the kind that make you come calling my name."

"And tomorrow."

"Tomorrow, we go our separate ways."

"And we'll never see each other again."

"That's right, Rain. One night. Just sex. No strings attached."

"I can do that." She nods her head like she's reassuring herself and takes a sip of her drink. "I can do that."

"Perfect. I get to have you tonight."

"Yeah. For one night. You get to have me, and I get to have mind-blowing sex with a guy rocking a sexy British accent."

"Then we have a deal."

"It's a deal."

We click our glasses together.

"Cheers," we say in unison.

CHAPTER 8

Tastes So Good

Noah

I NEGOTIATE MULTI-MILLION-DOLLAR BUSINESS DEALS FOR A LIVING. My superpower is my ability to control my surroundings and convince people to do things I want them to do. If they don't do what I want, I walk away. This holds for business and women. However, that's not what happened when I met Rain. This woman flipped the script on me; like a queen, she now holds the power. I'm not used to people challenging me. With the status I've risen to, most people don't. The way Rain handles me, shows she's not impressed or intimidated by me. How she handles me is sexy and intriguing and does things to my body. God, I can't wait to be inside her.

Holding Rain's hand, I lead her out of the restaurant. Directly across the street is the entrance to the Four Seasons, where I have a penthouse suite for the night. I'm too impatient to walk down the block to the corner, so I choose to jaywalk across the street instead. I pull her toward me.

Rain jerks her hand away from mine like it's hot when she realizes what I'm doing. "You're crazy. We're going to get hit."

"Trust me. I'd never let anything happen to you."

"Besides that, I'm not running in these." We both look down at her heels.

"Take them off," I command.

"No," she says, silencing me with a single word.

Closing my eyes, I take a deep breath to calm my nerves. I'm not used to hearing that word. Yet, coming from her mouth, the luscious lips I instinctively crave, I do the unthinkable—I cave. Pulling Rain to me, I cup her cheeks, then dip my head and crash my lips to hers in the most indecent public display of affection. It's urgent and feral; if I don't stop soon, I'll be compelled to take her against the building behind us. I want this woman. I need to slow the fuck down.

I force myself to pull away to regain my composure. Our breaths come rushed, labored, and I can tell by the look of desire in Rain's eyes that we want the same thing.

Dusting my lips against hers, I whisper. "Okay." Then I turn my back to her and drop to one knee. "Hop on," I tell her.

"What?"

"Hop on."

"You're determined to get me to ride you."

I shake my head. She says it to be funny, but it's not far from the truth. "Get on, woman," I command, and I'm not surprised when she does.

Determined, I swiftly walk across the street, through the lobby, and reach the private elevator in record time. My brothers would be shocked to see me carrying Rain on my back. Still, I can't help but enjoy the feeling of her arms wrapped around my neck and the sound of her lighthearted laughter. I'm not known for wild behavior, but this woman has me singing in the streets and supplying rides.

"That was insane," she says, her words tumbling out in a blissful rush. I can't help but chuckle at how innocent and uninhibited they sound. I kneel, and she slides off my back.

As soon as we reach the penthouse, she sets down her purse and walks toward the wall of windows that offers a view of the bay. She doesn't look around. Most women take in the interior surroundings and remark on how impressed they are with the décor before I haul them off to bed. They're likely hoping I'll see them again and that they maybe have a chance to snag a rich guy. I don't know much about Rain, but how she moves through my world tells me wealth is not new to her.

Rain stares out at the view of the moon reflecting like sparkles on the water beneath the night sky. Like a magnet, I'm drawn to her. Crossing the room, I stand behind her and wrap my arm around her waist. Holding her feels natural, like she belongs in my arms. Our eyes meet as she stares back at me in our reflection in the window. I've lived in Seattle for the past twenty years, so it's a view I'm intimately familiar with, but standing behind her, staring at the water through her reflection, the scene takes on a different mood, and I want her.

"You don't seem impressed," I tell her.

"You haven't done anything yet." Her words come as a challenge, and my dick instantly goes hard.

I dip my nose into her neck and bathe in her aroma, a mix of jasmine and honey that makes my mouth water. She tips her head, providing me better access, and I trail kisses down her neck to her bare shoulder. She turns her head to capture my lips, and I spin her around to face me and deepen the kiss, licking into her. Rain's lips are soft and moist. Kissing her is like tasting the juice of the sweetest berry, and I hungrily wrap my tongue around hers and suck. I can't get enough. I cup her face with my hands to control myself. If I thought my dick was hard before, now it's solid steel. The wolf in me wants to strip her naked, push her against the window, and drive right into her.

Restraining myself, I step away from Rain and sit on the sofa facing the window. I lean back and extend my arms across the back of the sofa.

"Take off your clothes," I tell her, and a slow, seductive smile forms on her face. She bites her bottom lip. The way she's staring hungrily at the tent in my pants, I know she's not shy. She wants me.

Rain's wearing a lavender cashmere sweater that hangs over her shoulders. She crosses her wrists near the edge of the sweater, curls her fingers around its hem, lifts her arms, and the sweater is over her head and off in one motion. It dangles from her finger and then falls to the floor. She's wearing a black lace strapless bra. Her nipples pebble through the fabric beneath my gaze, and I imagine sucking them into my mouth. She unfastens her black slacks, pushes them past her small hips, and they fall easily to her ankles, revealing silk panties trimmed with lace, matching her bra. I watch as she slowly steps out of her pants and kicks them aside. Tantalizing, she bends to take off her shoes, and I get a view of the shape of her breasts. They'd fit perfectly in my hand. My mouth goes dry, and I swallow.

"Leave those on."

She straightens on my command, and I lick my lips at the sight of her in black silk underwear and heels. This woman is perfection. I can tell by how toned her body is, the cinched waist, and the definition in her arms that she works out. Her legs are long and lean, and I imagine them wrapped around my back as I move in and out of her.

"The clock's ticking. Are you just going to stare at me, Nik?" She bites her lip.

"I find you surprisingly bold and beautiful." My eyes roam the length of her body. Stunning.

"Somebody's been watching too many soaps." She teases, and I can't help but laugh.

"And funny. Come here." I tell her, and she walks over and stands between my legs. Grabbing her hips, I turn her around and palm her perfectly shaped butt. I want to bite her there, but I refrain. I turn her again to face me, but don't let go. "I plan to take my time with you tonight. Is that okay?" She nods. Sliding my hands up her body, I squeeze her breasts, circling my thumb over her swollen nipples protruding through the fabric. She's so responsive to my touch. "Are you wet for me?"

"Soaking," she says, then takes my hand, lowers it down her body, and places it over the fabric, releasing heat between her legs. I slide my finger beneath the material and between her folds and rub. She's slick and wet and ready. Her breath hitches as I continue rubbing between her folds over her clit. I plunge my fingers inside her walls and she gasps. Reaching my other hand beneath her bra, I squeeze her breasts, alternating between them. Her chest rises and falls in heavy breaths. I increase the friction between her folds, curling my fingers, and continue moving them at a steady, even pace. Her mouth falls open as jagged breaths flow in waves from her lips. "Ahh. Ahh." Her walls begin to contract around my fingers, signaling she is about to come. I quicken the pace, pulling her climax from her, and her walls pulse around my hand, coating it in cum. "Nik." My name comes out in a seductive sigh, and I grin.

When her breathing settles and the pulsing stops, I remove my fingers, put them in my mouth, and suck them clean as she watches. "Hmm. You taste like ambrosia for the gods."

"Do I get to taste you?"

"Maybe. I'm not done. I'm going to make you come again, Rain. This time in my mouth, then again with me inside you." I say, then rip the silk underwear from her body.

"You're a Neanderthal."

"You do that to me. Hold on," I tell her. I take her hand and put it on my shoulder. I slide my other hand behind her leg, lift it, and pull it over my shoulder. Pulling her close, I kiss the skin on her stomach.

"Your skin feels like silk, and I can't wait to have your body wrapped around me."

I lean back slightly, then put my arm behind her to balance her. Nudging her sex with my nose, I inhale, and she smells like heaven. I don't know if I'll ever be able to get enough of this woman. Her body is like a siren calling me from the shore, and I follow the sound like a ship lost at sea.

"Your scent is intoxicating." I groan into her. I pull her sex to my mouth. I lick the length of her slit, lapping the vestiges of cum from her previous release. Her breath hitches, and her back arches. She's still sensitive, and I feel her body swell in response to my tongue. Tightening my grip, I palm her ass and pull her closer. Covering her mound with my mouth, I devour her like a king feasting. Biting, licking, sucking, darting my tongue in and out of her until she comes again on my face, screaming my name.

"Nik, oh god, Nik."

CHAPTER 9

Remember Me

Raven

Nik has a magic mouth, and I want more. I've already come twice before I've had him in me. Nik stands, bringing me with him. As he carries me to his bedroom, like saran wrap, I cling to him, then dip my head and kiss his neck, working my way up. When I reach his ear, I lick it, then suck his lobe. He growls my name, and it's wild, wanting. "Rain."

Once in the room, he gently lowers me, and my body brushes the bulge between his legs as he places me on the bed. He hovers over me, hand on either side of my head, staring hungrily down at me. I wrap my legs around him, keeping him close, craving his heat. His pupils are dilated, making his green eyes darker, and the look on his face, the raised eyebrow, slightly parted mouth, and intense gaze tell me this man is about to devour me. And I'm ready for it all.

"What are you staring at?" I ask knowingly.

He dips his head, sticks his nose to my neck, and inhales. "That should be obvious." He whispers in my ear, then traces it with his teeth.

"I want to feel you inside me."

He rolls his nose along my face and then hovers over me. I feel the warmth of breath against my skin—I want him. His lips are close enough for me to lick him, so I do.

"You're greedy." He licks back, but I want more. I need more. He untangles me from him, gets up, and stands beside the bed. Quickly, I remove my bra and heels. Impatiently, I watch him undress. First, he loosens his tie and places it on the nightstand. "I might use that on you later," he says in a heated promise of things to come. He swiftly unbuttons his shirt, and I'm blessed with a show of muscles that surrounds his chest and arms. The strong waves on his abs eventually form a v that disappears beneath his waistband. When he unbuckles his belt and undoes his pants, they fall to the floor, and I try not to gasp. The length of the rod rising to the top of his briefs is a promise I'll feel well into next week. He's huge. He takes off his briefs, revealing that he is all man, and I can't wait. My sex clenches and I desperately want him inside me…now.

I lick my lips in anticipation. "You shouldn't be so good at making me want you."

"I can say the same," he tells me.

He grabs a condom from the nightstand and kneels over me on the bed. He dips his head and kisses me. It's deep, urgent, and needy as we swallow each other's groans. He breaks the kiss and dusts his lips down my body, tracing a line down my neck, between my breasts, and then he takes a nipple in his mouth and sucks and licks. The cool air heightens the feeling when his mouth leaves my breast and then moves to the other, where he repeats the gesture—kissing, sucking and licking them like he did my mouth. My body buzzes in anticipation.

"Oh, Nik," I pant his name, and in response, he pinches one nipple while sucking the other. I can feel his thick rod against my folds and lift my hips to get closer. "You said you wanted to come inside me while calling my name," I remind him, and my eyes fall shut with need.

He leans back, and I hear the rip of the condom wrapper before I feel his length rubbing against the slickness between my folds. My body shivers—I need more. I push my hips, urging him, wanting to be closer—to be connected in only a way sex can bring.

"Hold on," he says, and in a slow push, he enters me, and I feel my body stretch to welcome him in. He moves in and out, slowly pushing in until I'm finally full of him.

"You're so tight and wet and mine." He doesn't have to tell me because I hear the cacophony of our bodies' sounds as he moves in and out. "Open your eyes," he commands, and I do. He leans and kisses me as he pumps into me. He breaks the kiss and looks at me. "I need you to come for me." He says, then increases the pace, and on command, my body contracts around him, and I fall. Before I come down from my high, Nik quickens the pace; his thrust becomes more urgent. The intensity of his grunts and curses signify that soon he'll find his release. "Rain." He growls my name. "I need you to come for me again, baby." His pumps come hard and steady, and as he asks, I come again, calling his name, and seconds later, he finds his release inside me in waves. "Fuck, Rain." He screams and grunts, and like he said he would, he comes inside me, calling my name. "Rain."

To say Nik, without a C, gives good love is an understatement. He took me three more times after he came inside me the first time. I lost track of the number of orgasms he pulled from me before I fell asleep wrapped in his arms.

When my eyes open, I see the light from the moon shining through the window, bathing the room in a silvery glow. The soft light casts shadows on Nik's skin, emphasizing the contours of his face. In the air, the smell of amber, musk, and sex combine in a concoction that can best be described as desire. Like an addict needing a fix, Nik is my new drug, and I crave his body. But as much as I hate to admit it, this man is not mine, and I need to get out of here. We only agreed to one night. So, I need to leave before I cave in and take him…again. Because Nik, without a C, is who he professed to be, a player, and he doesn't do tomorrows.

Careful not to wake him, I crawl out of bed and put on my clothes. I look around to ensure I have all my belongings and see his things spread around the room. The fastidiousness in me takes over, and I hesitate. There's no way I can leave this room looking like this. As I glance behind me, I see Nik is still fast asleep. I move around the room and gather his clothing, which leads me like a trail to the bed. I watch him. He looks so peaceful lying there. I want to lean down and kiss his face, but I don't dare. Instead, I carry his things across the room. Carefully, I arrange each piece on the wooden valet, finally folding his T-shirt and briefs and laying them on the shelf.

Although I'm almost at the door, I can't go without leaving behind a token for him to remember me by. I enter one of the rooms with a desk and grab some stationery. Retrieving the lipstick that matches my nail color from my purse, I generously apply it to my lips and press them against the paper. Placing the paper on his T-shirt on the valet, I take a deep breath and exit the room. Then, like I was taught long ago, I walk out the door, not daring to look back.

∾

It's three in the morning. The hotel where Nik is staying is within walking distance of my apartment, but I still call the car service to pick me up. When I arrive, I immediately go to my room, take off my clothes, run a hot bath, and soak. I am, in every sense, sore, satiated, and spent.

Following my bath, it doesn't take long for me to succumb to exhaustion and fall asleep. Later, my internal clock calls me to open my eyes before the alarm sounds. I glance at the clock to see it's almost six. This is around the time that Parker gets ready for work. I miss him, and our connection forces me to pick up my phone.

"Wakey-wakey," I say in my most cheerful voice and stifle a laugh as I watch him over FaceTime. He props himself up on his pillow and combs his fingers through his thick hair. He's so cute when he's grumpy.

"Rain. What are you doing?" His voice is low and rough.

"Calling you before you call me."

"It's too early. I would have called you in—." Parker turns to look at his clock, and I finish his sentence as usual.

"Three minutes." He closes his eyes, shakes his head, and sighs.

"You're up too early to be on holiday. I'm assuming you found some trouble to get into after I talked to you?"

"I did." My response is nonchalant, contrary to what I feel.

"Well, you'll have to fill me in later. How'd you fare this morning?"

"Not too bad. Anticipating a call with you helps quiet my mind."

"I would do anything to relieve you from going through this. But we talked about a potential solution you've yet to explore. Let me help you."

Parker suggested years ago that I seek therapy to help cope with my condition. I said no out of fear. Fear of opening old wounds, of finding out who I really am, who I could have been if I had sought help sooner. If I'm going to fix myself, I'll do it one step at a time. I'm a good attorney. My upcoming meeting is my opportunity to demonstrate how good I am which is the best place to start.

Parker's alarm blares in the background. He reaches over and shuts it off. "I need to get in the shower."

"Full schedule?"

"Court this morning, then several client meetings. You good?" he asks, searching for signs of the alternative.

"Yeah, I'm good."

"Then why don't you try and get some more rest and then find yourself some breakfast later."

"I will. I just called to see you, hear your voice, and say I miss you. And, of course, I like to think I'm a better alarm clock than that evil thing beside your bed."

"There's nothing better than waking up to you. Now get off the phone so I can get ready."

"I love you, Parker Page Esquire. Always."

"Love you too, Rain. I gotta go. Bye."

One of the many things I love about Parker is that he always knows what I need. Getting a little extra sleep before heading to breakfast is the right move. Especially after having Nik last night and again this morning, my body needs a quick dose of carbs and a shot of coffee.

Rummaging through my purse for lipstick, I find the flyer the woman in pink gave me for the new restaurant opening. It's around the corner from the apartment building, and I decide to walk there for breakfast.

When I arrive, I'm delighted to find that the restaurant has a modern rustic vibe. Near the back of the restaurant is a long white marble counter with glass cake displays containing a variety of treats, where people can sit and eat or have coffee. The worn grey teak tables scattered around the restaurant with leather-wrapped metal seating give it a slick feel. Along one wall is a series of booths for more intimate dining. The restaurant smells like cake, cinnamon, coffee, and everything tempting me to buy them makes my mouth water.

The server takes me to a table and gives me a menu. A wide variety of options make it difficult to choose, but I settle on eggs Benedict, an almond croissant, and a latte. While waiting for my order, I get out my phone and review the list I made of Seattle sightseeing options. Today's agenda will focus on the African diaspora. As I decide on each event, I double-check online to see if they're open and map out the day.

It doesn't take long for the server to return with my meal. The food is artfully arranged on the plate, so I position my phone, snap a picture, and text it to Parker.

Me: Took your suggestion, got some rest, and now I'm having this.

I glance at my watch. It's past eight. I realize that Parker is likely occupied with a court appearance or a meeting when I don't receive an immediate reply. I've witnessed his impressive performance in court, where he commands the room with his presence and exudes power when addressing the bench. The deep timbre in his voice while articulating his case is quite alluring. I attempt to take a picture of the restaurant to share with Parker when a tall figure catches my eye. I set my phone down when I realize it's…Nik?

When he enters the restaurant, he immediately spots me and walks toward my table. He's wearing dark-washed jeans, a long-sleeved sky-blue Henley, and a wide grin like the cat that ate the cream, and I know why.

"You didn't get very far," he says, then leans down and presses his lips to mine. Then, as if he's my man, he sits beside me. "What are we having?"

CHAPTER 10

You Don't Know Me

Noah

Even wearing a look of surprise mixed with irritation, Rain is gorgeous.

"I'm having breakfast. And I wasn't trying to get away from anything. Or anyone for that matter."

"Good." I break off a piece of her croissant and pop it in my mouth. Her eyebrows furrow, and she gives me an "I know you didn't" look. "Don't look at me like that. We're having breakfast."

"You missed the part where I said, *I'm* having breakfast. Besides, we don't know each other like that."

"Hmm. I beg to differ."

"Begging seems to be your default setting," she says, and I can't help but chuckle.

"Only with you. But I'm just saying we're past the point of being new, considering we've had dinner and drinks. And…as I recall, I had you for dessert. Remember the part where you came on my face calling my name? I'd say that quantifies how well I know you."

"You're—."

"Having breakfast with you." I eye the server heading toward the table. She knows who I am because, unbeknownst to Rain, I own this building and the one with the restaurant from last night. Before she reaches the table, I lift my index finger to stop her and tip my head toward Rain's plate. Understanding my request, she swiftly turns and heads towards the kitchen. Rain shakes her head, having witnessed the scene. She picks up her utensils and resumes eating. She may as well settle down. She's having breakfast with me this morning.

"I'm not going to ask what that was about. Because what I really want to know is, what are you doing here, Nik?"

"I thought we'd established that."

"After that. We only agreed to one night. Nothing more. That was the deal. You should have turned around and walked back out the door the second you saw me sitting here, but you didn't."

"I didn't want to."

"And I didn't peg you for a man that has the same meal more than once," she tells me, and she's right.

The women I have been with knew it was only for the sex. I made my intentions clear from the start. No dinners, no dates, no tomorrows. That way, no one thought there was a chance of a relationship with me. But something shifted when I watched Rain come beneath me last night. I felt something I couldn't describe when she called my name, and I want to feel that again. And when I tasted her, she tasted like honey, cream, and…more. More kisses. More sex. More time to experience everything Rain. Even now, my dick twitches at the thought of tasting her again.

"I've never had a meal like you."

The server returns with a plate of eggs Benedict and coffee, and sets it on the table. "Is there anything else I can get for you?" she asks. I gesture to Rain.

"The check," Rain says.

I look at the server and shake my head. "We're good. I'll signal you if we need anything else," I say, and she leaves.

"So, what do you want, Nik?"

"To have breakfast with Rain," I say. I cut into my meal and eat.

The food here is exemplary—I should know. This is the third restaurant they've opened in one of my buildings. I look at Rain and raise my eyebrow. She continues eating breakfast. We sit in silence for a moment while eating our meal. She's cute and carefree as she eats. I watch as she dips a piece of croissant in the yolk that runs onto her plate, and I wonder what she's thinking—besides the fact that I'm annoying her. Her lips are perfect, and I want to pull her into my arms and kiss her. That's when I'm certain I need to have her again.

"Spend the day with me."

She puts down her knife and fork. "What?"

"You heard my brothers on the call yesterday. I'm off for a few days. Spend the day with me."

She throws her head back and laughs, and I smile because her laugh is spontaneous and carefree. It reminds me of how she was with her friend on the call at the bar.

"What's wrong with you, Nik, without a C?"

"I'm still trying to figure that out. You. I suppose." I don't hide the truth. She continues to laugh, and I find myself feeling slightly agitated. Not agitated at her laughter, but because I'm losing control over the situation. I'm used to being in control. To having the upper hand. Used to power.

"You really don't get it," she finally says after she composes herself. I raise an eyebrow. "Nik, come on. When you first sat down, I said you don't know me like that. You said—."

I put up my hand to stop her because she can recite everything I've said since I met her. "I know what I said."

"But you're not listening to what I'm saying. I said you don't know me like that. I meant it. First, you walk in like you own the place—which, if I'm reading the room right from yesterday's dinner and today's interaction with the server—you either do or you know whoever does. Then you walk in here and kiss me like you're my man."

"It was a bit more than chaste, I'll admit. But you know from last night's experience that the kiss would have ended entirely differently if I were your man."

"That's beside the point. You assumed I wasn't meeting anyone here and proceeded to order breakfast. Do you even care whether I need to go to work following breakfast? What if I have a man waiting for me somewhere?"

"There's no way you have a man after the things I did to you last night," I say, realizing I need to rein myself in before I send her running out the door. What is it with this woman?

"Don't be Nik with a D," she says, then puts her napkin on the table. "Oh, by the way, the N is silent," she adds, and I can see she's on the verge of walking away. Fuck. Not again. I take her hand.

"Okay. I get it. You're right. I know nothing about you besides how good you feel in my arms." I want to say beneath me, but I'm doing my best to keep her here. "We agreed last night not to talk about personal things. And before you say it, I get that's not an excuse for what I said." I pause, carefully considering what to say next. Once again, I settle on the truth. "But it's rare for me to have free time, and I've never asked a woman to spend the day with me before. So, if you're available, I'd like to spend more time with you today. I'll leave you to fill in the blanks with any information that helps me understand how feasible that is." I feel more like I'm negotiating a business deal than a date.

"I'm not from Seattle, Nik. There's nothing for us following last night."

"Can you tell me how long you'll be here?"

"I fly out Monday," she says, and I feel hopeful that if not tonight, I'll get at least one more night with her. Because one night with Rain wasn't enough.

"Monday. Okay." I can work with that.

"Yes, and for the record, I'm not seeing anyone. If I'm with a guy, I'm with him—I don't cheat. I recently ended a relationship with a guy who cheated on me. And I'm not looking to jump into another relationship right now." Rain takes her hand out of mine, picks up her croissant, tears a piece off, and eats it. I detected a hint of pain in her voice when she said a guy cheated on her, and my instinct is to hunt him down and smash his face. But I don't tell her. Instead, I school my expression and nod in acknowledgment.

"Still sharing?" I ask, and she breaks off another piece of croissant. This one she holds to my lips, and like a peace offering, I eat from her hand.

CHAPTER II

Warning Label

Raven

I PUT A PIECE OF THE CROISSANT TO HIS LIPS. HE EATS IT, THEN licks the fragments of flakes from my fingers. The way he sucks my fingers, like he's savoring them, sends a shiver through me. I squeeze my thighs.

"Nik. What are you doing?"

"You have a habit of asking me to explain myself."

"Only when I want you to experience your bad boy actions through my lens."

He smirks, then says, "I just licked croissant off skin that's smooth as silk, and now I'm going to kiss a mouth that tastes like berries." When he's done, he cups the back of my head, dips his face, and kisses me in a display of affection that can get us arrested. He's salty, sweet, and warm, and the way he's sucking my tongue has my sex pulsing. Pulling away is my only option in the heat of the moment because I'll lose myself in him if I don't.

"Nik." My voice is barely audible.

"I love it when you say my name all sultry and flustered. The things you do to my body. Good god, Rain," he says, taking my hand and showing me by placing it in his lap.

"A man like you should come with a warning label," I tell him.

"You don't need a label if you don't plan to venture into danger. Otherwise, what's the point? Do you have to work today?"

"You don't give up." I sigh. "I'm on holiday this week, working my way through a list of tourist attractions in Seattle." A slow smile forms on his face, and I can see the wheels turning like he's hatching a plan. Then his eyes briefly shift from me, he gestures with his chin, and I watch as our server rushes to the table.

"Did you need anything else, sir?" she eagerly inquires.

"No. Thank you. Just clear this." he tells her. She is joined by another person, and within seconds, our entire table is clear of dishes, cleaned, and the servers have disappeared into the kitchen.

"Before you ask what I'm doing, I have a plan."

"At this point, I'm afraid to ask."

"What's on the top of your list?"

Reluctantly, I open my phone and pull up my list. "There's a lot of things on the list, but these are at the top. City Tour of Seattle, Mount Rainier, African diaspora experiences, Space Needle, Jazz Alley Supper Club, and Seattle Harbor during the day or an evening sail."

"I'll arrange it, and we'll do everything together."

"What are you talking about, Nik?"

"All you have to do is say yes. I'll make all the arrangements." Nik looks at me with the same interest and excitement from last night, and I wonder if this is what he's like when he takes on new projects.

But that's my fear. I don't want to be someone's project like something that needs fixing, and in the end, when everything is resolved and goals are met, everyone goes their separate ways. My life is a mess as it is, and I still have a lot of unresolved things to work through. Family issues, my co-dependency with Parker. The things I need to say to him but haven't.

Yeah, I'm a broken mess with too many wounds that Band-Aids alone can't mend, and there are some things I just can't fix. Things too difficult to talk about. Maybe that's why I can't solidify my relationships. Perhaps I'm self-sabotaging them—I don't know. But I don't want to feel like a project that needs fixing. I don't want to be the thing left behind after it's over when everyone brushes their hands together and goes, "Well, that's done," and walks away.

"No, nothing good can come out of this," I tell him, and before I can say more, his expression goes flat. He holds my gaze and pinches his chin. I think he's pissed. His back stiffens and I track his movements as he puts an arm around my seat, the other on the table, and faces me.

"Rain, I want to have an honest conversation with you about what I'm asking. Let's strip our emotions and talk. It sounds like you've been through a rough patch recently, but the guy who hurt you is a coward. I'm not him. I'm unsure if you're saying no because you're scared or don't want to enjoy our connection. The kiss we just shared leads me to believe you want more than one night, and I feel the same. Tell me right now if I'm wrong, and I'll walk away, and you'll never see me again. However, if you're scared, there's no need to be. I would never intentionally hurt you, and in fact, while you're with me, I'll do everything in my power to protect you. I get that you're not looking for a new relationship, and I'm not asking for that. I'm simply suggesting that we spend this week together and enjoy each other's company without any strings attached. So, talk to me, Rain. Tell me what you're thinking."

Nik's willingness to walk away shows he's in negotiation mode. The playful player is gone and replaced with a "we're making a deal" guy. I need to pay attention so I understand what I'm getting into. Because I don't want to get hurt again. Blake was showing me the signs of who he was, but I wasn't paying attention, and he was too much of a coward to reveal his true self—Nik's right. I'm scared. The brief taste I had of him scares me, and I fear that at the end of the week, I won't be able to walk away. I'm attracted to the power that Nik wields. The command and the confidence that he conveys are my catnip. Because only this type of man can withstand me. It's the same things that attracted me like a magnet to Parker. However, with Nik, I feel drawn to the excitement of challenging him in unexpected ways. The feeling I get when I do something that stops him in his tracks is contagious. It feels like I'm giving him something he doesn't know he needs.

"You're right. I'm rebounding from something that has me questioning my choices. Last night didn't help—I'm not one of those women you're used to, Nik. It was hard enough after what we did for me to walk away and forget. Because unlike everybody else, I don't forget anything. And sometimes, my thoughts and feelings get blurred, and unfortunately, I don't come with a reset button."

"Then we'll set boundaries for the week: at any point, you can walk away if it gets too much," he says it like it's a tap that I can turn the knob and shut off.

"That's easier said than done, but the best I can do is try," I say, sensing his relief as he hangs on my words. I decide to lay down some guard rails. "If we do this, we'll go by Nik and Rain, no last names. No talk about work."

"I may have to step away for…."

"For work? Yeah, I do, too—that's a given. No compromising our work. We both have real lives outside of this…whatever *this* is. Like before, what we share between us is sex, no feelings. We return to our lives on Monday and never see each other again."

"Seems reasonable." The way he says it, I can't tell whether he's placating me because walking away is so easy for him. He doesn't know he's not unique. I've known men like him. I learned from the best. If I have to drown myself in painful memories to get through it…to lose myself in order to walk away first, I won't hesitate.

"This is already hard enough for me, Nik. You asked me to tell you what I was thinking. When it's over, you can't just come to find me and claim me like I belong to you. You can't continue to delay the inevitable. We have to walk away. You have to let me go."

"Rain, the last thing I expected walking in the door was to find you here. Same as yesterday. I don't hunt for women, but I also can't pretend I'm not happy you're here. Because I want another night with you. And knowing you're here until Monday, I want all those nights and days with you. With that in mind, I have some things to add."

"I'm listening."

"If we do this, we share the same bed every night."

"What? That's ridiculous. We need some level of separation."

"No, Rain. That's not part of the deal. You'll pack your things when we leave this restaurant and come with me," he instructs, and I don't see that coming from the man with no tomorrows.

"Nik, that's not a good idea. We can't just—."

"It's non-negotiable, Rain. If we do this, I have all of you or none of you. You can walk away now if you don't want that."

Contemplating my response, I extend my hand and lightly tap my fingers on the table one by one. Spending a week in Seattle with my sister before diving into the biggest meeting of my career seemed like the perfect solution to reconnect and recover from a breakup with my cheating ex. Having a one-night stand with a sexy green-eyed god whose magic mouth offers more than a sexy British accent wasn't part of the plan. Now he wants more time. Six more days. What's the worst that can happen?

"Okay, Nik. Anything else?"

"You'll provide me with your list, and I'll arrange all the activities. You don't spend so much as a dime during our time together."

"You're making it seem like we're a couple."

"Well, technically, you have met my brothers. For this week, I suppose that's what we are. This brings me to my last condition. You have to stop saying no just to goad me. Only say it when you mean it."

"No."

"Rain," he growls. He grabs my wrist and pulls me toward him. "This is what I'm talking about. You're just saying it to push my buttons. I promise I'll never ask you for something you can't give or would not be willing to give. So, only say no when you mean it. That reminds me— we're a couple without drama," he says finally.

When I think he's done, I push away from him and reach for my purse. He grabs my wrist.

"What are you doing?" he asks.

"Making a warning label."

CHAPTER 12

A Day with Rain

Noah

SEATTLE IS KNOWN FOR ITS RAINY DAYS—OVER FORTY PERCENT OF our days are filled with rain. So, it's ironic to ask for a day with a woman named Rain and even more surprising that I get to spend the week with her. Like yesterday, any day with Rain is a good day.

It doesn't take long for us to collect our things. I packed mine before heading to breakfast. Rain chose to meet me in the lobby of the Four Seasons. She didn't disclose where she was staying, but it doesn't matter. For the next five nights, Rain is staying with me at my new lake house.

I'm waiting to welcome her as she enters the lobby, and her presence immediately catches the attention of other patrons. She has donned the perfect outfit for our outing: oversized beige slacks, a black belt accentuating the waist I want to hold, and a graphic T-shirt paying homage to Jimi Hendrix. As I approach her, I need to bend down to greet her with a kiss since she's wearing Converse instead of her heels. This woman is beautiful, and my attraction to her is magnetic. I constantly have to keep myself from touching her, but I can't. Palming her butt, I pull her into me, and I know she can feel hard evidence of how much I want her.

She pulls back and looks up at me. "Wow. Miss me much?"

"Something like that. Let's get your things in the car," I tell her. A hotel staff member follows us out and loads her things into the car awaiting us.

Rain wanted to get a sense of the African diaspora in Seattle. There aren't many of us here, but like everywhere, lay traces of our fingerprints as our people sweep across the land where many of our ancestors have settled.

Seattle is where my father was born. It's the reason he worked so hard to get back here and reestablish roots. He wanted a place for his sons to call home and continue growing branches on the tree of his father and forefathers. As for me—it took a while, but I get it. I understand how our community issues stem from our diaspora constantly being ripped away from our homes. I've experienced this. It's why I give back to my community. To create jobs, so families like mine aren't forced to leave to pave a better way somewhere else. I partner with organizations to purchase land for the African diaspora community, so our people can have access to homes with cheaper rent, retail space, and the things needed to build their own legacy. That's why I work so hard—not just for me, but for others like me. But in the process, I've given up things, too. Like creating close bonds with people outside my immediate family. Like building my own family. Like creating a space to call home.

I turn toward Rain, the woman whose presence profoundly affects me, making me reflect on my life. I could spend the rest of the week providing her with the whole Pacific Northwest African diaspora experience, but her time is limited—her list is long. Compromising, I'll condense her day to the things she highlighted and add in a few things I think she should experience.

Our drive to the Central District takes us through a neighborhood of mature tree-lined streets filled with homes clad with siding of every color. The sun shining through the trees casts shadows on the road, and as we drive, the view from the window becomes a hypnotic wave of light and shadow. I watch Rain as she takes in the scene.

Our first stop is the Northwestern African American Museum. When we arrive at the three-story red brick former Colman school building, the parking lot is almost empty due to the early hour. The driver pulls alongside the smaller outer building to the right to let us out. When I help Rain from the vehicle, she hands me her phone and walks away from the building toward the spiraling concrete path that forms the shape of a guitar in the middle of the park.

"Take my photo in front of Jimi," she calls over her shoulder as she cuts across the center of the park through the grass toward a free-flowing lavender and purple metal art installation. By the time I finish giving instructions to the driver, Rain is halfway through Jimi Hendrix Park adjacent to the building. When I finally catch up, she's posing, one hand on hip, in front of the installation constructed in Jimi Hendrix's likeness, waiting for me.

Rain is a beautiful mix of entertaining and adorable as she strikes several poses, first a peace sign, then an air guitar, and like the dutiful photographer, I capture each moment on her phone.

She reaches her hand out. "You want me to take a picture of you?" I shake my head. Not because I don't want to document the moment, but because I live discreetly. There's no reason to keep random pictures of myself.

"Let's go in," I tell her, taking her hand and leading her up the concrete path to the entrance of the building. The discreet purple and white museum logo alongside the words Northwest African American Museum is the only thing that provides a glimpse into the building's purpose. "This is a historic building."

"A former school, right?"

"That's right. It was the first school in Seattle to accept black students while also hiring black teachers. After years of being deserted, this building fell into disrepair. Then, this group took it over, and it was the longest occupation of a building in the US. It lasted about ten years."

"That's a long time." She's right. The lengths our people need to go to stay in our community and maintain a piece of land in America is heartbreaking.

"It is. It's because of them, their defiance, that our people were able to maintain control of this property."

"It's such a beautiful building," she says. She's right. The bones, the structure, and the location are perfect.

There are so many things I want to share with Rain about my connection to this building, but I can't. We agreed not to talk about personal or business things, or all of the things that would matter if she were my woman. So, I don't tell her that my company makes annual donations to the museum or that we sponsored exhibitions in the past. I don't share that the owners of the Black-owned architectural firm that designed the museum are friends of mine. I can't tell her any of the things I'd like to share, but it feels surprisingly good to have her here. To have her see this amazing place.

I open the door. "Ready?"

"Ready."

We walk into the bright, airy, off-white foyer with high industrial ceilings and a large purple and white NAAM logo hanging like art above the entrance. I follow her past the NAAM welcome wall label, through the double metal doors, and into a dimly lit, long, narrow, industrial putty-colored hall. Rain's eyes go back and forth as she takes in the forty-foot wall lined with photos, mementos, and stories documenting the journey of people of African descent who helped build the Pacific Northwest.

"I have no idea which direction to start," she says, standing in front of a monitor playing a welcome video.

"We can head in this direction," I say, gesturing to the right. "These walls tell the history of our people making their mark in the Pacific Northwest. Then we can make our way back down the hall to the other side where the stories continue."

Watching Rain while she walks the hall, scanning the walls and consuming knowledge of our people, is satisfying and sensual at the same time. Knowing that she'll remember these stories, these people, this place, this moment forever feels…powerful. She's a combination of beauty and brilliance that has me captivated.

"I had no idea the number of people whose names I recognize on these walls have come through Seattle," she says.

"Eye-opening, right?"

"Every city I visit, I learn something new and inspiring about our people."

"Because we weren't taught our history in schools unless we were fortunate enough to have teachers that looked like us."

"Yeah, there's a group of people out there trying to erase and rewrite our history. The color of my skin…our skin, tells the story of colonization. We're living proof of a past that can't be erased. We are survivors." Her voice rings with conviction.

I take Rain's hand, lace our fingers, bring her fingertips to my lips, and kiss them. Her hands are delicate and her skin is soft. I flip our hands and reveal the similarity of our skin tones. She's so lovely.

"No, Rain. They can't erase us."

That's why my brothers and I give a portion of our profits to organizations dedicated to preserving our community and its culture. But Rain will never know that about me. She'll never know about the hundreds of interns we hire from within our community to provide them opportunities to learn from the best in the business. She'll never know that my money isn't just spent on fancy dinners, fast cars, and frivolous interests.

Instead, we wander into another room containing a special art exhibition of women's portraits, allowing me to take in the only woman I want to see…Rain. I can't seem to get enough of her. She crosses her arms in front of her and tips her head to the side in a way that is seductive as she studies a piece of art. I walk up behind her as she looks at the mixed-media portrait of a woman with an afro adorned with pearls and other adornments. I dip my nose into her neck, inhale her essence, and kiss her skin. If this woman were mine, I'd bite the piece of skin between her neck and shoulder and mark her, letting the world know she belongs to me. But Rain isn't mine, so I don't.

"Not interested in her?" she asks, pointing to the portrait.

"Not in the least. I'm more interested in you and trying hard not to pull you into the restroom and take you against the wall." She reaches behind her and places her hand on me, finding hard proof.

"You need to put this thing on a leash. We still have more to see."

"Be careful," I growl in her ear. "You already have it on a tight leash if you haven't noticed. And if you keep touching me like that, the leash will break."

Rain surprises me when she turns in my arms, pulls my face to hers, and kisses me. She opens her mouth to receive my tongue. I lick down into her, and she tastes like warm caramel sauce on a sundae, and I want to strip her clothes and devour her. Breaking the kiss, I take her by the hand and fast walk towards the entrance, pulling her behind me.

"Wait," she calls out, but I don't stop walking. I can't.

"That's not our word," I say as we continue toward the door.

I keep walking until we're outside. As soon as the driver sees me, he opens the car door. I help Rain into the car and slide in beside her. Inside the car, I slip my hand into hers, but I don't speak; I don't pull her onto my lap like I want because if I do, I won't be able to control my urge to be deep inside her. Instead, I maneuver my phone and play "Angel" by Jimi Hendrix and let that play in the background as we ride. The six minutes it takes to get to my lake house are painful as my body craves her.

When we arrive at the house, I ask the driver to leave our things inside the foyer. Quickly, I help Rain out of the car, press the code for the entryway, and lead her through the courtyard, to the front door, and into the house. I don't stop to give her a tour; I take her to the bedroom, shut the door, and cage her against the wall with my hands on either side of her.

"I meant what I said back there. Now, take off your clothes."

Rain is silent while she undoes her slacks. She stares at me with a look of satisfaction wrapped in a slow smile that I want to lick off. Instead, I dip my nose into her neck and suck and lick while she removes her underwear and slips out her shoes. I lean back, giving her space to remove her T-shirt and bra while I pull a condom from my wallet and throw the wallet on the bed. Then I unzip my pants, freeing my raging cock, and cover it. Rain bites her lips, and I capture her mouth in mine, thrusting my tongue in and capturing hers, and I suck like she's giving me life. Slipping my fingers between her folds to test her readiness, I'm not surprised to find her drenched. In a swift move, I lift her against the wall, position my raging steel between her legs, and sink right into her. She gasps. It's hard, rough, feral, but her body sucks me in with greed, and I pump into her while her body keeps in time with each thrust.

"Oh god, Nik. Ahh. Nik." Rain screams my name, coming hard and fast around my shaft as I slam into her.

"That's it. Give it all to me," I tell her as I continue thrusting through her release. The look of pleasure on her face only makes my dick turn to stone, and I relentlessly increase the pressure pumping into her.

"No," she says, and I freeze mid-thrust.

"Rain, are you asking me to stop?" I watch her face, and her eyes fly open with surprise.

"It's just so much. I don't think I can come again."

"Do you want me to stop?"

"What? No. Don't stop."

"I promise you can handle this, and you will come again. This time with me," I tell her. Slowly moving in and out of her, I gradually increase the pace until the room is filled with the sound of my body crashing into hers. And this time, when she comes, it's to the sound of me calling her name as we find our release together.

As good as it felt taking Rain against the wall, we aren't done. We finally make it to the bed, where I ravish her body and taste her from head to toe before we finally make it to the shower, where I take her again.

Rain's body is addicting, but I need to give her a break, or we'll end up spending the day in bed—she's that amazing. So, I give her space to finish getting ready while I go to my office and check my messages.

Just like he said, my brother Mak has things under control. So, there's nothing for me to handle except a reminder from Jewel that I haven't sent her my receipts so she can process our expenses for the month.

The last time I was late, she reminded me that the head of finance reported to me and that I was setting a bad example. I can't argue with that. I take out my wallet, pulling out the bits of folded paper I've stashed there. Unfolding them, I come across the receipt from the bar where I met Rain last night. I don't know why I kept the receipt other than I found it intriguing that she took the time to doodle a heart alongside the word "thanks." What kind of woman does that? Certainly not the type I'm used to.

Maybe it was meant for me to find, or perhaps it was for the bartender because that's just how Rain is—thoughtful. Anyway, I kept that and the Four Seasons' stationery with imprints of her luscious lips wearing the same color I kissed off her that night. That was the night she left me craving her body. It's my first time wanting a woman for more than one night.

I continue pulling out receipts, snapping pictures, and forwarding them to Jewel when I come across the warning label Rain made for me on the back of the restaurant flyer.

Sitting beside her, I remember thinking this woman had a way of walking out on me to the point where I wanted to handcuff her to me whenever she was around. So, I pulled her into me amidst her goading me, but she pushed me off and reached for her purse.

"What are you doing?" I asked.

"Making a warning label."

Rain took out a pen and a small flyer. She turned the paper over and began to write.

"You're serious," I said.

She continued writing while I took advantage of the time to stare at her, taking in everything that was her. Her delicate hands. The natural glow of her skin. Her kissable lips. She's beautiful outside and in. And she's utterly unaffected by me, and it's refreshing. People tend to be intimidated by me. By how I carry myself, how I talk, and my status. Not Rain. When she was done writing, she held up the flyer and read it to me.

"Warning. High voltage. Caution: contents hot. Here, I drew five chili peppers to represent how spicy hot you are—no scratch that…ten." She briefly flashed the paper at me to see before she laid it back on the table. I leaned in to see what she was doing. Alongside the pictures of chili peppers, she drew five more. She picked up the paper again and continued reading. "There. Ten chili peppers. All objects are absolutely larger than they appear. Lastly, and this is the most important Nik, I'm including an NC-17 – Adults Only warning."

I laughed at the last one and she smiled at me.

"Should I continue?"

"No. I get the point," I told her. She handed me the paper, telling me I needed to always keep it on me. Then I kissed her.

I open my office drawer and put in the mementos except for the warning label, which I return to my wallet. Then I head back to the bedroom, sit on the edge of the bed, and wait for Rain to finish dressing.

"You have anything in this place to eat?" she asks, stepping into a strapless lightweight denim dress that's fitted at the waist and then flares at the bottom. She stands between my legs while I sit at the bed's edge. "Zip this, please." She turns her back to me. I zip her, turn her around, pull her into me, put my face to her stomach, and inhale. I need to be careful because being with Rain is more dangerous than having a sweet tooth.

"Let's have a snack, and then I'll take you on a tour around the house so you can familiarize yourself. But we need to leave soon. I have a few other places to take you to before we head to the restaurant. So, save space for dinner."

"Where are we going to eat?"

"I made reservations at a place from your list that I'm sure you'll love."

"Please tell me it's Communion."

"It is."

CHAPTER 13

He's the Type of Guy

Raven

Whenever I explore a new city, I like to understand the legacy our people left behind. Through mediums such as art, music, food, or plays, I get a glimpse into the lives of those who came before me. Following our visit to the Northwest African American Museum, Nik took me home and ravished me, reminding me how good he makes my body feel. Then afterward, he gave me a brief tour of the lake house.

His house is spectacular and the ultimate display of pure modern design. The walls, floors, ceiling, and all the surfaces are bright white and sleek. The picturesque windows overlooking the crystal blue lake are framed in black and make the view pop. The interior is three levels that all have a front row view of the lake. Two patios snake their way through a lush green landscape, past a vibrant blue pool, down several more levels to the boat launch. I can envision elaborate parties hosted poolside or intimate dinner parties in the house. I have a feeling that when this week is up, I will miss this place. It feels like home.

Nik tells me about the owner, her life, and how he found this home. Staring at him, I see a man unlike the version of Nik I experienced at the bar. This is a side of Nik that seems to be looking for something deeper, and I wonder why he's hiding behind the player façade. But I suppose that's none of my business, since this is all temporary.

Because Nik lined up a lot of activities for me, our tour of the house is brief. After the tour, Nik takes me uptown to the Seattle Center to the Seattle Repertory Theater to see the archway and walkway constructed in honor of August Wilson, the playwright.

Although the sun is shining and the temperature is unusually warm for Seattle, the streets are cool due to the shade provided by the trees lining the block. I keep forgetting that the amount of rain this city gets annually contributes to the trees being so lush and green. I grab Nik's hand, and we walk around to the side of the building to see what he wants to show me.

"This is the August Wilson Way portal," he says with pride as we stand in front of what looks like a freestanding oversized doorway that's been weathered with time. It seems strangely out of place, unattached to a building, outside amongst the trees at the start of a path. Attached to it is a wide faded-red-painted door that stands slightly ajar. Instead of looking through a glass window on the door, there is a faded black and white picture of August Wilson wearing a suit with his arms folded across his chest. It's a bit whimsical and surreal at the same time.

It looks exactly like a photo I saw online, and I'm reminded of a quote I came across while researching his work. "I believe in the American theatre. I believe in its power to inform about the human condition, I believe in its power to heal, 'to hold the mirror as 'twere up to nature,' to the truths we uncover, to the truths we wrestle from uncertain and sometimes unyielding realities."

"Take a picture of me in this doorway." I shove my phone into Nik's hand before I pull away from him, stand under the archway, and strike a pose.

"Did you know his mother wanted him to be an attorney?" he asks, unaware of the irony in his question.

I hold my finger up in a peace sign. Then I fold my arms and strike a pose like August. "Yeah, I read about that. It's a good thing he had a mind of his own, or we wouldn't have so many well-written poignant plays by him."

"I agree. His plays hit home for me in so many ways. Do you have a favorite?"

"I've only seen a few, but yeah. *Radio Golf.* It has so many layers that I can relate to. Politics and law versus passion and friendship versus family. So many things resonate with me. I think he was saving the best for last with this play. How about you?"

"Same. *Radio Golf* is my favorite, maybe for different reasons. Particularly the issues with city redevelopment and gentrification impacting the Hill District in the story. Later today, I'm taking you back to the Central District. What happened to Seattle's Central District almost parallels August's story in *Radio Golf.*"

"I can't wait to visit. Did you see the play live on stage?"

"No. I read it in school. Do you have a favorite line?"

"Yeah, quite a few, actually. But one in particular hit me hard. When Hammond finally realized that he had to do the right thing by Old Joe and said, 'You got to have rule of law. Otherwise it would be chaos.' For some reason, it made me cry. Maybe it was the poignancy of August's words capturing the reality of the African diaspora, or it could have just been how the actor delivered his line, perhaps all of the above—something about it touched me. What was yours?"

"When Old Joe says, 'They got fried chicken.'"

I swat Nik on the arm, and we both break out in a hysterical laugh.

"You're so smooth. Anyway. I love his work. Thanks for bringing me here. This is a nice spot."

"Yeah, it's peaceful here. Sometimes, we have to step outside the daily grind to appreciate the creativity of others and…life."

A woman walks past, pushing a dog in a baby basket. I raise my eyebrows to Nik. He shrugs, then puts his arm around my shoulder. We walk down a path that eventually opens into a park with a view of the Space Needle in the background. Nik and I walk on the grass and sit and watch as kids play at a fountain near the edge of the park. It's hard to believe I just met this man—he's so easy to be around.

"This is a nice park, Nik. We could have had a picnic here."

"We could have." His voice is sullen.

I look at him curiously. "What? Not your thing?"

"You know I'm not that guy," he says, but I press anyway.

"Not that guy to do it or didn't think of it?"

"Both."

"What kind of guy are you?"

"This kind." He holds me in his arms, lays my back on the grass, dips his head, and kisses me senselessly. I get lost in the moment with the echo of kids playing in the distance, the smell of fresh cut grass, the sound of water spraying from the fountain, and the warmth of Nik's body at my side, the taste of him. It all feels so perfect.

His hand starts to edge toward the hem of my dress, but he stops, breaks the kiss, and stares at me, eyes blazing with desire. He knows he's on the brink of going too far. He wants me, and I want him too, but this is not the place.

"You're so beautiful," he says. He dips his face and nuzzles his nose in my neck, and I sense he's pacing himself, calming down before he loses control again.

I lift my hand and rub it on his head, feeling the texture of his hair that's too short to grip. Yeah, Nik. You think you're not that guy, but you are, I say to myself and smile. And we lay like that for the longest time, just enjoying holding each other. It feels natural. That is until I feel something bounce off my head.

"Ow." I touch my head and laugh because I'm not hurt, but startled by the disruption.

"Sorry," two little kids say in unison as they collect the rubber ball beside me and then run off. Nik lifts his head and touches my forehead.

"You okay?"

"I think you need to kiss it better." He dips his head and kisses my lips.

"Well, you are way off the mark, but I guess that'll do."

"Don't worry. I'll be on the mark later." He smiles wryly, then sits up and helps me up in the process.

"Are you okay if we head out now? I still have some things to show you, and I don't want to miss our dinner reservation."

"Sure. Since we're on the August Wilson kick, what do you think about watching *Fences* later tonight with me?"

Nik stands, holds a hand down, and helps me to my feet. He texts the driver, and then we start walking toward the street.

"We can make it a movie night. I'll pop some popcorn," he says.

"Do you even know how to make popcorn? I'm not getting a man who's good in the kitchen vibes from you."

Nik looks down at me and rolls his eyes. "Rain. Come on. Yes. I can make popcorn as well as other things." He pulls me tight.

"Okay. I believe you. Not. You know how the saying goes: the proof is in the pudding. In this case—the popcorn."

"Let's go." He opens the car door, helps me in, and slides in beside me.

Our next stop is back to the Central District. Nik wants me to experience the neighborhood and see the impact of gentrification in Seattle. When the car stops, we are in front of a colorful six-story multi-use building that spans almost half the block. The brick, combined with vibrant orange and purple dropped against beige square cladding, stands out in the mature neighborhood. Across the street are mostly two-story homes with muted-toned siding.

"This was the site of the former Liberty Bank, the first Black-owned bank in the Pacific Northwest. It was opened in response to redlining and general disinvestment in Seattle," Nik tells me.

I can see by the various structures lining the block: stores, restaurants, and houses, that this neighborhood has undergone a lot of transitions over time.

"This building is huge. It looks nothing like the old one-story bank that I saw online."

"Yeah. This is pretty phenomenal, isn't it?" he says. I hear a hint of pride in his voice signaling there's more behind his simple comment that he can't tell me. Since Nik started showing me around today, I get the sense he has strong ties to building a better community for our people.

We walk around the corner and go across the street to get a real sense of the scale of the building. A few older gentlemen are standing to the right of the building, chilling and chatting. I wonder what they're talking about. Maybe they're reminiscing about what happened back in the day or gossiping about who did what yesterday.

Holding Nik by the waist, I watch the scene unfold in front of the building like a movie. Young mothers from the neighborhood pushing strollers greet each other near the restaurant's outdoor seating while the dinner queue gets longer near a metal stand that says, "Wait here to be seated." A guy who's a few shades lighter than me sporting a large, flowy seventies afro is holding the hand of his date, a woman with long, dirty blond hair, as they walk up to the queue. There's a very mixed crowd waiting to get in, and I sense the energy of people excited to break bread together at this place aptly named Communion.

"Are you ready to go in, Rain?"

"Ready." I take his hand in mine.

When we get across the street in front of the restaurant, I'm struck by how vibrant, sexy, and cool the atmosphere is. The patrons are chatting it up, laughing, clinking glasses filled with various colorful liquid libations. Tables are covered with dishes layered in delectable offerings of deviled eggs, greens, and wings, and I already know I have to read the menu to discover all the other things. The smells emanating around the room make my mouth water.

Nik and I are seated by a hostess wearing a summery Limoncello-colored dress at a table near the center of the restaurant with a view of everything. When the hostess leaves, I take a moment to observe the scene before our server appears. Tony! Toni! Toné's "It Feels Good" is jamming as the waitress, whose beautiful brown skin pops against her magenta bob, tells us that the menu can be found online by scanning the QR code on the table.

"Can I get you a drink to start with?" she asks. Her smile is warm and welcoming, and I realize right away that I'm in a place where I belong. Where I can relax and be me.

"Uhm, what do you suggest?"

"Have you been here before?"

"No," I tell her. "It's warm outside. A refreshing cocktail with vodka in it could work."

"I think you'll like 'Hey Auntie.'"

"Hey, Auntie? That sounds cool. What's in it?"

"Vodka, ginger, pear, lime sour."

"We'll take two," Nik says. Then the server tells us she'll give us time to view the menu and will return to take our order.

I can feel Nik watching me with his sexy, bad-boy self, but I'm preoccupied with the restaurant vibe. Doing what I came here to do— seeing just why this place is attracting patrons like a magnet. "Wanna Be Startin' Somethin'" by Michael Jackson is now playing as I watch our waitress go to the bar and have the bartender prepare two salt-rimmed glasses with ice topped off with a slice of lime. He hands her the glasses, and then his attention is drawn to an open window that overlooks the outdoor seating. I see him mouth the words, "I love you, buddy," as he places two fingers over his heart. Looking to see who he's talking to, I see a little brown boy who, by all appearances, looks like he could be his son, wearing a backpack and holding a purple lunch box, leaning over the wooden barrier and waving back. I wonder how lovely it would have been to grow up surrounded by people who care in a neighborhood like this. Then, our waitress passes in front of my view on her way to a glass front refrigerator, where she retrieves two unlabeled bottles that look like lemonade, before returning to our table with the items.

"Have you decided what you want?" she says, setting the items on the table.

"I haven't looked. Nik, did you read the menu, or were you watching—?"

"I got this." He proceeds to order for us, knowing I was too preoccupied. After he orders, I give my sexy companion all my attention.

"As you can see, I'm people-watching."

"I see that. Did you find what you were looking for?" He takes the cap off my bottle, pours the content over the ice in my glass, and then repeats the same with his.

"Yeah. This place, these people, this neighborhood. It says a lot without words. How do we stop this from changing more than it has?"

"You mean cultural displacement? How do we stop high-tech companies from coming in and driving up home pricing when all we really want is better sidewalks, better lighting for safety, and access to light rail transportation? It takes power and money, Rain. People like us with money to invest in a better future for the diaspora. Money to protect these lands, like this building, and secure our future."

"You're right." I take a deep breath. "Without buildings like this, where a group of African American investors purchased property to build something affordable for the community, we suffer the fate many have following the pandemic, where the people returning to retail space don't resemble those who left. People like us. I'm sorry. I don't mean to get too deep." I reach for his hand and he kisses my fingers.

"It's okay. I get it," Nik says as our server returns with a shrimp toast appetizer.

"This looks great." After plating a piece of toast, I cut into it. "You know, this is the first meal we've planned."

"Consider this our first date." Nik lifts his glass and taps it to mine.

"Says the man that doesn't do dates."

"To the woman who is my only exception," he adds, and I hear in his tone that he means it.

I like Nik, but by his own admission, he doesn't do dates, so referring to this as one is confusing. Maybe I should feel privileged that he thinks about me this way. Although I shouldn't read anything into it. In a normal situation, it would be nice to be sharing firsts with someone. Parker and I shared so many firsts, but our situation was different. We were two people on a path to living a life together, to make memories as a couple, that is, until we weren't. Perhaps Parker and I were only meant to be friends. Or…maybe I don't know how to be more. Maybe hooking up with Nik was a mistake?

"Rain." The sound of my name pulls me back into the moment.

"Nik. We said we wouldn't delve into anything personal, but your accent makes me curious how you acquired it." I don't tell him that whenever he opens his mouth to say something, I want to kiss him, which is crazy. I've never been attracted to accents before. Living in San Francisco, full of people following the technology trends, exposes me to others coming to live in the area from all over the world. More than half the people I interact with now have an accent—my former bosses are British.

"I'm British-American. My mum is British. My dad is American. I spent the first twelve years of my life in London."

I'm not surprised to hear him say he was born in London. If we were sharing business information, I would disclose that I worked for Soala Technology's London office after law school. But then I would have to share what led me to London, and that would take me down a rabbit hole of my life with Parker—to uncover secrets long since banished to the back of a drawer with used birthday candles, rubber bands, and broken pencils.

"You'd think you would have lost your accent by now."

"You'd think, but I travel back often—no chance of losing it. You, on the other hand, have a West Coast vibe. When you're not goading me, I can hear it. It's easy yet confident. Something I've only come across with women from Northern California. I'd say San Francisco."

"I'd say you're correct. So, I've met your brothers. Who, I might add, are very handsome. Any sisters?"

"We said no personal."

"Personal, identifiable things. Like I said, I met your beautiful brothers."

"No sisters."

"Which might explain the way you are with women."

"Rain." My name comes out in a controlled breath. I sense he doesn't want to discuss this. "You haven't experienced that side of me to know what I'm like with other women."

"I think I have."

"No, Rain. You haven't."

"I have when you practically dragged me out of the museum and took me against the wall at the lake house."

"Not even close."

"I find that hard to believe, Nik."

He pins me with a stare.

Our server returns with our meals, clears the other dishes, and disappears. I take a sip of my drink. Nik is still eyeing me. I raise an eyebrow, signifying I'm waiting for his response. "Well," I finally say.

"As I said, not even close. I didn't tell you to get on your knees, did I? Because if you were one of those other women, I would have taken you to the restroom and told you to get on your knees. I would never have let you kiss me; I would never have forfeited six minutes of pleasure, which is the time it took to drive to the lake house. I would have never eaten you like cake. And Rain, I certainly wouldn't be here discussing this. So no, you don't know what it's like to be one of those women. And if I'm honest with myself, you never will."

Well, hell. What do I do with this information? When Nik followed me out of the bar, I sensed he was stepping outside himself, but I hadn't realized just how far until now.

"You mentioned kissing me."

"Don't get hung up on this," he warns. "You're a smart woman. You know exactly what I'm saying. The intimacies I've shown you don't extend beyond you. Rain, you're the exception to every rule. So let it go. Accept this." He reaches over, cups my cheek, leans in, and kisses me hard. I'm lost in his kiss until the vibrating of my phone on the table shatters the moment.

"You need to get that?" he whispers against my lips. I pull back and glance at my phone. It's a message from Parker:

Parker: Hey. Just checking in. Got the photo you sent. Hope you're good. If you have time to talk before the morning, call me.

I smile at the message. "No. It's my friend."

"Parker." His name comes out with an irritated punch.

"That shouldn't bother you. Let it go." I use his words. "Back to this dragging me out of the museum. Next time, wait until I'm done with my tour. The wall part was good, though."

"I might make another rule."

"Which is?" I ask, knowingly walking into his bait.

"No PDA because it unleashes something I can't control in me. You should be glad your phone interrupted us." I smirk because he's serious. I've seen what our heated kisses do to him. "But you already know that, don't you, Rain? You know exactly how I'll respond. You know exactly what buttons to push. You're tracking every movement, the twitch of my lip, the lift of a brow. Just how far does this thing you have go? No. Don't answer that. How many people did we pass coming to our table?"

"Eight."

"Wearing blue?"

"Three."

"How many people have you encountered in your life with my scent, Rain?"

"One. You. I can't identify the spice you wear."

"Because it's custom. What did I do the last time I woke up to you, before…before you left me the other night?"

"Before you rolled over on me or after we were done?"

He pauses a second, pondering my question. While he thinks, I take a sip of my drink. "After." The distant look in his eyes tells me he's remembering the moment.

I know the exact moment, the moment it felt like something…more. But I'm unsure how he'll respond when I recite it. In my experience, people say and do what they want, but it's another thing to have someone repeat that back to you. To this day, Parker is the only one that can handle it.

"You sure?"

"I mean what I say."

I take a deep breath. "The aftershock of your release passed from you to me. Your breath was labored, then you growled and said, 'Oh fuck, Rain.' You slid out of me and rolled on your back. Your face was wet with sweat. Your scent, a mix of sweat, amber, musk, and me, lingered in the air around us. Then you looked at the ceiling and rubbed your head like you were trying to wring water out. It seemed like you were trying to figure something out. I don't know what. But then you reached over and pulled me on top of you. I dusted your lips with mine because I love kissing you. You're right—I do it because it drives you wild. You held me and stared at me like you were trying to memorize my face, then—."

"Stop, Rain. Stop. Holy fuck, woman. Are you serious?" I nod in response but don't say a word. I'm not sure if the look on his face is anger, confusion, or something more ominous. When I would repeat things to Blake, he got all freaked out and was angry, so I tried to suppress repeating things he'd said or done. Nik must realize my confusion. "Rain—I didn't mean it like that. It's just...wow."

"There is no shut-off valve for this…thing, Nik. I told you."

Nik pushes a stray curl over my shoulders and brushes his thumb across my cheek. "Rain. You wild, beautiful woman. I swear, I've never met anyone like you before." He dusts his lips across mine. "Ok, new rule. In our short time together, I've figured out a few things you like, and I'm sure I'll learn more. But I need you to promise me you'll say something if I start down the wrong path. I don't care what it is. I want your recollections of our time together to be good. I don't want to figure out after the fact that you don't like something I've said or done. It'll be too late by then, Rain. You would have imprinted those memories. And despite the man I am, how I am—I can't for my life come to terms with doing that to you. You feel me?"

"I feel you." And I feel relieved. But I don't tell him, because despite what he believes about himself, he is the type of guy who considers a woman's feelings. A man who thinks about her needs. He's the type of man I can see myself falling for.

"Seriously. This is the exception when you can put your foot down on something, but not a false positive like when you told me 'no' against the wall."

"Yeah, that one came out wrong." His eyebrows raise. "I mean, it went in right, but I prematurely…well, never mind. You know what I mean. I won't do that again." I shut up before I totally obliterate the moment. But I'm left overcome with how his words reach beneath my skin and hold my heart.

Following dinner, we return to the lake house. Nik and I change into sweats and hang out on one of his many decks overlooking the lake with a drink in hand. Today was the first day I felt like I was on holiday since I arrived in Seattle. Spending the day exploring the museum and walking excursions at different points around the city was enlightening. Even more enlightening has been watching Nik seamlessly navigate the day with me. The brash, bold, entitled version of him is still there, but following our discussion about imprinting things on my memory, he's been a lot less crass. I watch him as he sips his drink. He catches my gaze and holds out a hand, gesturing for me to join him. I sit on his lap, and he wraps his arm tight around my waist.

"Did you have a good day?"

"You caught me reminiscing about it. I'd say it was almost perfect."

"Almost?"

"We still have a movie to watch, and you have some popcorn to make."

"Oh, don't worry. I got you covered," he says. He takes a sip of his drink and then tips the glass for me to sip before placing it on the table beside him. I feel buzzing beneath us, and we both reach into our sweats for our phones. It's not mine. Nik holds his phone up.

"Nik, man. How's it going?" I recognize the voice of his brother Rok on FaceTime. Nik pulls me into his chest and extends his arm.

"Good, man. I'm busy."

"Hey, Rae. Good to see you again. You're a godsend. My brother never looks so relaxed."

"Hi, Rok, with a K. Where's the baby?" I ask, and Rok laughs.

"Safe to say he's still buried in spreadsheets. After that, anything goes."

"Did you actually need something, Rok, or were you just looking for Rain?"

"Actually, I need Nik for a minute, Rae. Will you be okay for a few?"

"Sure thing, Rok. Nik, I'll get the movie cued," I tell him. I wave to Rok before heading indoors.

I make my way to the small sitting room I discovered while wandering the house earlier that doubles as a movie room. I hadn't realized a projector was overhead until Nik pointed it out when he gave me the tour. I pick up a black remote from the table in front of the fireplace and press the button to bring down the movie screen. Once it's down, I scroll through his streaming apps until I find one with *Fences*, and then I position a few throws on the couch before heading upstairs to make myself a drink. Nik comes up behind me while I'm at the kitchen counter, wraps his arms around me, and kisses my neck in a way that feels like we've been doing this all our lives. It's nice. Familiar.

"Is that your favorite spot?" I ask.

"One of them."

"Your big brother is cute."

"That's your response to me kissing you?"

I swallow a smile. "Well, he is."

Nik starts to tickle me, and I try to wiggle free. "Oh, really. Should I let him know you're vibing him?"

"Sure. No. No. Okay," I say to get him to stop, but he continues. "Okay, okay. He's cute, but you, Mister Man, are fine as fuck. And the kiss was smoking hot." He stops tickling me, gives me a quick kiss on the lips, then walks to the cupboard and retrieves a pan to pop popcorn.

"We have a movie to watch. Butter or no butter?"

"Butter."

CHAPTER 14

Looking for Rain

Raven

As dawn breaks, I gaze out the window to the tranquil view of a slate waterfall surrounded by lush green foliage, providing seclusion from a city still sleeping across the lake in the distance. It's not yet six in the morning. It's that time in the morning when my mind begins to race and memories of my former life fight to be seen. I need to seek shelter from my thoughts.

Thankfully, Nik is still fast asleep, face down, his strong arms wrapped around his pillow. Cautiously, I get up, trying not to wake him. I slip into a T-shirt and steal away to the small sitting room that doubles as a screening room overlooking the lake. I walk onto the room's outdoor patio, take refuge in an oversized lounge chair, and pull my knees under my chin. As usual, I'm about to call Parker to wake him, but my phone rings first.

"Hey, handsome. I was just about to call you." Parker's hair lays in thick, wet strands on his head, and I can tell he's fresh from the shower. Recognizing the painting behind him that I brought means he's perched himself on the occasional chair in the bedroom.

"Hey, beautiful. I need to head out early today, so I figured I'd call you. How are you?" He stares, unblinking, reading my face.

He's so handsome. Sometimes, I wonder what he ever saw in me.

I trace the line of his perfectly angled jaw with my eyes and smile. Focusing on him helps me center my thoughts and snuff out remnants of my morning terrors. "I'm okay now that I'm talking to you."

"Where are you, Rain? I don't recognize the space you're in. I can see the cityscape in the background," he asks, eyebrows furrowed. I know he's worried.

"I'm at a lake house with a friend."

"Lake house where? Text me the address." I hear the sudden shift in his voice.

"It's nothing, Parker. I'm just here for a few days. I'll be fine."

My eyes shift to the door as I see Nik appear. He tips his head toward the hallway and then leaves. I look back at Parker. He notices my attention is diverted.

"Was that him?"

"Yes. Parker, it's nothing."

"Rain, I'm worried, is all. You just got out of a situation. I don't want to see you hurt again. And I'm surprised to see that you've left the city. You usually keep me posted on things like this. Text me the address where you are or turn on your locator."

"It's not a big deal, Parker. Everything's fine."

"Rain, I don't know this person. It'll make me feel better if I at least know where you are. What if something happens? I need to be able to get to you. We've been down this path before. I'm just looking out for you." I look back to the door to make sure Nik is gone. "Rain?" Parker says. I shift my eyes back to the screen.

His eyes are studying me with anxious sweeps, I'm causing this; I'm acting out of character. Years ago, Parker and I made a series of promises to each other. We would keep each other informed of our whereabouts.

Regardless of the discussion's difficulty, we would always tell each other everything. Lastly, we would never deny each other *anything*.

Parker doesn't need to ask me where I am. He could easily use his resources to find me. But he believes in our connection enough to know I'll honor our agreement. If he asks, I'll answer. And whatever I tell him will be the truth. I focus on his face, and as much as I want to fight, I can't. His intentions are pure. He's Parker Page, and as long as he's in my life, I have someone at my back. He's proven that. I press my lips together, compose myself, and force a smile.

He shakes his head at my lame attempt. "Babe, you can do better than that, but it'll do. Now, swipe your screen and send me your location." I do what he says. I go to his profile, share my location, and then return to FaceTime. "We have a little time before I have to go. You want to talk to me and tell me what's happening?"

I take a deep breath and brief him on what has transpired since my conversation with him at the bar. Parker listens quietly, and the way he's sitting in his chair, staring at the screen flatly, I sense he's checking himself.

"You know I disagree with what you're doing. I need you to promise me you'll be careful, Rain. You say it's just good times, but you can get hurt. I want you to come home whole."

"I will," I tell him, but I don't know whether it's true because I'm not perfect. But Parker's seen it all: the pleasure, the pain, yet through it all, he remains by me.

"You know you mean the world to me," he says, lowering his tone. He's struggling to keep himself in check. I realize it's been stressful for him to watch from the sidelines these past four years as I navigate one failed relationship after another.

"Yeah. You've told me. Parker, isn't it time for you to get ready to be brilliant?"

"Yeah, I like to think I'm brilliant whether I'm dressed or not. Which reminds me, Mom will call you this week to discuss the birthday party she's throwing me. It's more like a private gathering than a party. There'll be some people there that she wants us to meet."

"She'll use any reason to have a big party. Why call? She can just text. Besides, it's a few months away."

"It's a themed party, so I assume it's to talk about what you and I should wear, brief you as usual on the crowd. And I think she wants to hear your voice. Although I keep reminding her that we're no longer a couple, she's in denial. You can't blame her, though—she loves having you around. You're like the daughter she never had." I get it. She's like the mom I wish I had. But I don't tell him that.

"I suppose the way we behave doesn't help. Don't worry. I'll be ready for her call. Hey Parker, I'm sorry for being so difficult."

"You don't have to apologize. Now I need to get ready. I'll talk to you in the morning. Love ya."

"I love you, Parker Page, Esquire," I tell him, end the call, and then go upstairs searching for Nik.

I thought I'd find Nik in the kitchen, but I find him sitting on a chair on the deck near his pool, looking out over the water. I walk behind him, throw my arms around his neck, dip my head, and kiss his cheek. He reaches up and pulls me around to his front until I'm sitting astride him on the chair.

"The view of the lake is lovely, but this one is spectacular," he says, looking at me. He brushes my hair behind my ears, cups my face, and kisses me. It's soft yet brief. "Your call go ok?"

"Yeah, just a check-in," I say, although it's a lot more than that.

"You had me worried. You seem to have a habit of leaving me when I'm sleeping. It's unfortunate because I wanted to wake up inside you." He kisses me again. This time, it's hard, deep, and urgent. He groans into my mouth, and I feel his manhood rise between us. He reaches beneath my T-shirt and slides his fingers between my legs. "And you're ready for me," he says. He stands with me in his arms. He carries me back inside and lays me on the day bed. He removes his briefs, gets a condom, sheaths his shaft, then kneels over me. He dips his head and kisses me. "I promise we'll get to coffee, but first...." He doesn't finish his statement. He positions himself between my folds and fills me.

CHAPTER 15

Unleashed

Noah

RAIN SAYS I SHOULD COME WITH A WARNING LABEL; SHE SHOULD come with security because I can't stay off her. After I had her on the day bed near the pool, I took her upstairs and had her again in the shower. Twice. If I weren't committed to touring Seattle with her, I'd lay her out on the kitchen counter. Instead, I watch her devour her breakfast. As slim as she is, you'd never know how much she eats.

"This is a beautiful kitchen. The sleek white, modern design is one of my favorites, and it doesn't detract from the view of the crystal blue lake as it meets the cityscape under the cloudy sky…. Oh my god, Nik…it's spectacular. I feel like I never want to leave. I don't know if you rented this because I don't see any personal effects, but you certainly have good taste, whatever the situation," she says. I don't correct her to tell her it's mine and spending the night with her was my first night here. We agreed we wouldn't talk about such things; besides, it serves no purpose to tell her. I watch her go to the patio door and look out at the lake. She looks like she belongs here.

"You should eat. We need to leave soon."

Outings with women are foreign to me. Yet, preparing for the day with Rain feels comfortable, like a well-loved T-shirt, and we easily slip into activities that feel organic. It doesn't take us long to get ready.

Rain brings clothes appropriate for our day on the water. She places her things near the front door, but I pick them up and head toward the patio.

"This way, Rain."

"We're taking your boat?"

"No, we're taking that." I point to a blue and white seaplane landing on the lake in front of my dock.

"Nik, this is insane."

"There's more. Come on," I tell her. We head down to the dock, board the plane, and head to our next destination. The way Rain is looking at me with wonderment wrapped in seduction is everything I want to see.

It won't take us long to reach our connection point. She holds my hand the entire flight while I listen to her discuss our plans for the week. It seems a simple gesture, but I've never had a reason to hold a woman's hand at leisure. Not only is the gesture unusual, but being interested in a woman enough to converse about anything other than work feels strangely odd but easy with Rain. Occasionally, I point out landmarks and points of interest until I see our destination come into view near Bainbridge.

"Look down, Rain."

"Nik. Tell me that's our ride," she says when the yacht where we'll spend the day comes into view.

There are moments in your life when you don't know what you're missing until you've experienced it. One of those is watching Rain's face light up upon seeing the yacht. The one hundred and thirty-foot, three-level charcoal grey and beige lacquered-looking vessel that sits in the water in front of us is impressive by any standard. The yacht can accommodate eight, and I would have normally invited my brothers, but this trip is for Rain.

"That's it. We'll spend the day on the yacht, travel through Puget Sound, and then out to the Salish Sea. We can return home late tonight, or if you want, we can stay on the yacht overnight. The island here is small, but if you want, we can visit it." I barely finish talking when Rain throws her arms around my neck and kisses me all over my face. It's playful and innocent, and the moment stirs something in me that makes me want to do whatever I can to elicit that type of response from her again. I cup her face in my hand and kiss her. Once we break the kiss, I help her out of the plane, and we maneuver our way across the dock toward the yacht.

"This is a lot to take in, Nik, but thank you."

"I'm glad you're excited about today."

When we reach the dock, a crew member collects our belongings, we board the yacht, and I give her a tour.

"We can start on the upper deck, then go up one level to the sky deck, then make our way back down to the main deck. Does that sound like a plan?" The crew leaves us to go to their various stations as they ready the boat to sail. I take her by the hand and lead her up a spiral stairwell near the stern of the main deck to the upper level.

"This is the upper deck." I gesture toward the patio view of the water. "Just beyond these lounge seats, if you look over the rails, below us is a swim platform. If you want to go for a swim after we reach open water, I can have them drop anchor for us."

Rain turns to me, drapes her arms over my shoulders, and shoots me a curious glance. "It's bad enough you keep sweating all the products from my hair. I think I'll pass on swimming in the sea.

You're trouble enough." She laughs, and it's infectious, so I laugh too. "Don't laugh. It's true. If my hair were as closely cropped as yours, I'd take you up on the swim." She rubs her hand back and forth over the short waves on my head to prove her point. Her touch alone activates my body.

"Careful." I pull her tight against me so she can feel what she does to my body and dip my head into her neck. "I might end the tour here," I whisper.

"Don't you dare. You promised me a tour."

She pulls out of my arms, and despite my desire to have her, I turn her away from the water view toward the inner deck. We step into the large outdoor dining area with a ten-seater teak dining table overlooking the water.

"This is the upper dining area. Our main dining is just below us on the main deck. Beyond those doors is the salon, and beyond that are four guest sleeping quarters."

"This boat is perfect for entertaining. Do you host events?"

"Sometimes. Mak has hosted quite a few. Mostly, my brothers and I go out for a day to relax. But you're right; this is a great place to have a party or get away with family for a few days."

"I suppose Rok gets the main cabin when you're all here together."

"Depends on who's here. Either him or my parents. Age before beauty, you know."

"I've only seen your brothers. You're all handsome. I can only imagine what your parents look like."

"Was that why you eventually agreed to dinner with me? Because I'm handsome?" I take her by the hand and lead her up the inner stairwell. The motives of the other women I've been with were predictable to me, but Rain is different. The way she presents herself: confident, witty, and intelligent, is nothing like those other women. I'm keenly aware that men like me are not her type, so why she agreed to the initial one night, not to mention the rest of the week with me, is intriguing. Clearly, she sees something she likes, and I'm okay with that.

"Your bold, over-the-top arrogance caught my attention," she says when we reach the top, and I know she can see the surprise on my face. "What? You know how you are."

She's right. I am those things—I have to be to make multimillion-dollar deals, driving billions in annual revenue for my company. It's who I need to be to get results, to maintain power.

"Knowing who I am is not a surprise. It's you admitting it was the attraction."

"I think I proved I know how to handle a man like you, Nik. Remember you were chasing me? I allowed myself to be caught." She smiles wryly, but she's right. I went out of my way to get time with Rain. Something inside of me must have known she was worth the effort. Ever since this woman walked into my life, I've been questioning who I am. She makes me want to try to be the type of man a woman like her would date, and I don't recognize myself. I've been so hard-driving and focused on business, I haven't stopped to be with a woman in this way. I put that out of my mind long before I met Rain.

"What about my sexy accent?" I pull her to me and whisper in her ear. "What if I tell you everything I want to do to you in my British accent? How I plan to kiss you starting at your toes and suck and lick my way up your thighs, paying special attention to—."

"What are you doing?"

The way she pulls away from me and stares me down draws a laugh from me. Rain is so lovely, and her straightforward way of handling me is addicting.

"Isn't it obvious? Trying to get to the good part."

She walks over to the Sky Bar and takes a seat. One of the crew members immediately helps her.

"Would you like a drink, Miss Rain?"

"Champagne for me and…." She turns to me. "What are you having, Nik, without a C?"

"I'll have the same. Thanks." I walk over to her but don't take a seat. Instead, I lean against the bar and stare at her, wondering what she does for a living. She's bold yet playful and was right when she said she could handle me. Rain handles me as well as my brothers do.

"Don't look at me like you're going to eat me. Just kiss me already." That's all she has to tell me. I dip my head and give her an earth-shattering kiss. And I swear I feel like I'm trying to devour her soul before I force myself to break the kiss.

"Rain," I whisper against her lips, and I don't care if a crew member is watching. They're paid to be discreet. "I want you so bad. But you know that's my permanent state with you."

"When we finish my tour, you can have all of me." She smiles against my lips. Then she sits straight and grabs her glass of champagne that the staff must have placed down while I was ravishing her. "Here." She hands me my glass. "Let's toast."

"To my days with Rain," I say, because if the days to come are anything like the last few days, these will be the most memorable ones of my life.

"Cheers."

"Just let me know when you're ready to continue the tour. Would you like something to eat while we're here?"

"We can eat later."

She takes a few more sips, but her eyes never leave mine while she drinks. She winks and then smiles. I furrow my eyebrows, and she shrugs her shoulders. Then she holds my hand while sipping her drink, and I trace circles with my thumb over her wrist. Rain picks up our hands and places them against my cheek, and I can't help but smile, and she does the same. Kissing the inside of her wrist, I hold her gaze. Then, finally, I pick up my glass and take a sip. When I realize what's happening, I catch myself.

She's pacing us—pulling me into the moment, slowing our tempo. Helping me take it all in. Because she knew I couldn't see past wanting her. When she realizes I understand her intent, she smirks.

"Why can't I have you now?" I ask aloud, not understanding how we know what each other is thinking.

"Because we have time. I want to enjoy this lovely boat."

"How did you do that?"

"You mean, how did you tell me what you want, and I say no without saying no? I just followed your lead. You spoke to me with your body, Nik. I saw you do the same thing with your brothers over FaceTime in the bar the night we met."

"I don't get it."

"You grabbed my hand. Made me wait. Then, your brothers started questioning you. You didn't say a word. You just pulled me into you and changed the angle of your phone so your brothers could see me. Do you recall talking to them about me?"

"No." I only remember looking down at her, thinking how perfect she felt beside me.

"We all do it, Nik. Some of us are better at it than others. You answered Mak's question and introduced me to your brothers without a single word. The dialogue that happened was between your brothers and me."

"You're going to be the death of me, little lady," I tell her, because Rain makes me reflect on what I say and don't say. Every gesture and word, every blink of the eye, means something to her, and she's processing it all, storing it permanently. I don't know what to think about it.

She drinks the rest of her champagne in one final gulp, and I do the same.

"Let's go," she says. I help her from her seat and lead her back down the spiral staircase until we reach the main deck.

When we arrive, Rain heads straight to the side of the boat to stand by the rail.

"This is lovely," she tells me.

The blue waters are calm, and we watch the shore become progressively smaller the further we move away. This is where she wants to be, and that's okay with me. Rain wants to watch the yacht move into open water, so as much as I want to take her to the cabin and have my way with her, I don't. Instead, I stand behind her and hold her as she enjoys the sea view and watches as the city disappears in the distance. The blue sky stretches across the horizon until it touches the water. And although I've spent time on the yacht with my family watching this scene, experiencing this with her makes it feel new to me. It makes me wonder whether I'd have experienced this with someone else sooner had I not lost someone with whom this could've been possible. But I don't want to think about that because I have Rain.

She turns in my arms. "Thank you," she says. She stands on her toes to kiss me.

"What do you think? Can you see us spending the night on the yacht?"

"Of course. However, I wasn't expecting anything this elaborate."

"It is a beautiful yacht. I don't spend enough time here."

"You should. This is relaxing."

"The crew is at our disposal. We could spend a chill day on the boat. We can get some time at the pool before lunch if you want. Or we can hang out on the deck and drink. There are also plenty of games on board, as well as offboard water equipment. Maybe we can try out some of the watercraft. Or I can take you back to the cabin and ravish you. That's not to say I won't do that anyway."

"Let's hang here for a while. Then I'll change. The lounge chairs looked appealing. It's been a while since I've had the opportunity to relax." She leans over the railing and looks out to sea again, so I rest my chin on her shoulder and do the same.

As I hold her close, hints of jasmine and honey surround me, making me thirsty for a woman in a way that only Rain can quench. I want her now. And it's taking all my willpower not to drag her to the cabin and sink into her on the bed, the table, the shower. But I promised her a memorable experience, which means allowing time to enjoy the sights and all the amenities this vessel offers her. And she's already not so subtly called me out at the bar. Greedily, I tighten my arms around her waist, put my nose into her neck, and inhale her essence as she looks out to sea.

"Nik?"

"Hmm."

"The sky has been so clear since I arrived. Is that typical for this time of year? Look, I can see the entire city," she says, trying to turn in my arms, but I grip her tighter.

"No, Rain," I say, and I feel her writhing in my arms.

"No, it's not typical, or don't turn around."

"Both."

"Nik, let me lose." I loosen my grip. She turns and places her hands on my biceps. "Kiss me." I dip my head, hover over her slightly parted lips, and study her face. The thirst in her eyes has me in such a chokehold that I fear if I give in and quench her thirst, she'll drink the final thread that's holding back the wolf, and I'll be permanently unleashed. She's waiting for me to close the distance as our breaths mingle with the sea air between us. She smiles, and it's bright and warms me like the sun. "What are you doing, Nik?" She lifts her arms, wraps them around my neck, and closes the distance. She meets my unparted lips with hers. It's not enough for her. She pulls back, and her soft lips sweep mine as she starts to speak, making me want to lick into her. "Remember you told me to tell you if I didn't like something?"

"Yeah, beautiful. Did you think of something?"

"I don't like Nik on a leash." I study her face for a second. She wrinkles her nose, smiling up at me, and something in me snaps.

I press my lips to hers, lick into her, and suck and kiss her until her lips are swollen. Desperate to be deep in her, I grab her hips and pull her up until she wraps her legs around my back. Tangled, I swiftly take her to our cabin and toss her on the bed. Rain is insane, unleashing me like this. She knows I can't resist the need to be buried deep within her. Our clothes scatter across the room as we take them off.

"Get on your knees and bend over," I command. And she turns away from me and gets into the position. I get on my knees on the bed behind her and reach between her legs and stroke her sex, and oh my god, this woman is fucking drenched. I lick my lips because my desire to sink into her is overwhelming. I widen her legs, put one hand on her back, and lower her down further so I have complete access to her sex. I grab a condom, cover myself, and rub my length through her slickness, and then, in one push, I'm in.

She gasps as I fill her full in one pump. I grab her tight around the waist, and I pump in and out, and it's fast and hard, and my body slaps against her hips as I pump into her sex, and she's moaning and calling my name.

"Yes, Nik, more, harder," she calls out as I pump even faster, harder, deeper. I feel her body clench, fast and hard. Rain comes around my dick, coating it, making it even slicker, and I pump faster. It's hard and feral, and I feel the start of something building in my body.

"Come again, Rain," I growl. As I pump in and out, she comes around my dick again, and her response pulls my climax from me. "Fuck," I call out, pumping and growling as I hold her until I empty everything into her. "Rain."

"Nik."

I collapse on her back, roll to the side, and pull her over me.

CHAPTER 16

You Look Different

Raven

UNLEASHED IS MY NEW FAVORITE SIDE OF NIK. I HAVEN'T HAD THIS much sex in a day since my time with Parker. I think Parker still has a leg up on Nik, which may have to do with me knowing Parker much better and a lot longer. However, nothing is lacking in Nik's stamina. Yet, in the back of my head, sits the reality that this is short-term, so I should enjoy it for what it is.

While Nik is in the shower, I walk along the main deck and into the salon, where light floods in from the windows on either side of the room. Like everything on this boat, it's elegantly designed. The high gloss champagne-colored wire-brushed white oak walls, wood-paneled ceilings, and wooden tables all have the same hues. The mix of caramel leather seating combined with rich charcoal velvet cushions complements the room. An oversized limited edition black and white abstract print hangs on the back wall. The hand-blown custom light hanging over the indoor dining table matches the domed lights on the coffee tables. The space is so lovely that I could sit here forever lost in my thoughts.

I sit on one of the couches, prop my back against the armrest, and stare out of the contoured windows that beautifully frame the seascape. I take out my phone and proactively call Parker's mom, Janis. Janis is a beautiful, tall, slender woman who, even at her age, could pass for a model. It's not hard to see where Parker gets his perfect looks. Parker's family is lovely and treats me like part of the family. Sometimes, I wonder what my family would have been like had I been raised by two parents instead of one. Parker offered to help me research my family background, but I told him no. I might reconsider it.

Janis picks up right away. "Raven, darling. It's so good to get your call. Parker must have told you I would reach out soon."

"He did, Mrs. Page. How are you? I look forward to hosting the charity auction alongside you again in December."

"I'm good. I'm also looking forward to hosting it with you. It's one of my favorite events. Which is why I told Parker I wanted to speak with you. His birthday is coming soon, and I've invited some important people to stop by while they're in town. It could be worthwhile for you and Parker to meet them. So, I wanted to make sure you're there."

"Of course, Mrs. Page. You know I'd never miss Parker's party. He mentioned it might be a themed event."

"Yes. That's what I wanted to talk to you about. Your invitation should be waiting for you when you return home. The dress code is vintage Hollywood. I've already chosen something for Parker, and I envisioned you wearing this platinum dress I'm having made. I hope you don't mind. I recall you mentioning how stressful it was trying to find something for these events. I'd love to see you in it alongside Parker."

"Wow, Mrs. Page. That's so generous of you. Although you could have had your stylist send a few things." And in typical fashion, controlling, but she's so wonderful, I don't add that. Besides, she's been a better mother to me than my own, and that means a lot to me.

"Oh, wonderful. I'm so glad this worked out. When are you back, darling? I want to take you to lunch, and I can arrange for you to have a fitting for the dress that day." She asks a question I'm sure she has the answer to.

"Parker is picking me up from the airport Monday afternoon. I'll be working in the city for the remainder of the week."

"Perfect. Then I'll make all the arrangements and send you the details. Oh, and I have Parker over for dinner again next weekend. I'd like you to come, too. Darling, until then, have a nice time in Seattle. Parker tells me you have a big meeting upcoming. I'm sending you positive vibes."

"Rain, there you are." My head snaps toward the entrance, where Nik is leaning against the door. I hold up a finger.

"Sorry about that. Thank you again. I'll wait for your note," I say, and I end the call, hoping Janis didn't hear Nik in the background. I would not want to upset her. Janis is beautiful and pleasant yet controlling. She only wants what's best for her son, and seemingly, in her eyes, that's me. Janis Page wants to see her son married. Not *just* married, married to me. Her actions, constantly creating situations for Parker and me to make appearances together, show she'll stop at nothing to make that happen. Still, I wonder what a woman with such power and status sees in me that I don't see in myself.

Nik walks over, pulls me to my feet, and kisses me deeply. "Sorry about that. You have any more calls?"

"Not at the moment."

"Ready for lunch?" He turns me in his arms so my back is to his chest, then whispers in my ear. "Because that, little lady, is our lunch waiting for us." He points beyond the salon door to the outside dining table, neatly arranged with an elaborate lunch spread.

"Looks like I'm ready for lunch."

Nik walks me over to the table. He helps me to my seat and dismisses the staff. I smile at him, and he dips his head to kiss me before sitting beside me. He's so considerate and far from what I'd expected from a bad-boy billionaire.

If I hadn't provided Nik with my favorite foods in advance, I would have been a bit overwhelmed by the spread. An array of toast shrimp sandwiches with thinly sliced fries, salad, fresh fruit, cheese and crackers, and champagne are on the table.

"This is lovely, Nik. Thank you."

"Let me know if you need anything else. I can signal the crew. So, what do you think about us taking a couple of jet skis out on the water and having some fun after lunch? Or, if you want, I can take us out on the chase boat."

"The chase boat sounds cool."

"You're not afraid of speed, are you? Because the boat can get up there. But don't worry. I won't let anything happen to you."

"You haven't given me any reason not to trust you so far. You mentioned something like that when we struck our deal. Is that normally how you respond when talking to women?"

"What do you mean?"

"When we made our deal, you promised to protect me. Is that normal for you?"

Nik sets his fork down on his plate and watches me with wonderment in his eyes. "No, Rain. I don't recall ever saying those words to anyone else. Somehow, it felt right to say them to you. Now that I've spent time with you, you've become a part of my life, my circle. We'll never see each other again after this week, but you need to know you'll never be absent from my world. Because there is no forgetting you, Rain. If you ever need me, call me. I'll be there."

Wow, just wow—I didn't see that coming. If I didn't know any better, I'd think Nik was trying to make me fall for him. In a way, I think I might be.

"Nik." I reach over and touch his hand. "I don't know how to respond to that, but thank you. Can I ask you another question?"

"Like anything I say would stop you. Go ahead."

"Why is Rok so surprised about me? Why do you look different to him? And he seems intrigued to see me every time you have a call with him."

"Do you have any non-soul-searching questions for me? Forget that. Those might be worse." He chuckles. I eat while I wait for his response. "Seeing you two days in a row with me could contribute to his fascination with us, and the fact I've made a point to bring you into my calls with my brothers is another. I'm a private guy. Women don't get a real glimpse into my world or who I am outside the bedroom. They don't get to know the real me. I'm not on social media. They can't look me up and say, oh yeah, I was with him. They never get to meet my brothers unless I approach a woman while I'm out with them. Even then, they don't know who I am. And after that, I don't see them again—but you know that part."

"Why do you look different?"

"Like I told you before, it's you. You don't get the version of me I am with those other women."

"So, is this the real you? Rok seemed relieved when you answered."

"Honestly, Rain, I don't know. Maybe once, a long time ago. Since I met you, I've been trying to figure that out. I've been driven and focused for so long. It's allowed me to have what I want most."

"Which is?"

"Power."

Maya Angelou said, "When someone shows you who they are, believe them the first time." So, when Nik tells me he's using his bad boy, "I don't care about anything but power," façade to help him focus and achieve his goals, I believe him. I also think he's wrestling with the man he presents when he's around me, so I don't probe him further. As much as I like him and want to get to know him better, I have to remember he's not my man.

Following lunch, the crew readies the sleek black chase boat, and then Nik helps me into it. It's a powerful machine, and I let Nik take us at full throttle. Like a scene from Miami Vice, the boat tears through the water, bouncing up and down as it goes. Nik takes us out to sea with the wind blowing in our faces. The exhilaration makes me forget everything but Nik's strong arms steering the boat. I can tell by his broad grin that he's enjoying this, too, and I wrap my arms around his waist and stay that way until he brings us back to the yacht.

"Nik, wow, another amazing experience. You have some skills you've been holding out on," I tell him once we're back on the yacht, heading to the cabin.

"Yeah, I promise you I'm not holding out on anything. Want me to show you?" He laughs, and before I can respond, he picks me up, takes me into the bedroom, and tosses me on the bed. I land hard and laugh even harder, but he crawls on top and kisses the laugh right out of me. He breaks the kiss. "And she goes quiet." He whispers against my lips.

"Because you, Nik, without a C, take my breath away," I tell him because it's true. He does take my breath away. I close the distance with a kiss. And on cue, I feel Nik's body respond between us, and I want him. I cup his hips in my hands, pulling him to me, trying to get closer when I feel his phone vibrate in his back pocket. Damn.

"Fuck," he growls, reaching into his pocket. I see Mak's face on the screen when Nik swipes the phone. He kneels over me, and I'm right—he's hard as a rock. "You're timing is impeccable," he tells Mak, and I hear the irritation in his voice. He looks down, then dips his head to kiss me. "Tell me this is important, Mak."

"I need you on a plane," I hear Mak say.

In a rush, Nik gets up and walks into the study to talk.

CHAPTER 17

No Hesitation

Raven

WHEN NIK RETURNS FROM THE DISCUSSION WITH HIS BROTHER, I can tell by his tense facial expression and the tick in his jaw that he's torn between duty and desire.

"Come here." Nik's eyes narrow, his voice is strained, and I sense him struggling to rein in the Nik reserved for those other women. I go to him, and he dips his head to my neck and inhales. As he begins to trail kisses along my neck, I turn to capture his lips to reclaim the Nik I've come to know. Our kiss turns desperate and heated, and his body rises against me. I break the kiss in a pant.

"You want to take me now or talk to me?"

"I want you, Rain."

He doesn't have to say anything else. We strip off all our clothes, and I give him what he needs…me.

Nik is on his back, and I'm wrapped in his arms when I hear my phone buzz before reaching across him to silence it. He stirs a little, but he's too tired to open his eyes after our day of leisure. Whatever happened between him and his brother, he sought me out to get a reprieve, and I gave it to him. After all, that's what this week is about…escape. Nik and I went three rounds before we decided to nap. He was going for round four, but as good as he felt in me, my body needed a break, so I curled into him. And as I knew, he couldn't resist holding me.

"Nik." I raise my head and kiss the corner of his lips; my breasts are pressed against him. "We should get up," I whisper against his lips. He turns to his side, bringing me with him, locks his lips on mine, and I feel him rise thick against my body.

"Woman, you should have let me sleep," he growls.

"We can go all night, but I suspect your brother will be looking for you. You want to talk to me?"

"I want to bury myself in you."

I dust my lips against his. "Talk to me, Nik."

He sits up with his back against the headboard and pulls me up and into his side.

"I have to attend a meeting at nine tomorrow morning, so I need to fly out early. It's a show of good faith about how serious we are in making a deal happen."

"What's the problem? You need to be there. So be there."

"You."

"Nik, we promised we wouldn't compromise on our normal lives."

"It's not that."

"Then what is it?"

"It's the first time I felt myself hesitate regarding work. I need to be there without question, but my immediate concern was you."

"No hesitations. Nik, I'll be fine. Regardless of the circumstances, I'll be touring with or without you this week." It's true. I can manage on my own, but it's been a lovely escape to allow him to take control for this brief time.

"Listen. You and I are not done. I already have tomorrow all planned out for you. As for me, I have a jet, so I'll leave in the morning and attend my meeting. I'm sure the organizers have lunch planned afterward, so I won't be able to get back here in time to spend the afternoon with you. But I'll be back to take you to dinner at the supper club."

"Okay." I'm unsure what he wants me to say because I never expected this.

"Rain, I'm serious about this week. I want this to go smoothly. I can't be with you for the full day, but I've arranged for a cook to prepare breakfast for us tomorrow before I fly out. That way, we have some time together in the morning. Later, the driver will collect you and take you to start your tour, then afterward, he'll pick you up to take you to the restaurant I've arranged for your lunch."

"You really have thought this through."

"I'll be back no later than four. Then I'll sink into you before we head out to dinner." I swat him in response. "Okay, make that a few times." I shake my head.

"So, I don't suppose we're spending the night on the yacht."

"That depends on how much sleep you want to get." Nik pulls me to his lap so that I'm straddling him. He wraps his lips on one of my breasts and sucks, and my sex throbs.

"I imagine this boat is spectacular when lit up at night. I want to enjoy an evening on the sea before we head back to the house," I tell him.

"Okay," he says against my skin, then takes my other breast in his mouth. "Then I'll have you now." He licks and sucks, then repeats it again, alternating breasts. "Then we'll dine outdoors on the deck." He rolls me off him and onto my back and hovers over me. "We'll take in the evening view as we head back to the shore." He says, dipping his head and kissing me. It's sloppy and wet, and I want him.

"Nik." I grab his length. He lifts, pushes my hand away, grabs a condom, swiftly opens it, and then stretches it over his erection. He nudges my leg with his leg, giving him space to access me. He positions himself between my legs, holds my gaze, and pushes in hard and deep. "Ahh." I groan, and he dips his head and swallows it with a kiss. He moves in and out, over and over. I lift my hips, pushing into him, fingers pressed into his shoulders, and I can't help but come. "Oh, Nik."

∾

One thing for sure is that Nik is a man of his word. He took me twice before dinner. We had a lovely dinner on the outdoor deck, which felt magical at sea. Then, on the way back to the shore, we sat in the lounge on the outdoor terrace and made out under the stars. We got so riled up that back at the house, we went at it like rabbits before finally falling asleep. Despite having to come back to the house, the night was perfect.

This morning, I'm up earlier than usual. Instead of waiting until six, I'm up at five thirty to have my call with Parker. Parker suggested our morning routine years ago to help me. Our calls temporarily relieve me of the secrets that only Parker knows lay thick like cobwebs in my head. Over the years, Parker and I have become one-half of each other. So, I was surprised to hear a hint of something I didn't recognize in his voice this morning when he realized I was still at the lake house. We didn't talk long, but it was long enough. His message was clear.

"Rain, don't get lost in whatever it is you're doing. I need you to come back to me whole. I love you." That was the last thing he said this morning before I told him I loved him and we hung up.

Parker's worried about me, and rightfully so. I need to get out of the clouds—to remember I have a life outside of a man with no tomorrows. Because Monday morning, there will be no hesitation. I will seize my opportunity and crush my meeting.

Immediately following my call with Parker, I shower. It isn't long before Nik wakes and joins me, then takes me against the wall before we get clean.

I'm dressed before Nik since my dress code calls for a day of leisure. I head toward the smell of yumminess coming from the kitchen. The cook is busy finishing up. I sit at one of the counter stools and check my phone while waiting for Nik. There are a few missed texts and several urgent emails. Shoot. I need to hop on a conference call with Alejandro later this morning, and it appears my sister is back, and there's a cryptic text from Blake. Wait. What?

The coward: Call me when you get this.

That's it. That's the damn message, you jerk. You can't be for real, I say to the phone. I should have blocked Blake. I don't respond to the coward. Instead, I type out a message to Alejandro.

Me: Nine o'clock is good. Talk to you then.

The scent of amber, musk, and spice wafts around me long before I feel Nik's lips on my neck and his body pressed to my back.

"Hey, beautiful. Ready to start your day?" Nik releases me and sits on the stool beside me. He looks absolutely edible in his dark blue suit. Wow. I've only ever seen him in slacks and a shirt at most, besides his jeans and a Henley. Neither of us had any reason to be overly dressed on holiday.

"Um, can you stand a second and let me get a look at you? Because holy hell, Nik, you're fine."

To my surprise, he stands, but I only get a brief look because he pulls me to my feet and kisses me hard. It's the kind of toe-curling kiss that makes you forget your name. And for me, that's a hell of a kiss. Then, because I'm in a haze, he helps me back to my stool and sits beside me again.

"Now, are you ready to start your day?"

While I gather my wits, the cook places a plate of shrimp and grits in front of each of us. Then, puts several platters along the countertop in front of us. I add eggs and pastry to my side plate, and Nik adds bacon and some fruit to his.

"I have a conference call to take in a bit, but yes, I'm ready. I don't know why you're so mysterious about my tour." He reaches into his pocket, pulls out a phone, and hands it to me.

"Here. Keep this on you."

"What's this for?"

"We didn't share our info. You can reach me with this if you need anything. There are three numbers in there. If you call me and I don't automatically pick up, one of the others will."

"What?" I scroll through the phone. It says Nik, without a C, Rok, with a K, and Baby Mak. I smile because the thought of grown men with coordinating nicknames is so ridiculous that I can't help it. "Are you serious, Nik?"

Nik is unphased. "Three seconds." I look at him with raised eyebrows because I have no idea what he's talking about. "That's the longest it will ever take for someone to respond to you."

"Oh, shoot, you are serious."

"I am. Tell me all about the tour when I get back. I can't wait to get your reaction. Now eat."

We eat and shoot the breeze about the restaurant scene in Seattle. Before I know it, it's time for Nik to head out. He gives me the code to the house and the driver's number and kisses me senselessly before he leaves.

Home

Noah

"I need you on a plane." Fuck. Mak's words come out in a whoosh, and I'm sucked back into a reality I'm not ready to be in. Because for the first time in years, I find myself attracted to a woman on a deeper level. A woman I want to get to know better.

I look down at Rain to check her expression for signs of annoyance but don't see any. I give her a kiss. Spending time on the yacht with Rain is more enjoyable than expected. And right in the thick of things, my brother calls. If Mak calls me on holiday, then whatever he wants is important. I walk into the study next door to take the call in private.

"Talk to me, Mak."

"Sorry to interrupt, man."

"You have my attention. Use it."

"I reviewed what you sent me and ran the numbers."

"And.?"

"I'll approve it."

"So, it's a go."

"Yeah, but to get in on this, you need to meet the owner face to face."

This is excellent news. I pitched to acquire a San Francisco building that's coming up for sale. It's within reach. I'd never thought we'd simultaneously have this many big deals in the works.

"Why?"

"It's an off-market deal, and from what I uncovered, this property has sentimental value to the family."

"That's no way to deal, Mak. If they can't find the right bidder to scoop it up, they're at risk of bleeding money and defaulting on their loans."

"They put together a shortlist of people they're willing to talk to. You're on it."

"Fuck—can you go? Or Rok?"

"They want you."

"And this fits within our model, class, tenants, top ROI, everything?"

"I went through everything. If we can land this deal, the revenue and the total square footage alone will boost our overall portfolio, putting us one notch closer to our goal, Nik. One more deal like this, and no one can touch us. The preliminary meeting is tomorrow at nine."

"Who else am I up against in this meeting?"

"You and three others make four, but only three of you tomorrow. It's in your email. There is one private meeting happening. I don't know who they are."

"Find out."

This could be huge. Knight Development Corporation could be the top commercial real estate developer sooner than I'd anticipated, between the deal I'm working on for next week and this one. When my brothers and I took over the company, we committed to scaling the business beyond what our father had. The sacrifices we've all made to get to this point are about to pay off if we can land the next two deals.

"I will."

"You said this was personal for them. Put Rick on this and have him get the name of the fourth bidder. Send me all the personal details of those involved in this deal. I need to know about this family by tomorrow night. I don't care what it costs," I tell him.

If Rick is on this, I'll get a leg up to closing this deal. Rick is the investigator we use for our special projects. With the instant revenue we can generate securing this property, this deal just made the top of the list.

"What about Rain?"

"What about her?"

"I was surprised to see her." I raise an eyebrow, shooting him a questioning gaze, but then he says, "In a good way, man. What does this mean? Are you finally settling down? She's a beautiful woman, Nik, and, from our brief interactions, a one-eighty from your usual suspects." The reality of Mak's words hit me hard in the throat, cutting off my oxygen. The need for air is strangling me, so I leave the study and walk outside along the deck. "Where are you going, man?"

"I'm listening, Mak. Tell Jewel to update the arrangements from two to one—Rain has carte blanche. I'll be back by dinner. And no, I'm not settling down."

"But if you did…."

"But I'm not."

"If you did…."

"I'd never do that to her," I say, trying to hold the clip in my voice. I need Mak to move on.

"We see the way you look at her and how you're spending so much time with her, Nik. Even you have to admit—you're different with her. You two look like you belong together. You're less grumpy."

"I'm not grumpy. I'm focused."

"I'm just saying, grab hold of her and let that past shit go."

"I'll admit. There's something different about her. But we're done after this week."

"Man, I never thought I'd hear myself say this, but you should reconsider that. Give this thing you have with her a chance."

"Listen, are we solid for tomorrow?"

His expression goes flat, resigned to abandoning his train of thought. "Yeah, we're good."

"I gave Rain a private line to you and Rok. If that call comes through—."

"We know the drill. We got this."

MAKING DECISIONS THAT IMPACT THE SUCCESS OF KNIGHT DEVELOPment Corporation and the thousands of people who depend on us is hard but necessary. Telling Rain that I would be unable to spend the day with her was even harder. I don't know what I expected, but when I told Rain I had to travel in the morning, she reminded me of our original agreement not to let our affair interfere with our personal lives or business. In the end, Rain is right. I need to go into my day without hesitation, so instead of sinking into her at home, I find myself in San Francisco, walking into a meeting with Wade Wallace to discuss the Wade Building.

"Mak, I'm heading up now. Any news from Rick?"

"No. You said you'd give him until this evening. He'll have something for you by then. I have something that might be even better."

"What's that?"

"Chase's birthday party. Did you RSVP?"

"No. I'm with Rain this week. I don't see how our cousin's birthday party plays into this."

"He checked in, wanting to confirm we'd be there. I probed—turns out Jude Wallace is attending and hoping to see you there. Jude's your inside track to Wade."

Fuck. I hadn't plan to attend, but if Wade's son is interested in chatting with me this must be related to the deal.

"Okay, have Jewel RSVP on my behalf. Add Rain as my plus one."

"Consider it done. Do you need anything for the meeting, or are you set?"

"Set. You said it's an introduction."

"Yeah, they want to know who's serious about this."

"There were no sharks on the list you sent, so this is personal."

"Then be real. You know what family business is like."

"I'll call you afterward. Stepping out of the elevator now."

"Later, man." I end the call.

The receptionist greets me as I step off the elevator. "Mr. Knight. Nice to meet you. I'll show you to the conference room." She shows me to an interior room.

I recognize the other bidders that Mak sent me information on. Kurt Whitmire, out of Miami. He and I crossed paths around the time I made my first deal. He's a stand-up guy, but their company valuation is much smaller than ours. Then there's Christopher Mays. He's an up-and-comer out of New York in one of the most challenging markets.

I shake their hands and take a seat. It isn't long before Wade comes in, and I presume the person with him is his attorney.

"Gentlemen, thank you for coming. I want to keep this meeting brief. I'll be truthful: I'm old school and intend to separate the wheat from the chaff," he says. You could hear a pin drop because this is a bit unconventional. In a situation like this, no one wants to go against the grain. "By now, you all know I'm selling the Wade Building, my labor of love. You've read the data I sent, so you know your long-term potential and understand the automatic revenue you'll have walking in." We all nod in agreement. "What I'd like to do as a next step is get your proposal for how you'd take this building forward. Here is a list of things you must agree to if you're the lucky bidder."

The attorney slides a document across the table to each of us. I don't look down. I lock eyes with Wade because that is all that matters—his attention.

"Gentlemen, everything you need to know about delivery and timing is noted in the document. I plan to schedule follow-ups one-on-one over the next few weeks. I won't be taking questions. When we're done here, my team will meet with you," he says, then gets up and leaves.

I already know that the rest of today's meetings with his team are useless to me. My team has already dug deep into the numbers, but I go through the motions and present a good face. In the back of my mind, I wish I was back with Rain. Mak could have handled this portion of the meeting.

Two things came from this that I can use. One is that I need to be on Wade's side, and two, I need to stay ahead of the competition. The people present are newer to the game than I am, but I won't underestimate their abilities. I need to find out who the last player is in this game and how I overtake them. Because the fact that this individual was exempt from being here today meant something, and I need to find out what that something is.

The meetings last well into lunch, so they bring meals for the last meeting. As soon as lunch is over, I head to the airport to get back to Rain.

Once I'm on the plane, I call my brother. "Mak, I'm headed back."

"Everything is all good, Nik. Rain will be back by the time you're home." The second the words are out of his mouth, I feel the pressure that's been clinging to my chest since I left this morning release, and I can breathe.

Home. I'll be home soon.

CHAPTER 19

All That Jazz

Raven

AFTER NIK LEAVES, I HEAD TO WORK IN HIS OFFICE AT THE BACK OF the house. I contemplate calling Parker about Blake's text but think better of it. He's already worried about me handling the situation with Nik. I don't want to add this additional burden. I'll try to control the coward, as Nik calls him, myself. Then there's my sister, who wants to pick up where she left me stranded. Hard pass for the moment. I will try to see her before I go, but on my terms. I should be more reasonable, but I'm not feeling it. I have bigger fish to fry.

When I outlined the potential scenarios with Alejandro that could derail the contract Ross Enterprises is working on to secure a real estate developer for their corporate expansion, I anticipated an issue would surface. I hate when I'm right, but it's always good to be prepared for the worst-case scenario. Now I need to meet with Alejandro on the issue, so I settle into the lake house office and log into my video call. Alejandro doesn't hop on right away, so I pick up a pencil and sketch the Space Needle from memory. This city has the loveliest views, and for once, I'm glad to have perfect recall because this week has been spectacular.

When my boss finally shows up on the screen, I don't waste time and jump in. "Alejandro, I've reviewed everything that came through this week. The real estate developer wants confirmation that Ross Enterprises is scandal-free. Otherwise, they don't want to do business with them. I confirmed that Miss Ross hasn't violated her former employment agreement with Soala or her existing one with Ross Enterprises. That means that the article appearing in the British media is making false claims. I need to provide proof that they are false and secure a retraction. But to do that, I need to understand the source. Which involves talking to the media company. If I can sort this out and shut down the media angle, this will alleviate their client's concerns about the ethics clause, and the deal can go through."

"Right now, this is the one thing pending," Alejandro says. "The property developer has an outstanding reputation. They also stand to forfeit millions if this deal doesn't go through. We lose, too."

"I understand that. I have a few days before the meeting. Let me work on this. Once I have what I need, we can take it to their general counsel for final review," I tell Alejandro. I can tell he's stressed about it by the look on his face. In the end, he trusts that I'll solve this. If I don't have a solution, Parker will, since entertainment and media law is his area of expertise.

Following my meeting with Alejandro, I use the time to get some work done before the driver comes to collect me. When the driver arrives, I try to inquire where the tour will begin, but he insists Nik wanted it to be a surprise, so I sit back and enjoy the ride. It isn't until we drive into a private warehouse that I understand what's happening.

Once we stop, the driver helps me out, and I'm greeted by a man named Jim.

"Hi, Ms. Rae. My name is Jim, and I'll be your pilot for the day."

"Jim, nice to meet you. Where are we going?"

He turns and gestures for me to do the same. I see a slick black helicopter. "We're getting in that and heading for Mt. Rainier. Then I'll take you around the city and surrounding areas before returning."

"That sounds amazing."

"Great. First, I'll take you through the safety procedures, then we'll get going."

I am weighed, I sign some documents, and Jim takes me to the sleek black aircraft. It doesn't take long for me to get strapped in with a headset on. The ride to Mt. Rainier is stunning. It takes us about thirty-five minutes to get there, and the snow-covered mountain is a sight to behold. I hopelessly try to capture a few moments via my phone, but the unobstructed view with my eyes is too tempting.

After taking a pass along the mountain, Jim starts back to Seattle. Once we are over the city, we fly past various landmarks, including the Space Needle. Viewing the city spread below me is like viewing a living map. The waters are so blue, and the landscape is dotted with skyscrapers. It's spectacular. I only wish Nik were here to experience this with me.

When we finally land, I go through all the necessary safety precautions to exit the helicopter. My car awaits me, and I replay the sky tour in my mind during the ride back. Nik knew what he was doing when he arranged the tour, and I'll be forever grateful for his thoughtfulness in doing so.

The driver takes me to the restaurant Nik arranged for my lunch. Due to the hour of the day, I decide to eat light. I'll see him in a few hours before we head to dinner at the jazz supper club. While eating my meal, my phone rings, and to my surprise, it's Parker.

"Rain. How are you?" I can see from the textured walls that he's sitting on the couch in his office at work.

"Hey, Parker. I get to talk to you twice today."

"Yeah. My meeting ended early, and I was thinking about you. How did your day go?"

"Mixed...but cool."

"What does that mean?"

"Well, I need your advice on how to handle the British media. And I had a fun tour around the city today. So, you know, mixed."

He presses his lips together in response, and I'm happy to see him a little more relaxed.

"Okay. What's happening in England?"

I tell him the problem I'm trying to solve. Like me, Parker's spent time living and working in England. I'm confident he'll see an angle to solve this I might not have considered. Plus, he has a lot of connections. I can tell by the serious look on his face he's already thinking through how to solve my issue. Usually, I could figure this out on my own, but the meeting is on Monday, and time is of the essence.

"Can you tell me the name of the media company?" he asks, and I nod. I watch as he types something into his computer. I can see the reflection in his eyes. He's scrolling through something. "I'm familiar with them. There's no conflict of interest between us and them, so that's a bonus for when I reach out. Our agreements are still in place, so let me work on this and get back to you." Parker and I may not work for the same company, but we wanted protections in place in case our paths crossed legally so our companies have NDAs on file.

"Parker, you don't have to do this."

"Dealing with a shady news media outlet making a false claim against an exec at one the world's largest companies is not anything you want to get your hands dirty with, Rain. They could easily turn this on you, making you their next target. They're just out for blood. That could get you pulled off this deal. We don't want that. I'll yank the necessary chain, and this will snap back in place. Based on what you shared, the media company stepped out of line, not your client. I'm looking at the article now. This appears to be some disgruntled former employee of Soala feeding information to them."

"Yeah, June and I worked there together."

"Now that she's a big fish at Ross Enterprises, someone's looking to cash in. That's why you need to let me handle the media outlet. I've got this. I'll reach out to Soala's legal team."

He's right, this is just about the money, and if they'll come after her, making false claims, and if I insert myself, they'll come after me. Me… it's not until he says it that I realize how far I've come. My client, Ross Enterprises, is one of the largest companies in the world. I represent them. Oh my god—this is real. I'm finally making my mark.

"I owe you, Parker."

"Just be happy. I don't want you to stress. You good?"

"So much better, thanks to you."

"What's happening with the situation you're in?" he asks, and I feel his mood shift. I understand. It's always the hardest part—discussing other men with the man who was the love of your life.

"It's fine, Parker. Dinner tonight, but trust me, I've been listening to you. I'm trying to keep things in perspective and will be back on Monday. You better be there waiting for me."

"With open arms. Tell me you've got this under control."

"I have this under control."

He sighs. "If you need anything, call. Be safe, and tell me you love me."

"I love you, Parker. Thanks for your help. Have a good evening."

After the call, I request the bill from the server, but she tells me it was already settled. Nik meant it when he said he didn't want me to spend money. On the ride back to the house, I go through my to-do list. I still need to text my sister and let her know when I'll hook up with her. I'm not ready to deal with that, so I put my phone back in my purse. I have the driver take me down the road to a quaint neighborhood to Leschi Market so I can get some snacks. Nik's version of snacks is a full-blown meal. There's no way he shopped for himself. The confused look on his face when I mentioned buying sardines was priceless.

The ride back to the lake house is short. I'm exhausted from the day's activities, so I decide to take a nap so that I'm rested for the night ahead. My rest doesn't last long, because Nik arrives earlier than I anticipated.

"Rain." I feel the warmth of his breath sweeping across my cheek, carrying my name in a whisper, accompanied by a warm embrace.

CHAPTER 20

Protect Her

Noah

Although productive, the two-hour return flight from San Francisco to Seattle was agonizing. My desire to return to Rain competes with my need to secure my business deals, further build our firm, and positively impact the community. I use the time to catch up on work and have our team draft a response to the document from Wade Wallace. This deal is essential. I want it more than anything, and I'll stop at nothing to lock it down and make it mine. Or would I? Rain has me questioning myself and my priorities.

The emotions I felt when Mak told me I would be home soon caught me off guard. It hadn't occurred to me that that's where I was heading... home. To my new home, to a woman named Rain, whom I serendipitously met and who made me want to be a different man in the few days we've spent together. To be a man that comes home to a woman like Rain. A woman who's beautiful, smart, and sassy and dines on sardines and crackers. This all feels so new, real, yet familiar in a personal way, and I don't know if I'm ready for that. Not yet. I don't know what I'm doing. All I know is that arriving home early is the highlight of my day because Rain is right where I want her, in my bed at home.

I don't hesitate to strip off my clothes to have my woman. The one who's mine for the week.

"Rain," I whisper, then slide under the covers and wrap my arms around her. She feels soft and warm, like heaven on earth. Like home.

"Hey, how long have you been here?" she asks, all sleepy as she turns to face me.

"Long enough to get naked," I tell her and kiss her like there's no tomorrow, but I need to see her beautiful face, so I reluctantly break the kiss to look at her. Rain is so beautiful and giving, and I don't know if I'll ever meet anyone like her again. My body is hard for her, but I don't take her…yet. "So, how was the tour?" I ask.

"Good enough that I might have you three or four times before dinner." She says words that make my heart race and my dick ache for her. Rain desires me, and I desperately want her back.

"Wow, that good? I guess we better get started." I kiss her, and it's wet, wild, and wonderful because Rain is all those things and more. I can't get enough and sink into her as our bodies bang over and over until we both find our release.

❧

After having Rain as often as she'll let me, she forces me out of bed and into the shower. My desire for her is insatiable, but I promised her dinner and a show, and I'm a man of my word.

Once I finally get some clothes on, I watch her in the mirror. She is stunning. I walk up behind her, hold her, and dare to think about what it would be like to do this every day. When I think about it, I'm not even sure I have what it takes to sustain being who I am around her. If we weren't in this temporary situation, would Rain want a man like me? During the short time we've been together, I've shown her a side of me that I didn't realize was buried deep inside. Rain also caught a glimpse of the man I am without her. The man I needed to be to become the success I am. The type of man that would break her heart. But I tuck the former version of me away, because I have her for a few more days.

One of the must-do things on Rain's list was to see a show at the Jazz Alley Supper Club. I secured front-row seats for the show. Before the show begins, I catch up on her day. I inform Rain that we're invited to attend Chase's birthday party tomorrow evening. Surprisingly, she seems okay about it, but I shouldn't be surprised. Like Rain pointed out the day I met her, I was used to a particular type of woman. Rain shows me what it's like to have an independent woman on my arm. She is tough, stubborn, and has a wild streak that smooths out those edges. I enjoy the combination because it makes her spontaneous and sexy.

"Sounds like fun. I can't wait to see what Chase looks like. Does your whole family possess the sexy gene? You guys, oh my god…," she starts to say, but I can tell she's getting flustered. Her unfiltered way of being is cute, and it makes me want her even more.

When I tell Rok he is going to eat this up, and Mak, well, he's my baby brother, he is used to women reacting to him like this by now, but I know because it's her, he'll still get a kick out of it. They really like her, but she is on borrowed time, and they know it.

Our evening at the jazz supper club is going well until we leave, and on the way home, Rain discloses her concern about her ex-boyfriend.

"The coward texted me demanding that I call him." The crack in Rain's voice signals that her disclosure makes her uneasy. An intense surge of heat crawls up my neck, and, at this moment, I understand what it means for your blood to boil. I don't know what it is about this woman, but my instinct is to protect her at all costs.

"Who is this guy, Rain?" I snap involuntarily.

"We said no names."

"Our names. What's his?" My words come out as a demand. I'm doing everything within my power to restrain myself. This coward needs to leave Rain alone.

"I can handle this. I'll deal with him when I get back home. But thank you for offering to help. I wouldn't have mentioned it, but it was weighing on my mind. I can't control how my brain associates dates with events. Especially negative ones. A week ago today, Blake was with another woman. He told me he was somewhere else."

"Rain, you should not have had to go through something like that. Let me take care of this situation for you. Any man who's willing to be deceitful in his personal life won't stop there. This man needs to be dealt with."

"No. I got it," she tells me, and despite my anger and instinct to protect her, I have to respect her wishes.

The afterglow of sex, when Rain wraps herself around me to catch her breath, is one of my favorite moments. When she's tucked away in my arms with her breast pressed to my side, legs tangled around me as our sweat mingles and our heartbeats sync. For those few minutes, she belongs to me, and I watch her, savoring every second. I don't want to close my eyes for fear that the moment will end. Because when I fall asleep, I lose a piece of her as moments slip away. Sometime in the early morning, she steals away to her favorite room. I know she's talking with her friend, but I don't ask about it, and I need to remind myself that she's not mine to claim. Because Monday will be here way too soon.

I surprise her by making breakfast instead of bringing in the chef. I don't recall the last time I made anyone breakfast. It feels good doing that for her. Seeing the way her face lights up is my new favorite thing.

"Who would have thought you could cook?" Rain tells me.

"We had this discussion before. However, don't get too excited. It's only eggs."

"Eggs or not, I appreciate it. Thank you."

"So, what are your thoughts about this party we're attending later? I understand it's last minute, but if you don't feel like going, I can arrange for the cook to make dinner for you tonight."

"It's a party. I have every intention of going. But I need to figure out what to wear because I already wore the only party dress I brought."

"We can add shopping to our agenda for today. How's that sound?"

"Sure. I have some things brewing at work that I need to attend to this morning, but afterward, we can go shopping if that's okay?"

"Works for me." That'll give me time to take care of a few things Mak sent me to review. But I don't say that to her.

While Rain takes refuge in the sitting room with a view of the lake where I found her the first morning in this house, I head to the office at the back of the house. I notice a drawing on my notepad when I turn on my laptop. It's a sketch of the Space Needle that Rain must have drawn when she was working here yesterday. She's so creative, and I wonder if she's an artist. I rip the page from the notepad. I think about putting it in the drawer where I keep the other mementos. I lift it to my nose and inhale. Jasmine and honey. These bits of her will be the things that will remind me of our time together. They'll remind me of a woman who, in less than a week, did something I didn't think was possible. She stole my heart. Instead of putting the sketch away, I slide it into the corner of a photo frame holding a picture of my brothers and me. Hmm, my brothers…. I have a feeling that after they meet Rain, they'll be more attached than they already are. But I can't think about that now. I need to get to work.

My first order of business is to ensure we're on track with submitting documentation to Wade Wallace's team. My team assures me everything will be submitted on time. As requested, Jim gives me a detailed brief on Wade and his family situation. From the file, it appears Wade is taking his property out to bid because his sons don't plan to take over with development portion of their business, to their father's disappointment. Jude and his brother Jayden are expanding their media corporation and are in the final stages of a business acquisition. I can only imagine how my father would have felt if my brothers and I turned away from the legacy he'd built. But my dad doesn't have to worry about that. He gets to relax and watch his sons continue to grow his legacy for future generations. Having this bit of information gives me an idea of how I can get an edge over the competition. We have a proven track record of success and a commitment to continuing our family legacy. That's right up Wade's alley.

In addition to the Wade Building bid, I have another deal in the final stages for next week, which leads me to jump on a call with my brother.

"Mak, talk to me about the upcoming development agreement. I see our attorney has raised a few flags."

"It's not on our end. Our client was named in a lawsuit that was picked up by the media."

"Then our standard protocol overrules. We won't do business with them. The ethics clause in the agreement states they can't engage in unethical behavior. If what the media states is true, they breached the agreement before it was even inked. We can't be linked with a company involved in a scandal. The value of our brand reputation alone is worth more than any deal can bring in for us."

"Got it. I just wanted to ensure you're okay with my approach before I go back to them and tell them the deal is off if they can't fix this."

"You have my approval. Give them an ultimatum. Fix it, or we walk. Get Rok's sign-off and let me know if anything changes."

"Will do."

"Anything else?"

"No. We'll see you two tomorrow. I'm looking forward to meeting Rae."

"Yeah, Casanova, be on your best behavior. Later," I say and end the call.

By the time I finish work, I check in on Rain and find her wrapping up whatever she's been working on. She's a lovely sight I could get used to in my life, sitting on the lounger typing on her iPad. I walk over, dip my head, and kiss her deeply to recapture all the moments I've missed over the past hour.

"Miss me?" she asks knowingly.

"Seems I can't hide the fact."

It's been a while since I've missed anything. When we left London years ago, I remember how hard it was to be away from everything and everyone I'd grown up around. Focusing my energy on my education helped me overcome the feeling of loss. I liked the discipline that required me to stay focused in school to master various subjects while concurrently learning American history. It didn't matter what the subject was. I liked learning and gathering knowledge—keeping my mind preoccupied. I also liked the consistency of going to a familiar place—school, home, football practice, time with my family, and Dad's office. Getting back those things I thought I'd lost. The routine of it all grounded me. My dad told me knowledge is power, and that kept me focused. He said people can take everything from you but can't take your knowledge; therefore, they can't take your power.

"Don't try. Isn't that what we're here to do…enjoy us?"

"I think you put some juju on me the day I met you."

"Here, I thought I was using repellant after how strong you were coming on to me."

"What?" I feign ignorance.

"You know all the bad boy lines you were throwing at me. I distinctly remember you telling me you can't come inside me while calling me Rae?"

"Okay. I recall that and delivering on my promise by coming inside you and calling out Rain. No regrets." I pull her to her feet, grab her hips, and pull her into my hardened body so she can feel what she does to me. Dipping my head, I kiss her hard. Rain wraps her arm around my neck and licks into my mouth, returning my passion. I break the kiss. "Rain, I want to come inside you again, calling your name."

She swallows. "You can call me Rain anytime." Her words come out in a rushed breath. I lift her until she's straddling me and carry her to the bedroom. And like I did the last time, I come inside her, calling out her name.

Despite the extracurricular activities, Rain and I finally get out of bed and get dressed so I can take her shopping. I arranged for a stylist at Nordstrom to meet us and show her a broad selection of party and evening dresses. Watching a woman try on dresses is a new experience for me. On the rare occasions I'm at the store, I see men taking their women shopping, and the man is usually trailing behind, seemingly bored. Watching Rain, I feel far from that. I have a prime seat in the dressing room as she slips in and out of clothes. First, she tries on a simple black sheath that is sexy yet conservative, then a gold shimmery number that I can see her wearing at a New Year's party, and next is a long crocheted gown with crystals sewn into it, which I plan to secretly purchase anyway. I also like how she looks in the yellow ombre slip dress that would work well at a summer cocktail party or a wedding. Chase's birthday party is not formal. However, the women in attendance will likely be decked out in whatever they wear.

"What about this one?" she asks, turning around in a silk strapless green dress that sits above her knees. She looks great in everything she has tried on so far.

"Not that one," I tell her.

"Seriously? Why?"

"Because you look absolutely fuckable in that. And I might just take you right here in this dressing room." I walk over to where she stands on a raised platform surrounded by mirrors. She turns around to try to see her reflection from all sides in the mirrors bordering the small room's walls. Standing behind her, I kiss her neck as we stare at our reflection in the mirror. We make the perfect-looking couple, and I imagine us having beautiful babies. The thought lingers in my head. It is the first time I've thought about having my own family. Rain is the type of woman a man wants to start a family with.

"You wouldn't dare."

Challenge accepted. I unzip the green dress, and it falls to the ground. "Nik, what are you doing?" she half-heartedly protests.

"Showing you how much I appreciate seeing you in that dress." I turn Rain to face me, pull her close, and kiss her. It's slow and sensual and all the things it shouldn't be in the dressing room. We both get caught up in the kiss, and I slide my hand between us and down her silk underwear. I push two fingers in and move them in and out while massaging her clit with my thumb. Her body responds in rhythm with my movements until I feel the beginning of her contraction around them. As my fingers continue, her response intensifies. I mask Rain's groans with a kiss until she comes on my hand in the middle of the dressing room. Watching her when she's flushed from desire is the most beautiful sight.

"Nik." She pants. Then she steps out of the dress and walks me backward to the chair until my calves bump into it.

She puts her hands on my shoulder, guiding me to sit. Then Rain kneels in front of me and frees my raging cock. She sweeps her fingers along my length before wrapping them around me. Then she licks the tip like a popsicle, and I want to explode because I'm so wound up. After licking, kissing, and tasting me, she wraps her luscious lips around me, takes me deep to the back of her throat, and I groan. "Fuck."

She works my shaft, sucking hard, in and out, and I feel the rumbling of my release pushing through me. "Rain, I'm going to come," I warn her, but she doesn't stop. My balls tighten, and I thrust up, exploding in her mouth, and she takes in every drop like it's giving her life. "Fuck," I growl. When she's done, I pull her to my lap and hold her there until my breath is under control.

"We're getting the green one," I tell her.

CHAPTER 21

A Matter of Seconds

Raven

WHEN I BEGAN THIS WEEK IN SEATTLE, I NEVER EXPECTED TO HAVE a one-night stand, let alone a week-long affair with a man I barely know. Now, I'm attending a birthday party with his relatives while still trying to maintain our anonymity. The party is on the top floor of a glass and steel building with a view of the city, and there is a bar in the center of the room. High tops and other tables are dotted around the room and dance floor near the DJ, who's pumping out R&B tunes mixed with afro beats through the speakers. The place is teeming with women with barely-there dresses and high heels and guys suited up.

The room is crowded, but as soon as we walk in, a tall man, whom I recognize as a slightly older version of Nik, heads towards us. I know immediately it's Rok. He's about an inch taller than Nik and just as gorgeous.

"Hey, brother. Mak and I have been waiting for you. And this beautiful creature...," he says, taking my hand and bringing it to his lips. "I think I need to bow down to you." He kisses my hand, and honestly, I want to melt. He's so smooth, and his perfectly chiseled face is "I'm having your fifty-eleven babies" kind of fine. I think my mouth is open by the way he's smirking. I snap it shut. Shoot.

"Hi, Rok, nice to meet you finally. You caught me mid-drool?" I touch my lips and smile mischievously because I can't hide the truth.

"Yeah, I get that a lot." He laughs and pats his brother's shoulder. "She keeps looking at me like that, and I'm a snatch her up, man," he jokes.

"Rain, stay away from him. He's dangerous." Nik dips his head and claims me with his lips. And I know I'm exactly where I belong.

"Where's Mak?"

"Making his rounds, checking out the sights. You know. Don't worry, like a moth to a flame, he will find this one in a matter of seconds." Rok lifts his chin toward me. Nik rolls his eyes.

"It's a good thing I found her first. You talk to Chase yet?"

"We caught up when I arrived. He's waiting for you but got pulled into a conversation with Drew. I need to hit Drew up for a second. Let me send Chase your way. Lil Sis, I'll see you in a bit. Stay out of trouble until then." He dips his head and surprises me by kissing me on the cheek. Then, he winks at his brother and disappears into the crowd.

"I'm going to have to keep you and Rok separated," he teases me. "I'm getting jealous."

"Right." I rise on my tiptoes to kiss him—letting him know just how into him I am, and when I feel him deepen the kiss, I pull back because I know Nik can't control himself.

"You are trouble, aren't you?" He smirks and adjusts himself. "Speaking of, I see Chase heading our way."

I watch as a man who favors Mak but with a dimple on his chin walks toward us. He's hot and has a swagger that says he's the birthday boy and here for sin.

"Hey, Cuz, glad you made it." He takes Nik's hand, and they pull their arms to their chest and bump shoulders.

"Yeah, my brothers were hitting me up hard," Nik says, and I notice Chase staring at me. Nik notices, too. "Hey, man, let me introduce you to Rain."

"Rain…" He pauses. "We get a lot of that here in Seattle, but nothing as beautiful as you. Good to meet you."

"Nice to meet you, Chase."

"Listen, Nik. I need to make that introduction we discussed. You know the dude only came here to see you," he says, then turns to me. "Rain, you okay for ten? Because I need to steal your man here. They'll fix you up at the bar but don't worry, I'll come to find you after I settle Nik in, and my cousins are floating around here somewhere."

Nik pulls me into his side. "This won't take long. Will you be okay for a bit?"

"Absolutely. I'll grab a drink then go find your brothers." Nik dips his head and kisses me. "Don't worry. I'm sure they have eyes on you," he says, but I don't know what he means by that. It doesn't matter. It's a party, I'm on holiday, and I'll have a good time no matter what.

Chase begins to walk away with Nik, but he turns back. "I like that you have my man on lock." He winks, and they disappear into the crowd.

Knowing what I want, I orient myself and walk straight to the bar. The crowd is thick, with people gathering around the bar. I could easily push my way through, but I get distracted when a purse hits the floor near my feet. The woman in front of me at the bar accidentally dropped it, but she didn't notice. I reach to retrieve it, but someone else is already reaching for it.

"You dropped this."

I freeze. I recognize the voice, and not from Seattle. I take a deep breath and straighten.

CHAPTER 22

Find Me

Raven

WHEN I STRAIGHTEN, I FIND MYSELF FACE TO FACE WITH FUCKING Blake Wallace, the coward. How the hell is he even here?

"It's not mine." I lift my chin to the bar, and he places it there.

"Didn't expect to see you here," he says. Bile begins to rise in my throat at the sight of him.

He's the last person I expected to see here. When I left him sitting at the restaurant a week ago today, I told him I never wanted to see his face again. I remember the smug look he gave me after I confronted him. I tried to tell myself that the restaurant manager must have been mistaken about seeing Blake the previous night.

Now, Blake is standing in front of me, acting like nothing happened. Only an egotistical jerk would think I'd want to talk after I've rejected him. An egotistical jerk like…. My mind flashes back to my college days, like Kevin. Kevin was the last egotistical jerk who dared to walk up on me like this at a party. *"You and Molly look good out there,"* he whispered in my ear. I still recall the scent of beer mixed with something that smelled like cheap hotel soap rolling off him. The burn of bile battling its way to the surface brings me back to my current dilemma. Blake.

"I'm not here for you." My voice is calm but laced with finality.

"No, I didn't think you were after you sicced your hound on me. About that—."

"Don't you dare bring him into this discussion. You're the one who fucked up."

"Where's your sidekick anyway?"

"I'm not discussing anything with you. Walk away, Blake. This won't end well," I tell him, and he knows from experience that I mean what I say.

When he doesn't walk away, I take out my phone like I'm preoccupied and begin a text message. Nik told me that if I needed help, I could contact him and his brothers. Nik is entrenched in a meeting, and I don't want to disturb him. I don't want to ask for help from them, however, I also don't want a scene with Blake. And I certainly don't want him to drag Parker's name into this. Because I can't keep my mouth shut if Blake starts something. I refuse to do this with him right now, so I do the next best thing—I text Rok.

Blake doesn't take the hint to leave me alone, and his voice grates on my ears like fingernails on a chalkboard above the crowd's noise.

"So, you really going to pretend like I'm not here?"

God, what did I ever see in this man?

Me: Find me.

I press send on the text, trusting Nik that someone will respond in less than three seconds. For Blake's sake, I pray my message doesn't roll to Nik. I count to myself. One.

"I got you, beautiful." The words come as a whisper in my ear meant only for me, and I immediately recognize the silky-smooth sound of Baby Mak's voice. It's my first time seeing him in person, and I understand why his brothers refer to him as Casanova. His seductive voice alone will make your panties drop, but his face is…perfection. He slips his hand around my waist and then kisses my cheek. "Hey, Sis. Ready to go mingle?" he says so Blake can hear. I nod.

"I was talking," Blake barks, snapping me out of my dreamy Casanova haze.

"And now you're done," Mak says flatly, eyes narrowing.

"Rae, like I was—," Blake starts up again.

"Listen. I'd ask your name, but I already know it. And when I know the name of someone who's a nobody, that's bad news for them," Mak says. I'm curious how he knows Blake.

"I don't know what you think you know."

Mak sighs, and his beautiful face takes on an ominous appearance. "Blake. Here's what I know," he says, and absent is the silky-smooth panty-dropping tone, replaced by a deep clipped timbre. He steps forward. He gently guides me behind him but doesn't let me go. He looks down on Blake, who's a few inches shorter. "In three seconds, you'll be walking out that door. Forget you ever knew my Sis. Oh, Blake, I'll tell your boy Jude you had to bounce," he says. I feel myself being pulled away. When my back hits a muscular chest, I crane my neck and see Rok.

"I got you, Lil Sis. You can stand here for a front-row seat. This will only take a second," he says with a slight smirk. Then I notice Chase beside Mak and a group of other men I don't recognize surrounding them. I lose sight of Blake for a split second until I glimpse his back as he heads toward the door. And just like Mak said, he's gone in a matter of seconds.

"So, Lil Sis, ready to get this party started?" Rok takes my hand and leads me to the dance floor.

Once Rok and I take the dance floor, the song switches to *Golden* by Jill Scott. I'm still a little shaken by my encounter with Blake, and I suspect by the way Rok is looking at me like a doctor observing his patient, he senses it. Although we're dancing apart, he hasn't let go of my hand. He catches my eye.

"You okay, Lil Sis?" I nod. "What's Blake Wallace to you?" he asks. His voice is steady and calm. There's a slight edge to it, but I don't think it's meant for me because he obviously knows Blake. I just don't know if that's good or bad.

I close the distance, putting my hand on his shoulder so he can hear my voice above the noise.

"He's my ex. The one who cheated on me." He nods, looks over my shoulder at something or someone, and then his eyes shift back to me.

"He won't return here, but I can make sure he doesn't hassle you again. Say the word. I'll take care of it."

"It's fine, Rok, thank you. I was just surprised to see him here, is all. I feel bad it caused a scene."

He smiles down at me. "You caused a scene the second you walked in the door. I'm sure my brother has already told you how lovely you are. No one was paying attention to Blake. Anyway...." He takes my hand and twirls me when the song changes again. "You let me know if you need my help, Lil Sis."

"I will."

CHAPTER 23

Hey, Jude

Noah

IF THERE'S A MOMENT THAT MARKS A MILESTONE IN MY LIFE, THIS IS it. She is the first woman I've formally introduced to my family. While my brothers have met Rain over FaceTime, this is the first time they'll meet her in person. They're likely hoping this is the start of something long-lasting, so I should remind them to cherish this occasion. Who knows if it'll happen again?

Upon our arrival at the party, my brother Rok approaches us, and I introduce him to Rain. Right away, it's obvious Rok's striking looks take Rain by surprise. It's clear that she's impressed by his larger-than-life imposing figure. When I think about it, I should feel self-conscious, but I don't because I sense by the way she's holding on to me that Rain is secure in her choice. Yet still, I find it cute. If she's crushing on Rok, I can only imagine what will happen when she meets Casanova. The effect my baby brother Mak has on women is a mystery to me.

We chat with my older brother for a while. Rain's magnetic personality makes it easy for him to connect with her. Other than her blushing, you'd never know she hadn't met Rok before today. As my brother heads off to find Chase, I look down at Rain, who's standing at my side. She's so beautiful. I hate leaving her to attend this meeting, but this potential deal with Wade Wallace is important.

"You are trouble, aren't you?" I bend and kiss her head. "Speaking of, I see Chase heading our way."

It's been a few weeks since I've seen him. We typically get together for family holiday events or if our paths cross in business. On rare occasions, like recently, Chase joins my brothers and me for a drink on a Friday after work before heading into the weekend. In our family, Chase is the one we refer to as "the connector." He knows a lot of people. And if you need to find a guy about a thing, to take care of something, he's the one to call. Which is why I'm about to meet one of Wade Wallace's sons.

I follow Chase out of the main room and into a smaller room across the hall.

"Jude's over here. I'll introduce you two, then you can get back to your girl."

"Thanks, man. I appreciate you all for keeping her company and for setting up this meeting. Save me some cake," I tell him. I see Jude before he sees me.

"Jude. I found Noah. Noah, this is Jude Wallace. I'll let you do your thing. When you're done, make sure you join me for a birthday toast and some cake."

"Noah. Nice to meet you. I've heard a lot about you. I think my dad secretly wishes he had a son like you," Jude confesses. I'm taken aback at how upfront he is during our first interaction. I shouldn't be surprised by his honesty because of who his father is, but you never know.

"Call me Nik. It's good to finally connect. I'm sure your dad appreciates the man you are. You and your brother are making a name for yourselves. But now that you mention it, that gives me some insight into why I was among the few invited to meet him. So, what's the situation? Why the cut for the meeting?"

"My brother, Jayden, and I are expanding our media company. The real estate development space is not our forte. We worked with Dad to hire some young blood into the ranks, but at the end of the day, he wants to retire."

"And you and Jayden won't transition to take it over."

"No, man. Media is my blood. I'm sure you know what it's like when the right thing hits you, which is unfortunate because there's no next generation beneath us yet. He's looking for someone passionate about this type of work. You and your brothers and a few others made the shortlist because of how you manage your business. He's been watching you."

"Good to know my reputation precedes me," I say as the private line in my coat signals. It can only be Rain. I pull it out and see her text to Rok:

Rain: Find me.

Fuck, fuck, fuck. What in the world is causing Rain to reach out? The heat crawls up my neck at the thought of her needing help and me being in here instead of with her. My first instinct is to end this meeting and go to her. But I need to trust that my brothers have this under control. This is my worst nightmare coming true. Not having control over the situation—I don't know what I'd do if something happened to Rain. I feel a sense of helplessness I haven't felt in years, and I don't like it. My phone buzzes again.

Rok: All good. Mak's with Rain.

I read the text but feel only slightly relieved because I don't know what caused Rain to reach out in the first place. I take a deep breath and remind myself that my brothers are out there. I have complete faith that my family will protect her. The way Rok and Chase looked at Rain like she was one of us when they met her tells me I have nothing to worry about. However, my need to protect Rain is overwhelming. Let it go... they got this. I struggle to tamp down my feelings and focus on this deal. The sound of Jude's voice pulls me back into the meeting.

"Listen, man, stay on the straight, jump through his hoops, and you should be good. If you have questions about navigating my dad's oddities, drop me a line."

"Good to know. I appreciate it. Was this one of those hoops?"

"Your question shows me you're on top of this," he says in subtle confirmation.

"I have one more question."

"Shoot."

"What do you know about the fourth bidder? I found out this person had a private meeting with your dad."

"On that note, you know more than me. I wasn't aware of the private meeting. I can look into it and see if I can get a name."

"I'd appreciate it, man, but I'm not asking you to overstep."

"Nah, I'm glad you brought it to my attention. Jayden and I need to be on top of these things," Jude says. I can tell by his look that he's thinking about what I said.

Jude and I hash out a few more logistical items related to the development deal that I should consider. Then, we discuss Knight Development Corporation's potential to work with his media company.

"I'll put you in contact with my head of PR," I tell him before we conclude our meeting. We shake hands, and I leave to find Rain.

When I arrive in the main room, I spot her, as I suspected, with Rok. They are on fire on the dance floor, and she looks so happy, shaking her hips and cutting moves with my brother. He looks up and catches my eye, and the look he gives me confirms that I did good with her. I watch them dance a few sets, and when she sees me, she drags Rok off the floor toward me.

"I could have sworn I said we needed to keep you two separated, yet here you are delivering the smoothest moves out on the dance floor."

Rain laughs. She's out of breath. She slips an arm around my waist, but Rok still has her other hand. "This guy here. Wow. I did my best to keep up with him. Thanks for the dance, Rok," she says. Rok kisses her fingers before letting go of her hand, and Rain places it on my chest.

"Nik, I'm warning you, keep an eye out on this one because I'm coming after her. Oh, and we handled the situation."

I look down at Rain and inspect her. "Hey, are you okay? Want to talk about what happened? I saw your message come through."

"I'm okay, but it turns out my ex was on the guest list."

"Blake Wallace," Rok interjects.

Shit. Blake Wallace, cousin to Jude Wallace. How the fuck is Rain connected to him? Fuck, Fuck, Fuck.

"What the fuck. Where is he? Did he touch you?" I scan the room, but I don't see Blake. I turn to my brother. He knows I'm pissed. He shakes his head like he does when I get riled up in a meeting and he wants me to calm down.

"No," she says. "He was upset and wanted to argue, but I told him I wasn't talking to him. It's okay, Nik. He's gone."

I look at my brother for confirmation.

"He didn't touch her. Mak slid in and handled it, Nik. It was fine. Then I stole your girl." Rok talks like it's nothing, but I'm seething inside knowing Blake was here and tried to engage with Rain. However, Rok is the most level-headed of the three of us, and I need to take his lead and not give the situation more attention than needed. Rain is safe and seems to be having a good time, and that's the most important thing at the moment.

"I see that. Where's—," I start to ask about Mak, and as if conjured, he appears.

"Hey, Sis," he says, kissing Rain's cheek. "Did you save a dance for me because I have better moves than this old guy?" Mak gestures to Rok, and here we go. The competition is on.

"Nik, can you handle watching me dance with Mak for a song?"

"Or two," Mak adds.

"Or two…. We'll see how it goes, Mak. I don't know. You might be too smooth for me."

"Bring my girl back after one dance, Mak." I watch as Mak holds his hand out for Rain to take. Rok raises an eyebrow, giving me the "Are you sure about that?" look. Rain puts her hand in Mak's, but before she walks away, she turns and kisses me. I'm sure.

"Don't worry. I'll be back." She smiles, and it lights me up inside to know she's having fun with my brothers, and it's all good. I finally feel I can calm down.

"That's if I don't convince you otherwise. They don't call me Casanova for nothing," Mak says. He laughs as he takes Rain to the dance floor.

"So, what was the deal with Blake, Rok?"

"You were right calling him a coward. Although, at the time, I didn't know her ex was Blake. I watched the whole scene. He walked up to Rain and initially appeared to be helping her with something. However, she seemed annoyed, and it quickly became apparent she didn't want anything to do with him. When she couldn't diffuse the situation, she signaled us. Mak was already on the prowl for her when the message came through. Blake must have thought Mak was some chump and ignored him, but that only lasted for a second. Chase and the entire crew walked up to them, and I pulled your girl out of there so she could watch the action from the sidelines. I didn't know he was her ex until I asked how she knew Blake."

"I didn't know Blake Wallace was her ex, either. She wouldn't tell me his name."

"I doubt we'd handle this any differently if she had. You had to take the meeting tonight."

"Maybe you're right, but Rain may not have wanted to attend if she knew. And I doubt she knows of his business reputation. So, he left without a fight."

"You know your brother. Everything he does is smooth."

"Well, I appreciate you guys looking out for her. I saw the message come through while I was with Jude and was dying to come out and take care of it. I'm just relieved to hear the outcome."

"We had you covered. How did the meeting with Jude go?"

"I think we have a real chance, man. I'm researching one potential obstacle, but other than that, I feel good about this."

"Good. How does this thing with Blake play into all this?"

"It shouldn't. Wade Wallace operates with the highest standards. He doesn't approve of his nephew. It's the reason Blake doesn't work for him or his sons. He has no influence on this deal. Still, I need him to stay away from Rain."

"There's nothing you can do about that after this week. She doesn't want us to interfere."

"She told you that?"

"Yeah. Listen, I'll have Jewel put time on the calendar for Monday so you can brief Mak and me on this deal. I understand you're trying to spend as much time with Rain as possible before Monday. You may not want to hear this, but I still think letting her go at the end of the week is the wrong move."

"Rok, I had this discussion with Mak already."

"I know, man. I'm just saying."

"I hear what you're saying."

"No, you don't, man. If I had met her instead of you, we wouldn't be having this discussion. I'd be walking her down the aisle."

"Get out of here." The sincerity of his admission stuns me. He's Roman Knight. The older brother I looked up to all my life. He is the ultimate businessman and a confirmed bachelor. Although Rok hasn't settled down yet, he's been talking a lot about it and trying to get me to consider it. But I didn't think he was serious until now.

"No, man, I'm serious. You need to rethink what you're doing."

"I'll take it under advisement," I tell him to get him off my tip, because if I don't agree to consider what he's telling me, this discussion could turn into something more.

My brothers feel I've put up walls to protect myself. In a way, I suppose I have. The walls I've built have allowed me to focus on taking Knight Development Corporation beyond my father's dreams. And now, these walls will serve to protect Rain from me.

The sound of Rain's laughter pulls me from my thoughts. Mak whispers something to her, and she looks in my direction. He takes her hand and leads her back to me.

He's wearing a wry grin. "Man, you look like you lost something, so I figured I'd bring Rae back."

"Thanks again, Mak, for helping me earlier and for the dance," she says.

"The pleasure is all mine, Sis. If this one's too slow for you, come and grab me again."

"I got her covered, Mak. But she's right. Thanks for looking out for her." Mak and I bump fists, and then I escort Rain to the dance floor. "Okay, Rain, let's show them how to do this."

CHAPTER 24

The Queen Bee

Raven

Chase's party is a great way to kick off the weekend. Despite the brief blip with Blake, I dance the night away with Nik, his brothers, and Chase. Observing Nik interact with his family gives me a new perspective on what lies beneath the bad-boy billionaire. I witness a funny, sexy family man who loves his brothers.

Watching Mak and Chase work the room is also a sight to behold. Standing here, chatting it up with Nik and his brothers, I decide to get a better sense of how this Casanova thing works and I ask Mak what the minimum effort is for him to get a woman's attention. When he tells me he doesn't have to do anything, I stare at him dumbfounded.

"Try it. Choose someone for me." The silky-smooth sound draws me in.

"What?" I ask, confused.

"Just look at someone. Nod, wink, smile. Whatever signal you want to use. You're standing next to me, Rae. Look. They're all watching you. You're the queen bee. Pick someone for me," he says, like I possess all the power in the world.

Rok's eyes shift judgmentally between Mak and me. "You remember what I told you, Lil Sis."

"Stay out of trouble. But you qualified your statement by saying until you returned. You're here now," I deadpan, and he narrows his eyes and shakes his head. I'm sure his brother told him about my recall ability, but it's worth it to catch him off guard.

"Our girl has a point, cuz. Rain, when you're done, I'm next. I need someone nice for a change." Chase chuckles.

"That's not happening," Rok says, but I ignore him, and it dawns on me that this is what it must feel like to have brothers. Or even a sibling that paid me attention. It feels good. My sister and I never hung out in social settings together.

"Okay, Baby Mak, here goes." I study his face briefly, wondering what woman would pair beautifully with him. Mak's a younger, sexy version of Nik. Yet Mak and Chase favor each other so much they could pass for twins. I'm still contemplating his type of woman when Mak's eyes shift from the crowd to catch me staring at him. His lips curl into a sexy smile, and wow, he's so fine. Quintessential Casanova.

"Shit. Quit looking at me like that, Sis. I'm not in the mood to get my ass kicked for stealing my brother's girl." He laughs, and I roll my eyes at him.

Once I get over my Casanova haze, I turn and scan the room. I see this cute woman with shoulder-length silk-pressed hair wearing a pretty red couture cocktail dress. She looks a little shy, but I can tell by her demeanor that she comes from money. She's talking to her friends. Her friends are watching our interactions, so she turns to see what they're looking at. I catch her gaze and smile, and she smiles back. Then I just curl a finger at this woman, and she doesn't hesitate to walk right over to us. I'm stunned, but I play it off.

"What's your name?" I ask her as if cross-examining a witness.

"Melanie."

"Nice to meet you, Melanie. This is my brother, Mak." Mak smirks at me, and before I can hear his response to Melanie, Rok positions himself between me and my match-made couple and hands me over like a misbehaving child to Nik. I choke back a laugh. I like these guys. We play well together.

"Nik, Mak has your girl doing his bidding for him." Rok chuckles. Nik shakes his head and sweeps me off to the dance floor.

I never get to fix Chase up. Nik and I end the night so tired from dancing that we fall asleep in each other's arms when we return to the house.

CHAPTER 25

I Got You, Babe

Raven

IT'S A FEW HOURS BEFORE SUNRISE, AND I CAN'T SLEEP. MY MIND IS reeling with thoughts of this week and the potential end to whatever Nik and I are doing. I fall into my morning routine and sneak to the safety of the sitting room to call Parker.

"Hey, Parker. Good morning."

"Morning, Rain. What are you doing? It's five o'clock. This is early even for you." I can hear the irritation in his voice. He closes his eyes, reopens them, and focuses on me, reading me. "What's on your mind?"

"I just need to hear your voice. I miss you, Parker." If only he knew how much. I would curl into him and tell him everything I'm feeling if he were here right now. He'd tell me that everything would be okay. That whatever these feelings are, they will dissipate in time. That he's there for me now and forever. But I'd also have to admit I'm a mess and don't know what I'm doing.

Parker's looking at me like he's searching my soul, and I know he sees more than I'm telling him—because he always does.

"I miss you too, but Rain, I don't like the look on your face. Are you okay? Tell me what's happening in Seattle between you and this guy Nik."

The way he says Nik's name reminds me of the first time I had to tell Parker I wanted to date someone who wasn't him. By then, we had been apart three years, but the deal Parker and I struck years ago is not something anyone will ever understand. It was a deal between two inexorable people who loved hard and lost even harder. *"What's his name?"* Parker asked me. Those three words sealed the deal, and the dominos fell. Anyone I dated would have to meet Parker. But Nik is exempt because I'm not dating him. After Monday, I'll never see him again, and he'll never have to come face-to-face with Parker. I'll never have to explain who Parker is to me—that he's the only man I've professed my love to.

"So far, we've been enjoying ourselves touring Seattle, spending almost every moment together except when we step away for work."

"That's a lot of time together. You mentioned previously that this tryst would end this week. Has that changed?"

"No."

"You say you're enjoying your trip but don't sound like yourself. Have you developed feelings for him? Talk to me, Rain. I need to know what you're thinking. I promise I got you no matter what."

Parker wants me to open up to him, but I don't know how without the floodgates breaking and every thought from a lifetime of storms spilling out. Even now, I feel unshed tears fighting their way to the surface. Focus, Rain. Look at his beautiful face, closely trimmed beard, and piercing blue eyes you used to get lost in. I focus on Parker and use all the tools in my arsenal to pull myself out of the kaleidoscope of memories. It's enough to help me center my thoughts so I don't completely lose myself. But it's hard to tamp down my feelings. My face is hot, and although I stare into his eyes, they blur and become crystal blue waves before I feel the water run down my cheeks.

"Ah, honey. It's okay." He reins in his tone. "Please talk to me," he pleads, watching my distress unfold. If I can't pull myself together, he'll be here within hours. I need to focus, but memories of the past flood my mind, and everything feels like it's happening in the present all at once. I see my family, my dad, and my days with Parker, Blake, and Nik. It's too late—I'm spiraling. "Rain. Close your eyes, honey." His words cut through the noise in my head like a knife, and I close my eyes and concentrate on his voice. "Take a deep breath, Rain." I take a deep breath. "That's it. Again." I take another. "Good. Now, concentrate on my voice. Can you do that for me?" I nod, unable to find my voice. "Rain, I'm here. You're safe in the house overlooking a lake. Visualize the water, how it's sparkling under the sun's warm rays."

Parker continues describing the scene outside the window, guiding me through the scene as if he were here with me. His voice is like a beacon guiding me out of a heavy fog toward a clear path. When he senses my breath coming under control, he stops.

"Okay, open your eyes when you're ready and look around." I take a minute, then open my eyes. "Good. Now, tell me five things you see."

"I see you on my phone. I see a blue pillow. I see a beige throw. A painting on the wall. I see an unlit fireplace."

"That's great, Rain. How about four things you can touch around you?"

"My phone. The pillow." I say and pick up the pillow. Then, I rub my hand on the chair. "The lounge chair. My chest." I touch my breast.

"Okay. Enough of that. I think you're doing just fine." He laughs. It's warm, and I feel a sense of calm come over me. "Take another deep breath, then tell me how you feel?" I take a deep breath. "Are you okay to talk?" he asks again. I take another breath, wipe away the tears, then try to focus on what I want to say.

"Parker. I don't know what's happening. I think I'm developing feelings for Nik, but I don't understand them. Our time together is winding down, and I'm trying to enjoy the activities and not focus on feeling. We agreed to just this week, but I want more time."

"Time for what, Rain?"

"To see if there is more between us. To not feel alone. I don't know. When I arrived in Seattle…well, I was still reeling. Still stewing over Blake's BS. I shouldn't have come here until the day before my meeting."

"Tell me what you need."

"I should have come home, Parker. The minute my sister bailed on me, I should have come home. When I said goodbye to you at the airport, I felt like I was being torn away from something." Torn away from what? Parker? A sense of security? I shake my head because I need to pull myself together. This is why I should have taken his suggestion to go to therapy. To better arm myself with the necessary tools to deal with these heavy emotions on my own. To help me wean myself from calls like this.

"What are you saying?" The softness in his voice is gone. It's a valid question because I'm all over the map with my feelings and don't have a good answer.

"I don't know, Parker. Maybe I needed to talk through it with you. To figure out why I can't seem to make these relationships work. To focus on myself. To have time to heal."

"Do you feel you went into this thing with Nik as a rebound?"

"I feel a lot of things. Lonely, missing you, conflicted about saying yes to Nik. He's easy to be with, but how he is with me is not how he is normally."

"What's his normal state?"

I tell Parker about how Nik initially approached me like he was looking for a one-night stand, how he came across then, and how he's different now.

"Tell me he hasn't hurt you."

"No, Parker. He hasn't hurt me. I don't know if the player in him is real or if the way he is with me is real. But he's intentional about how he is with me."

"Which is?"

"Respectful, thoughtful, caring. Nik is completely focused on me when I'm with him like he's enamored." I tell him about how Nik told me to let him know if he does something I don't like because Nik doesn't want to create negative memories for me.

"Rain, it doesn't sound like you two have discussed seeing each other beyond this week. What's your plan?"

"I don't know. I've been asking myself a lot of questions."

"From what you said, you two behave differently than you normally would. If this were to go beyond this week, would he eventually be frustrated for becoming someone he's not? You said he's not this way with other women. Okay, you're the first. What are the other things he's learning about relationships he's yet to experience? Is that the role you want to play, Rain?"

"I'm not sure."

"But you should know these things, Rain. What emotional support are you receiving? Would you receive? What does he know about us?"

"Nothing." He doesn't know anything about my twelve-year history with the man I called the love of my life. Whose heart I broke because

I can't get my act together. He doesn't know about the one I compare every man to and who they all pale in comparison to.

"Does he know why you leave him every morning?"

"No, Parker."

I haven't told Nik that my brain can't handle the trauma from accidentally witnessing my dad leaving us without a word. The man who was my world. The one I looked up to, who I worshipped as a child. He doesn't know how he left in the wee hours of the morning when he didn't think anyone was aware. I knew. I can't unsee his step falter when he figured out that I was there…watching. *"Dad?"* I called out to him. He didn't even turn around. He just walked out of our lives like we never existed.

No, Nik doesn't know that I get up early to avoid sleep terror and that even then, there's no hiding. I can't stop the tape from replaying the scene every morning, marking the hour he left while I sit paralyzed, seeing my former self. That was the last time I ever saw him. No. He has no idea about that or other traumas that are triggered by reliving that one moment. He doesn't know how messed up my mind is. How every blip in my life feels like the searing poke of hot steel branding my brain. How every negative thought brings forth a wave of bile that I have to force down.

He doesn't know the relief I find in the sound of Parker's voice.

"Rain, I didn't mean to upset you."

"It's okay. You're right. If this continues, there's a lot to talk about."

"I'm concerned about you. This is insane. Does he even know you're on the heels of a breakup with Blake?" When he says Blake's name, my stomach turns because I haven't told him about what Blake did, but I need to before he discovers it himself. The situation with Blake needs to end, and even though he walked away from the party, it doesn't mean it's over.

"Can we talk about him?"

"About Blake? Why? What happened, Rain?"

"He was at this party I attended with Nik last night and—."

"Jesus, Rain. He what?"

"He was at this party and approached me upset about his exchange with you. I didn't ask about it. I told him I wasn't having a conversation with him."

"Oh my god. I'm sorry he approached you because of something I did."

"That's not your fault. That's how he is."

"Did he listen to you?"

"No. Blake was persistent, but Nik's brothers handled him, and he left without another word."

Parker closes his eyes a second before reopening them. "Nik's brothers? Where the hell was Nik?"

"He was there meeting with someone to discuss business," I tell him, and the look on Parker's face, like he's about to punch someone, is one I haven't seen since college. It was the night Kevin dared approach me, reeking of beer at a party and trying to make me leave with him. That night, I learned the extent to which Parker would go to protect me. I realized just how powerful his family was and the extent to which they'd go to take care of their own. That was the day many people's lives were forever changed for the worse.

"Listen. I'm going to solve this once and for all. You're going to get a call from Blake today with an apology like he was supposed to give you before. After that I promise that he will never show his face around you again. Take the call, and this will be done."

"But I don't want to talk to him."

"Take the call, Rain," he insists. "You don't have to talk. Just listen. I promise it's done after that."

"No, Parker. I can handle this. If you asked him to apologize, then fine—I agree, he needs to follow through with that. Before I left, I told you that's what I wanted. Will you step aside after that? Don't take any further action."

He takes a deep breath. This is hard for him because he can't deny me anything. "If that's what you want." It's what I want. To stop allowing him to step in, and handle this myself for once. I can do this.

"It is." I don't tell him he's the reason I want to be the one to set Blake straight. That I sense Blake's beef with Parker is not over. He's had one ever since I introduced him to Parker and he realized that Parker's family is the majority shareholder controlling the Wade empire. Parker could shut this down within seconds—but I want to do that. On the other hand, shutting down my emotions for Nik may prove more difficult than I can manage.

"Okay. I'll let you handle it, but Rain, what are your plans with Nik?"

"Honestly, Parker, I don't know. We promised to go our separate ways after this week. I walked away the first night. Even then, it felt difficult. The things you're asking me are questions I've asked myself. I've asked myself what's the attraction besides the power, the confidence, and the attention he gives me. I just want to feel like I'm needed, and I feel that way with him—like there are things I give him that no one else has. That no one else can."

"But what is he giving you? You said this is his first time doing anything like this. Did Nik tell you he wants to continue the relationship?"

"No," I say, and the tears start to fall again.

"Ah, Rain, say the word, and I'll be there in a few hours." His words are a promise of the comfort of his arms that if I ask for it, he'll give. And I desperately want what his promise will bring, but I won't ask.

"I…." I can't bring myself to say the words. To tell Parker to come to me because he will…he'll drop everything to be here in a heartbeat. He's done it before, but it's unfair for him to continue picking up after my mess. I made a mistake. I should have walked away from Nik before it became too much. Before I caught feelings.

"Hey, don't cry. You're not in this alone. I got you," he assures.

"I should have listened to you. Come back to me whole, you told me." But I was too determined to do my own thing versus looking objectively at what Parker was telling me—to realize he was protecting me from myself. It's been a constant battle, thinking I've got the situation under control when sometimes I need to settle down and listen.

"It's okay. When you get back, we'll talk and figure this all out. Don't overthink it. Listen, you still have your upcoming meeting, so you need to pull it together. I dealt with the media company, and they've retracted their claims. I'm forwarding you the confirmation statement now just in case you need it," he says and breaks away from the screen. When he returns, my phone pings with an email alert. "All you need to do now is lock down your clients at the meeting and show them what you're made of."

"Parker, I don't know what I would do without you."

"I'm committed to ensuring you never find out. So, this is the plan. Review what I sent so you can update your clients and close this deal for Monday. Take the call from Blake today. Like I said, I'm only telling him he owes you an apology. When you return, we can continue this conversation and discuss the next steps for both of us. Because, Rain, if I have to fucking put my thumb down on another man, I'll end up in jail, a psych ward, or both. I'm backing off, but this is hard," he says, and I can't help but laugh. "Seriously, Rain. I heard everything you said, and we need to talk. This stops here. We'll figure this out. Regarding Nik, I'm going to rein myself in for twenty-four hours and leave him to you to manage. Just note that it's a very short rein." He emphasizes the last sentence. "You know I have no issue securing the jet to get you. Say the word—I'm there."

Parker's alarm buzzes in the background. It's Sunday. I know his routine by heart. When he gets off this call, he'll go downstairs to his gym and work out for ninety minutes. Cardio. Hydrate. Strength. Stretch. Then he'll take a shower, after which he'll check messages before making something healthy to eat. He'll fit in time to be brilliant and work before going to his parents. I watch as Parker shuts the alarm clock off.

"You have to go."

"The only thing I need to do is talk to you. Nothing else matters right now. How are you feeling?"

"Better, because you make it seem so simple."

"It's not simple. I'm taking the emotion out of it. You think you can handle the next twenty-four hours?"

"Yeah. I think so. Thank you for the work you did for Ross Enterprises. This is a big deal for me."

"I got you, babe. Get your day started, get some breakfast, and don't hesitate to call me if you need me," he says, and then we say our goodbyes.

I mull Parker's words over in my mind. *I got you, babe.* Despite everything, the heartache, the headaches, the men, the memories, the mess—Parker has me. The question is, given the circumstances, would Nik do the same?

CHAPTER 26

It's Our Anniversary

Noah

TODAY IS THE LAST FULL DAY THAT RAIN AND I HAVE TOGETHER. When the clock strikes midnight, it will be Monday, our seventh and final day. Combing my thoughts, I think about how best to appropriately mark the day to make it memorable for Rain. It's times like this when I feel out of my element. The only milestones I've celebrated outside family events are business milestones like the deal we closed last week. I hope to celebrate a few more of those, the deal Monday being one of them. But today is about my final full day with Rain, and it feels more like we're observing an anniversary. That's it. We'll celebrate like it's our anniversary.

It's early. The sun hasn't made an appearance yet. Rain is having her morning call. It's a routine that's a mystery to me. If she were my woman, I'd discover her secret, but she's not, so I don't. Patience isn't my strong suit, especially when I want something, but I'll make an exception for Rain. For now, I know she'll return to my arms afterward. Then, I'll savor our final hours together before our agreement forces me to let her go.

The best I can do is focus on our plans for the day. One of the items on Rain's must-see list is the Space Needle. I've arranged for her to have the ultimate experience. As I send my final text to my assistant, Jewel,

Rain comes back into the room, and instead of sliding back into bed on the side she usually sleeps, she lifts the sheet off me, crawls on top, and straddles me. There's no hiding. I'm hard, but I need to let her take the lead if that's what she wants.

"How is it that you're hard like this, and I just walked into the room?" She reaches behind her, wraps a hand around my length, and squeezes. It takes all my willpower not to throw her on her back and push into her.

"I'm sure we've had this conversation already. This is my permanent state around you. The way I crave you, like berries with the sweetest juice, I'm ruined—no other fruit will satisfy me. Because no woman will ever taste as sweet as you." For whatever reason, I don't want to hide the truth from her. Because the truth is Rain *has* ruined me.

Rain bends, presses her chest to mine, and kisses me. Her mouth lingers like she's savoring my taste, and I wrap my arms around her and deepen the kiss, sucking and licking like a starving man into her. And I am…starved for the future days with Rain that will never come. Starved for all the moments we could have shared had I been the right man for her. Starved for a life I'll never have with her.

The need to have her is too much, so I flip her on her back in a fluid move, grab a condom, cover myself, and sink into her. What I feel for her when I'm unleased is greedy and uncontrollable as I move in and out of her with quick, powerful thrusts. Within moments, she succumbs, crying out my name as her body clenches around mine when she comes. But I know this is only the first because I continue pumping and swirling my shaft. And when she comes the second time, it's with tears in her eyes.

"Are you ok?" I pant, sweat dripping from my head.

"Yeah, it's so good." Her voice is barely audible. Slowing my pace, I move in and out of her and kiss her, enjoying how my body feels deep inside her as we savor the moment.

"Rain. Can you feel what you do to me?" I growl into her neck.

"Nik." My name comes out in a breathy pant. I continue with a slow, deep rhythm as I feel my release build.

"Come for me one more time," I tell her, quickening my pace and steadying our rhythm until I feel her body move in time with mine—until I can't focus on anything other than chasing the feeling that erupts within me. Then, together, we come hard, cursing and calling to one another, and it's primal and urgent, and I never want this moment to end.

"Rain."

∾

I DO MY BEST TO CONTROL MYSELF, BUT RAIN IS JUST AS INSATIABLE as me, so we spend the better part of the morning enjoying each other in bed and then again in the shower. If I'm honest, I think we were making up for lost time following the party.

"Okay, Nik, stand over there while I get dressed." She tells me to get my desire to have her under control. How our bodies fit together and how she feels when I'm inside her has me questioning my plans for today.

"Don't trust me?"

"That's the problem. I believe you when you say you can't control yourself."

"Touché. Are you excited about today?"

"Yes, I've been dying to get to the Space Needle. I think I have a thing for iconic buildings like the Transamerica Building in San Francisco," she says, not knowing what's in store for her today other than our destination.

We go to the kitchen and share a light breakfast of toast, fruit, and coffee. I use the time to update Rain on my idea before we head out.

"So, the plan is to spend part of the morning there, then have lunch."

"This is our last full day together. I have to say, Nik, when you told me you would make all the plans, I didn't know what to expect, but you outdid yourself. Everything so far has been amazing."

"It's not over yet. I was thinking we should mark today as a special event."

"Mark it? How?" she asks, lifting her cup to her lips before taking a sip.

"Like an anniversary."

"What? Like a wedding anniversary?"

"Well, I wasn't thinking that. More like the day we met. It'll be our seventh day in Seattle together when the clock strikes midnight."

A vision of my brother Mak sweating at the mention of a wife and kids flashes in my head. It's the second time I've given the idea of having a family another thought, but there's no way I'm ready to do anything like that. But being with Rain has me constantly questioning whether I am ready. Whether she's the one. Whether I should take our connection further. Whether I can be the type of man it takes. Whether my roots are planted deep enough to start a family.

"Okay, so our one-week anniversary. Basically, do what we would do on a normal anniversary as a couple."

"Something like that."

"I didn't take you for the type to celebrate an anniversary. Then again, you did surprise me by asking me to spend the week with you. I imagine this all feels strange to you."

She's right. The day I saw her sitting at the bar, I saw more than a conquest. I saw a woman of substance, one I wanted to get to know, and I became someone else going after her. I just knew I had to have her, and once I got her, it wasn't enough. I had to have more. To know her name. To understand her dreams. Remember, she's not yours to have, man.

"Questioning myself somewhat, but the time we've spent together has been good. You should know that. This is not something I typically do."

"You don't have to convince me. It's a lovely gesture and a great way to end the week. Although, you didn't give me much time to plan for anything. I want to do something special for you. Will we have time for me to pull something together?"

"Yeah. But I have some things planned that include items from your list."

"You're serious about planning. My gut tells me this is a skill you use in business."

"It is. It's what I'm good at, managing a project from start to finish."

"Don't say anything more. I promised not to pry into your personal affairs. So, what's the dress code for this morning?"

"Casual. What you have on is fine."

"And for later?"

"I picked up a little something for you to wear to dinner. I hope you don't mind. I didn't want you to worry about anything today."

"Nik, you've been so generous. You didn't have to do anything. But I appreciate the thought. I'm sure whatever you've chosen is lovely." She's right. However, she doesn't know that it's one of the dresses she already tried on that I liked. It was too elegant for my cousin's party but perfect for what I have planned for tonight.

"Finish up. We should get going."

The car picks us up at the house, and it doesn't take long to reach our destination. The Space Needle stands tall in the backdrop and gets larger the closer we get. When we arrive at the Space Needle Center, the driver enters the large circular drop-off point and parks in front of the steel and glass building. I help Rain out of the car and hold her hand as we enter the building and pass through the shop and up a ramp that leads to the elevator.

She looks around, confused. "Why are we the only ones here?"

"You have to know all my secrets, don't you?"

"Not necessarily, but I think you went above and beyond. Don't get me wrong, I certainly appreciate it, but this is unexpected." She raises on her toes and gives me a chaste kiss on the lips.

She thinks she's getting off easy, but I grab her by the waist and hold her tight against my body. Then I give her an open mouth kiss that's too inappropriate for public consumption and force myself to pull away before I lose control.

"Nik. You're trying to start a fire in here. Let's get started on our tour."

"You're right," I tell her and gesture for her to continue up the ramp, but she stops me. "You okay, Rain?"

"Yeah, but you're rushing me. I want to read the history wall."

"Lead the way."

I step behind her as she slowly walks up the ramp, taking time to look at the pictures and read the corresponding text, taking us from the concept to construction and, eventually, the unveiling of the building.

I try my hardest not to press my body against her because I'm already hard enough. She smells delicious, and our kiss still has me heated.

Eventually, we make our way to the elevator. She looks down over the empty building but doesn't question me again about it. I don't tell her I rented out the entire building for the morning. We have full access until twelve-thirty, then later again tonight.

Our tour guide joins us in the elevator and reiterates bits of the history of the building the we read on the walls. She tells us the Space Needle was built for the nineteen sixty-two World Fair, whose theme at the time was "The Age of Space."

"The Space Needle has the world's first revolving floor. You'll have a chance to see that," the guide tells us.

I jump in and add some obscure facts about several other World Fair buildings and the length of time it took to build them.

"I don't even want to know why your brain holds that fact," Rain says, and she's right.

The encyclopedia of information I retain about buildings and architecture is astounding even to me. It would be great to share more about that with Rain, but our agreement doesn't allow for much personal insight other than what's required to navigate our time together effectively. Still, sharing this part of me with her would be nice.

The elevator ride is impressive and fast as we arrive at our floor in a matter of seconds.

"It's just a thing I have for architecture," I tell her as she exits the elevator and walks to the floor-to-ceiling windows for an unobstructed view of the city.

"Wow," she says, staring out the window.

The moment is interrupted when my phone buzzes. I step back a few feet and slide it out of my pocket to see a message from Mak:

Mak: Outlined our concerns with the client. The deal will go sideways if they don't respond before Monday.

I did not want to get drawn into this on my last full day with Rain. In the distance, I see her walk through the glass doors to the outside viewing area. She's focused on something on her phone. She has something going on at work, so I expect that's what it's about. I wonder what it would be like to experience both sides. Rain is a beautifully complicated woman who, under other circumstances, I would like to get to know a lot better.

Me: You gave them the ultimatum. If they don't respond, pull the plug.

Mak: You sure?

Me: We can't risk the Wade deal because of this.

Mak: Understood. Will keep you posted.

I feel Rain's arm snake around my waist and her head presses to my back. I hadn't realized she moved from her original position.

"You look like you needed a hug," she says from behind me. I put my phone away and turn to face her.

"More like I need this." I bend and capture the luscious lips that are still mine until tomorrow.

She pulls out of the kiss. "Careful, Nik, or we'll have to break in the Space Needle."

"Kinda like the mile-high club."

"Something like that," she tells me. I recapture her mouth.

If I could spend the rest of today inside Rain, I would. She's that good—that perfect. Walking away from her will be the hardest thing I've done. The one thing I have to hold to is a promise always to protect her. To do that, I'll need to find out who she is. Before we go our separate ways, I plan to ask Rain her last name so I can watch out for her. Because if anything happened to her, I fear it would break me. One loss in a lifetime is one too many. Knowing that after tomorrow, I'll go back to living a life without her is a hard pill to swallow, but a sacrifice I must pay. Because my brothers and I have a business to build. We have a legacy to uphold.

Rain squeezes my arm. "Hey, we still have tonight," she assures me. "That we do."

The morning and afternoon are eaten away by our time lounging around the Space Needle, taking in the view. Then afterward, I take Rain for a casual lunch at a spot she wanted to try. There's a line, and we order and wait outside for it so we can take it back to the house.

"Well, that was a lovely surprise at the Space Needle. I didn't realize they served champagne and snacks."

"They usually have some things to cater to the masses. But what we had was prepared only for us."

"For a guy who's never done this before, you're pretty good at this dating stuff."

"I'll take the compliment. And this." I kiss her again because I can't get enough. Her phone rings. The look on her face is a mix of dread and annoyance, and I sense that whatever it is, she's not happy about it.

"I need to take this," she says and steps aside, but she doesn't go far. "Speak," she commands the person on the phone, in a voice I haven't previously heard her use.

I can tell she's upset, and I feel the same rage simmer within me that I did when she mentioned her issue with Blake. It was the desire to protect her at all costs.

I can't help but focus on her face. When I think about it, I've seen this expression on her before, and at that moment, I know who it is. Fucking Blake Wallace. I told Rain previously that a man capable of lying to a woman won't hesitate to lie in other situations. And there's nothing I loathe more than a liar. It's one of the reasons we include an ethics clause in every contract. Even before I knew his name, I sensed he was bad news. At the party, when I found out it was him, I had confirmation. He's notorious for his underhanded ways. I take a deep breath. Blake is no threat to me, but I don't know whether he is to her. Watching Rain, I'm torn between stepping in and letting her handle her business. The range of expressions her face goes through as she listens to him is about to break me, and I can't take it anymore. I take a step toward her and place a hand on her shoulder.

"Rain? Are you okay?" I ask, allowing her to leverage me if she needs to. She holds up her hand, signaling to me that she's okay. I step away, but not far, watching her as she listens, but she doesn't say a word. Finally, after a few moments, she ends the call. I walk over to Rain and brush the curls from her face.

"You don't have to tell me anything, but that was Blake, right? Just tell me if you need me to do anything. I'll take care of him once and for all."

Rain's lips form a tight smile. "Don't worry. He'll never bother me again." That's all she says, and then she walks toward the restaurant door. We collect our meal and go back to the house to eat it.

Our Mexican food meal is nice. I make margaritas to go with it. Despite Blake's call, Rain is upbeat and chatty.

"Rain, are you sure there's nothing I can help you with?"

"Nik." She stands and walks over to me. I let her stand between my legs. "The only thing you can help me with is celebrating our anniversary in peace. No more talk about you-know-who. Deal?"

"Deal."

She leans into me, and I hold her tight, savoring how she feels in my arms, like she belongs to me. I breathe in the jasmine and honey that I love so much, and my mouth waters, thinking about how she tastes.

"I still can't believe this is not your normal way of being," she blurts out. But it's not a question because I've told her the type of man I am.

"Don't. Try not to think about that side of me."

"So, I have a few more calls to take before heading out on my anniversary shopping trip. What about you?"

"I have a few things being delivered. For the most part, I'll be here waiting for you to return."

"Sounds like a code word for work."

"It's who I am. I'll check in on my brothers and see what they're up to. Want me to tell them you said hi?"

"Yes. Tell Rok and Baby Mak I'm sending them kisses."

"No," I tell her, because as it is, my brothers disapprove of me ending this after tomorrow. I can imagine their faces knowing she's thinking about them. Sending them kisses.

Rain kisses me, and it's sweet and gentle. "Send some of that to your brothers for me. And don't tell me no again."

During our meal, Rain steps away for one more call, and I use the moment to catch up with Mak and Rok in the group chat.

Me: Are we in or out on this deal?

Mak: Just received final word. It's done. We are good to go, and everything is set for Monday.

Rok: What's happening with Lil Sis?

Me: Tonight's the last night. We talked about this.

Mak: You dictated. We didn't talk.

Rok: Don't let her slip away.

Me: I'm not what she needs. Let it go.

Mak: Man, what are you doing?

Me: The right thing. Let it go. Don't you all have something else to do besides ride me about this?

Rok: Besides fight for our Lil Sis? No.

Me: Rain's on her way to the table. Chill.

I put my phone away, but my brothers aren't done with me, as evidenced by the barrage of buzzing in my pocket.

"Ready to go?" I ask. Rain nods.

"The car will be here for you any moment."

I arranged for her to have her own private car to take her to run her errands. Rain leaves, and like a warm blanket being removed, I immediately feel her absence. While Rain is shopping, Jewel stops by to deliver the gifts I had made for Rain.

"Rain must be special. You've never had me arrange anything for a woman that wasn't family."

"She is special." It's the only word to sum up what Rain means to me.

THE HOUSE ALARM ALERTS ME THAT RAIN IS HEADED TO THE FRONT door. The overwhelming sense of relief I feel knowing she's within reach reverberates throughout my body. I open the door, collect her bags, and toss them aside. The way she's looking at me, I can't help but pull her into me and kiss her. It feels needy and raw.

"Wow. Now that's a welcome home kiss."

"You've been gone a while, and in case you haven't noticed, I've developed an addiction to you." She's so beautiful. I stare at her and notice she's studying my face. I know she's memorized every feature, and the sudden realization that my image is forever imprinted in her memory makes me feel…I don't know… seen… alive?

Her voice pulls me out of the haze. "If you keep looking at me like that, you'll have to take me to bed."

She doesn't have to say more. I scoop Rain up, take her to the bedroom, and dive into her.

We go a few rounds before I untangle myself from her so we can shower. Following our shower, I retrieve the dress I had brought for her. Rain stares at me curiously as I unzip the long black garment bag.

"What's this?"

"This is your dress for tonight."

When the beige couture dress is revealed, she gasps. "Oh my god, I remember trying on this one. It's stunning, Nik." She takes the dress from me and lays it across the bed. "You really outdid yourself with this one." She rushes to me, jumps in my arms, and kisses me, and it's hard and heated, but I break the kiss, or we'll never get out of the house. My attraction to her is that electrical.

"Rain, I'm two seconds away from fucking you against the wall. You need to get down now." My voice comes out rushed and deep because my need to be inside her is too much. She slides down my body. The sensation of her rubbing against my cock has me unleashed, and I need to walk away. I grab her and give her a chaste kiss because it's game over if I do anything more. "Get dressed or get in bed," I tell her, and then I go to the closet to get dressed.

CHAPTER 27

I Apologize

Raven

It's my last full day with Nik. He takes me to the Space Needle, and the five-hundred-foot view of the Seattle skyline is simply spectacular. As soon as we get out of the elevator, my phone buzzes. It's a text from Ross Enterprise's chief counsel letting me know they are pleased with the quick resolution of their issue with the media in England. I don't hide the fact that Parker helped me. His influence and knowledge of the media are unmatched, and I'm grateful to have access to his brilliant mind. Now, I need my client's attorneys to send their final email to their external client confirming the ethics issues are settled and we can move forward. This deal is too important to me. I can only pray that nothing else pops up between now and Monday.

I look over at Nik. He has an intense look on his face, so I go inside, walk up behind him, snake my arm around him, and press my face to his back. I take a deep breath and enjoy the shape and firmness of his muscles beneath my fingers. It feels good, right, familiar.

"You look like you need a hug," I tell him, and he puts his phone in his pocket and turns to me. The look in his green eyes is pure desire. I feel it, too.

"More like I need this."

He grabs my hips, pulls me into him, then kisses me so deeply I feel it at my core. He rises thick against me, and I'm confident this could turn into something more than it should, so reluctantly, I pull away. "Careful, Nik, or we'll have to break in the Space Needle."

Nik and I joke around, kiss, and then I face the view. I stay pressed against him but lean back to see his face, giving him a few minutes to calm down because Nik is on fire. We stand there, holding each other, until I see the storm clouds in his eyes subside. I realize we're both searching for something, and I'm unsure if it's each other.

When the moment passes, Nik takes my hand and leads me around the sky deck, pointing out various districts and significant buildings. He's so knowledgeable about the city; I find it fascinating, and his enthusiasm for architecture is contagious. It takes a while, but we make our way around the entire floor until it's time for us to leave.

Following our tour of the Space Needle, we head to lunch at Carmelo's Tacos, which I've been dying to try out. We get in line, which extends outside the unassuming brown and tan brick building that bears the scars of graffiti. We both order tacos and get a side order of chips and guacamole. The place is small, so we order it to go. After we place our order, we step aside to wait for them to call us.

"Well, that was a lovely surprise at the Space Needle. I didn't know they served champagne and snacks."

"They usually have some things to cater to the masses. But what we had was prepared only for us," he tells me.

"For a guy who has never done this before, you're pretty good at this."

"I'll take the compliment and this," he says right before he kisses me while everyone in line watches. I hear my phone ring. When I see Blake's name on my screen, I freeze. My face grows hot, but not from desire. My heart is racing, and I can only think of how much I don't want to take this call, especially while Nik is studying me cautiously. I shift focus to recall Parker telling me that I don't have to do anything other than answer the call and listen to what he says.

"I need to take this," I tell Nik and step aside. "Speak."

"Rae." He says my name, but it comes out strained.

I understand it's difficult for a man of his stature to relay whatever he has to say to me. But that's the point—to stop being a coward and have the courage to tell the truth for once. To apologize. He cheated on me because he didn't respect me. I don't know what Parker said to get him to call and it doesn't matter.

It was bad enough that Blake did what he did to me. But he also tried to slander the one man who has stood beside me for twelve years. Parker once told me when we were in college that he didn't let people get away with disrespecting me because they'd continue doing it. That people will do what you allow—that, in essence, I was teaching them how to treat me. I didn't understand it until he broke it down for me, and I saw the aftermath of him putting someone in their place. He was right. People looked at and treated me differently from that day on. I got it.

Parker has been my saving grace so many times that it's time that I stood up for both of us. Blake owes me this apology, and my friend Parker deserves respect. If he speaks ill of him around me—he won't hesitate to do it around others.

Blake is not the kind of man who bends, yet…this will be the second time he's had to do so. Knowing him, he's pissed about it and won't let this go. I told Parker to let me handle Blake, and he did, but Blake just kept coming, and last time, instead of just coming for me, he came for us both. I need to do something about it.

"I'm calling to apologize for my behavior. A woman like you is a privilege for any man to have on their arm. Unfortunately, I'm not the kind of man that deserves someone like you. I was wrong to cheat on you. I was thinking about myself. You deserve much better. My actions at the party were deplorable and done out of spite. As for my issue with Mr. Page: I was taken aback when he called and asked me to apologize to you. It was a simple request, and I should have discussed my issue with him directly. Please forgive me. After today, you'll no longer hear from me. If we happen to be in the same vicinity, just know that it is only coincidental, and I will not go out of my way to approach you. I hope you can find it within yourself to forgive me."

A hand on my shoulder distracts me. "Rain? Are you okay?" Nik asks. Blake is still reciting his practiced monotone monologue on the phone in the background, so I hold up my hand, signaling to Nik that I'm okay. He steps back but continues to watch me intensely.

When Blake is done with his speech, I listen a beat to hear if there's more or if he's waiting for a response. When I met Blake, I was coming down from another failed relationship. He attended an event where I was receiving an award for my community endeavors. His company was one of the sponsors. I don't know what I saw in him. Maybe I thought he was a good guy because he was there. Perhaps I was attracted to his confidence. Maybe I was looking for something he didn't possess. Whatever it was, it was a mistake. I didn't really know Blake. Parker cautioned me, but I refused to listen.

Now I see what Parker saw all those months ago: a ruthless, self-absorbed jerk. I get that my relationship with Parker is hard for other men to compete with, but the bite with which Blake speaks Parker's name has the undertones of something ominous. Blake is not done.

I've known him long enough I can sense it. This is what Parker was talking about—that I need to teach people how to treat me. I thought Parker was being controlling when he took action against men that slighted me. Parker was only protecting me. I need to return the favor, and I know exactly what to do to put an end to this ordeal with Blake. Ignoring Blake, I type out a message.

Me: Mr. Wallace, do you have time for a call today? I'd like to talk with you about something.

WW: Ms. Nichols. Lovely to hear from you. I'm at your disposal.

"Well, that's all I had to say." Blake's voice pulls me out of my thoughts.

It's harsh, but I have no interest in talking with Blake. He confirms he finished, so I take his cue and end the call. The sooner I solve this thing with Blake, the sooner another chapter of my life will be closed, which is my signal to consider how to navigate my life moving forward.

I walk back to Nik, and I know he's been watching me with the look of protectiveness I usually see in Parker. Parker is the one constant in my life and has seen me through some tough times. This blip with Blake is minor compared to some of the things I've been through, and I appreciate Parker stepping in on this, but I've got it from here.

"You don't have to tell me anything, but that was Blake, right? Tell me if you need me to do anything, and I'll take care of him once and for all."

"Don't worry. He will never bother me again," I tell him. Our order is called and I head toward the restaurant door.

❧

NIK HAS ME ON A TIGHT SCHEDULE, AND I DON'T HAVE TO WAIT LONG before the driver he arranged for me arrives. This is a good time to catch up on personal items. I have my call with Wade Wallace to talk to him about his nephew, Blake. I met Wade through Janis Page and we've kept in contact. He indicated he's been frustrated with his nephew's behavior the past year, and this is his push to do something about it. He says just leave it to him. Then he asks me how it's going, balancing my time with the Page's events and my work life. Mr. Wallace is a family man whose been monitoring my career over the years.

Janis has been instrumental in ensuring I'm connected to important people in her network, like Mr. Wallace. Janis' unconditional offer of support reminds me that although she treats me like her daughter, I'm someone else's. And that my real family, which I've been so desperately trying to mend, is still broken. I message my sister to let her know I'll meet her later and make reservations for us online.

My mind wanders to Blake's apology. I need to update Parker, but I don't want to call and rehash the conversation, so I text him instead:

Me: Blake called to apologize.

My phone sounds, and I'm surprised to receive an immediate reply from Parker. It's the weekend, and he's usually preoccupied with his parents and their social events. His mom successfully tries to rope me into attending all her social activities when I'm not busy with my own. But I don't mind because she's introducing me to powerful people— people that I can learn from, network with, and, if needed…leverage. I realize she's been handing me the tools I need to stand on my own two feet.

Parker: Rain, are you okay?

Me: I'm fine, Parker. Missing you.

Parker: Same.

Me: You can just look in the mirror if you miss yourself.

Parker: Cute.

Me: I am, aren't I?

I'm expecting some witty retort, but my phone rings. It's Parker on FaceTime.

"You're stunning, Rain." He smiles, and I feel his warmth hug me through the phone.

"Parker, it looks like you're at your mom's house."

"I am. Now tell me how you're feeling."

"Fine now, but when I took the call from Blake, I wanted to throw up."

"That's a natural response considering the circumstances. However, I'm sure you didn't. But he apologized." It's not a question because Parker knows the outcome already. He knew Blake would call.

"Yeah, he did, but I didn't say anything to him."

"Good. That's over. You ready for Monday?" I hear his mom talking in the background to his dad. He has such a loving family. I wish I had that.

"Is that Raven, honey?" Parker shifts his phone so that Janis comes into view. "Raven, darling. I trust you received all the details for when you return." She smiles.

"I did, Mrs. Page. I'm looking forward to it," I tell her. Parker walks away from his family to give us privacy. "Be nice to your mom," I chastise.

"She was one second away from taking over the call. You didn't answer my question. Are you ready for Monday?"

"I am. I revised the agreement and sent everything to the in-house counsel. They were excited you resolved the media issue."

"That was a small fraction of the work. The rest was you. You know you're brilliant." My face warms at his compliment because despite knowing Parker for so many years, I still hold his opinion in high regard. After all, he's surrounded by an elite group of people. He's seen the best, so he's not loose with compliments.

"Well, thanks all the same." The car begins to slow, and I look out the window. We're a block from the mall. "Parker, I have to run a few errands."

"Okay. I just wanted to see your face. Let me know if you need me for anything. See you soon. Love you."

"I love you too."

Those words swirl in my head as I exit the car and enter the mall. Parker's been in my life for twelve years—almost half my life. I don't think I've ever stopped loving him. But how does what I feel for Parker differ from what I feel for Nik, a man I barely know? It's a question I tuck away for the moment as I go into the jewelry store I contacted earlier. They indicated they'd have my special order ready when I arrive.

Following my stint at the jewelry store, I go to a card store to find something I can use to document my appreciation of Nik. When I took calls in his office earlier, I noticed Nik saved my Space Needle drawing. I was taken aback because I didn't think he was sentimental. There are so many things I don't know about Nik that I probably would if we were a real couple. That's not our reality. For now, I'm enjoying the man I've come to know.

❧

My sister's place is out of the way, so I ask her to meet me for tea while I'm on my shopping excursion, hunting for something for Nik. I decide on this cute tea shop that sells teas and all the accouterments you could ever need to prepare and serve it. Walking in, I'm hit with a lovely, spicy, sweet smell. The walls are a deep greyish green, like a color you'd see in nature. I'm surprised to see my sister seated at a bistro table when I arrive. I go over and take a seat at her table.

"How was New Orleans?"

"Hey, Rae. It was okay. You were right. I could have gone anytime. Bram was busy with work most of the time, so I had to explore the city alone."

"Sounds familiar," I say with slight sarcasm.

"I know. I'm sorry about that. How was your week? Did you get through your list?"

"Yeah, I did actually. I still have my big meeting tomorrow. After that, I head back to San Francisco," I tell her, but this feels like mindless chatter. Am I being difficult or protecting myself from disappointment?

"Any plans to return to Seattle with your company?"

"I don't know. My clients are based in San Francisco. I'm only here because they're working on expansion plans in multiple cities, including Seattle. Nothing is final. Why?"

"I thought you might come back, and we could spend time together."

"Robin, are you serious? I'd have to think long and hard about that. I'm still pissed you bailed on me at the last minute. I only came here before my meeting to spend time with you. At your request, I might add," I emphasize the last part.

"I thought I was doing the right thing going with him."

"Like you admitted, you could have stayed."

"If you come back next time, it'll be different."

I blink. There is no way I'm related to this woman.

"With you, there's always a New Orleans thing, an 'I don't have time,' or 'I forgot,' or some lame excuse. I don't understand why you're being this way. It's me. I'm your sister, for Christ's sake."

"That's not fair. I'm trying."

"It's the truth. Is this why you wanted to spend time with me today? To talk about this? Because I'm on a tight deadline today," I tell her, struggling to keep my temper in check.

"You're right. I fucked up. What if I plan a trip to San Francisco?"

I sigh. "That's a start. But I need to go." I start gathering my things.

"Raven, wait."

I stand and look at her. "I need to be somewhere," I say and turn to walk away. Because I can't keep doing this with her. All these years I've been spending my time trying to find a way to connect with my sister, but the efforts have been one-sided. Enough is enough.

"You could have stopped him." Her words cut like a sharp knife, and I turn around.

"What?"

"Mom told me you were there when he left. That you saw him leave. You could have stopped him. You were his favorite. The one he cherished. I saw how his eyes lit up whenever you entered the room. You could have stopped him, Rae, with one word. You could have stopped him, and we'd still have our father."

As she says the words that cut into my core, I feel the sting of unshed tears pooling, and I have to sit to keep from falling. I take a deep breath, attempting to pull myself together as the early morning memory of the last time I saw my dad twist and tear like the serrated edge of a blade through my soul.

"You don't know what you're talking about. You weren't there."

"But you were. One damn word…that's all it took. You could have stopped him," she repeats. I close my eyes and open them again, trying to stay in the moment and not descend into the void.

"I couldn't stop him." The words fall from my lips, and I can't hold back the tears.

"But he loved you so much," Robin says, her face softening slightly as she watches my distress.

"It wasn't enough. I called out to him. He didn't stop. Whatever happened to make him leave, I couldn't stop it."

"You're lying."

I shake my head.

She's lashing out because she's hurting, too. She knows I'm telling the truth. I'm a lot of things, but no one, not even Robin, could ever say I'm a liar and mean it. And I see the shock on her face, realizing the truth.

"I couldn't stop him."

"Oh, God, Rae. I didn't know. She never told me. I…."

Using a napkin, I wipe my face, trying to pull myself together, remembering we're in a public place. All this time, my sister has been sitting with this in her head. Blaming me.

"Robin, we were kids. I was only eight. There was nothing I could do. To this day, I don't even know why he left."

"She never told me. I know you think she and I are close, but she never told me, Rae. You have to believe me. I'm so sorry."

"I know." I can see it in her face, hear it in her voice. And I know, slowly, she's releasing the wedge she'd been holding between us. But it's a big wedge and will take more than an afternoon's conversation to remove. I close my eyes and exhale.

Robin and I spend the next hour catching up, and she commits to planning a trip to San Francisco to spend some quality time together. There are a lot of years of bitterness to unpack and get past, but our conversation is a start to peel back the layers. Now, I just need to figure out what happened with my dad. Parker offered to help me in the past and I refused because I was scared. Now I'm ready.

When I return to the house, Nik greets me at the door. He's still casually dressed in dark blue jeans and green long-sleeved Henley. As soon as I pass the threshold, he takes my bags, sits them on the floor, pulls me by the waist toward him, dips his head, and kisses me until I feel dizzy with desire.

"Wow. Now that's a welcome home kiss."

"You've been gone a while, and I've developed an addiction." He stares at me as if reading my expression. Watching him watch me, I don't send him any unspoken words. I use the moment to memorize his features: the fullness of his lips, the curly texture of his facial hairs, the perfect symmetry of his facial features, the richness of his green eyes, and the color of his skin that mirrors mine. He's a beautiful man and all mine for the moment.

Earlier today, I inadvertently told Nik I couldn't believe this wasn't his natural way of being. *Don't. Try not to think about that side of me,* he'd told me.

But it's hard not to. He's generous and tender but still manages to be bold and commanding. All the things I love about him. Yet, I know what he means. The way he is with me is not who he is with anyone else. I wonder if there are feelings behind his actions, but it's a question that I'll never have an answer to because we don't have a future beyond midnight tonight. One week, just sex, no feeling, that's what we agreed to.

I break the silence. "If you keep looking at me like that, you'll have to take me to bed."

Nik doesn't say a word. He lifts me until I'm straddling him and carries me to his bedroom.

CHAPTER 28

Let It Rain

Noah

As the car stops, water streams down the window, and the street lights blur into streaks of muted watercolors. It's raining, but it won't put a damper on my last night with Rain because all I see is sunshine when I look at her. Surprisingly, this is Seattle's first rainy day since I met her. Maybe it's the universe expressing my feelings about my final night with her. So much of my week has been consumed with Rain that it's hard to remember my life before her.

Rain peers out the car window. "Nik, we're back at the Space Needle."

"This is where we'll have dinner," I say. I help her out of the car as our driver holds an oversized umbrella to protect her from the elements.

We enter the building and are greeted by staff wearing black suits who take us to the five-hundred-foot level. A series of strategically placed fairy lights leads through the dark corridor overlooking the cityscape to our dinner table.

"Oh my god, you didn't," Rain exclaims when she realizes we have the entire space to ourselves again.

"You didn't think I wanted to share you, did you?" I take her hand and lead her toward the lavishly decorated table with a chandelier hanging from the ceiling above it. "Take a look," I say, bringing her to the window to see the city lit up at night. I stand behind her and observe her reflection in the window. She looks spectacular in her dress, which I can't wait to take off later tonight.

"Beautiful," she says.

I bend, kiss her neck, and whisper, "You are." She turns in my arms and smiles, and it squeezes my heart. Before she can say anything, I kiss her. She opens her mouth to accept my tongue, searching desperately for hers, and I devour her. I wish I had brought a shorter dress to lift it and take her against the window.

Rain pulls away. "Nik," she pants.

"I know." I press my forehead to hers, willing my body to calm down. I hold her a moment, turning her toward the window so we see our reflections. "You're stunning in that dress. You look like a goddess. I'm doing my best not to rip it off you." She laughs at my admission.

"I don't doubt you. You're insatiable and an incredible lover."

"Because you're amazing, and your body is a godsend designed for me." I don't know how I'm going to give it up. I don't say. "You ready to eat?"

"Sure."

When we sit, the staff begin their dance, delivering champagne and a series of meal courses I had planned especially for Rain.

I hold up my glass and gesture for Rain to do the same. "Let's toast." She smiles, waiting for me to continue. "To the most beautiful girl that walked out on me."

"To a man named Nik, without a C, who begged me to stay. Cheers."

I touch my glass to hers. "Cheers, my beautiful Rain." We both take a sip of our champagne.

The staff continues to bring out food, and we spend some quiet time eating, staring, and enjoying each other's company, knowing it's our last night together. When we finish the main course, I signal the staff to bring out the dessert, and they return with a custom gold floral two-tiered cake that serves two.

"This is lovely, Nik."

"Rain," I hold out my hand to her. "Come sit with me." She stands and comes to sit on my lap. "I know this is unconventional, but I want this night to represent all the milestones we shared or could have shared if we were a couple. Like the first time I saw your face, our first date, our first kiss, the first time we made love, and all the anniversaries that would have proceeded today had I been that man. To all the birthdays, holidays, and special moments and occasions we would have celebrated. This moment honors you, Rain. The woman who made me wish I was a better man."

"Ah, Nik." Rain kisses me, and I feel a tear roll down her cheek when it meets mine. I break the kiss and wipe her tears.

"I didn't mean to make you cry."

"It's okay. I wasn't expecting you to say something so sweet, so intimate. I want to celebrate the man who's filled my week with a lifetime of sweet memories, amazing sex, and cherished moments I will never forget for as long as I live. Thank you for showing me the man you hid away. He's beautiful, thoughtful, and caring. And he has fine ass brothers."

I laugh, then pull her to me and kiss her deeply, and I know she can feel me rise against her. I reluctantly break the kiss. "Rain. The things you do to me. Here, I have something for you." I reach for the gift near the cake and hand it to her. "Open it."

Her hands move with caution as she opens the gold-wrapped gift. First, she pulls the red bow, then she peels back the paper. When she finally unwraps it, she smooths her hands across the square, flat, black velvet box.

She lifts the lid, revealing a platinum charm bracelet. "Nik," she squeezes my neck. "You didn't have to do this."

"I wanted to commemorate the day with something special."

She leans back and examines each charm. "Oh, Nik, let me guess what these are for."

"Okay. I'll hold them up, and you tell me what you think." The first charm that I hold out is a cocktail glass. She laughs.

"That's for the first time we met at the bar, and you paid for my drinks."

"The night you walked out on me."

"You were being such a jerk." I hold up another charm. This time, a hand curled into a fist. "That looks like the black power symbol. Ah, our day at the museum." I nod. Next, I hold a coin imprinted with a cityscape. "This is easy, it says Seattle. I saw the whole city from the helicopter. I get it. Each charm represents something I experienced with you."

"That's right."

She takes the bracelet from me. "I don't see anything that represents sex."

"Don't be sassy."

"Whatever." She looks at the charms. "So, this music symbol is for the night we went to the jazz club. This yacht is for our day on the sea. This dress…is it for tonight or—."

"For the dresses you tried on and the one you settled on to wear to the birthday party."

"The day you gave me an orgasm in the dressing room."

"Well, maybe I was thinking about what I got."

She smacks my arm.

"And this one—The Space Needle for today. But what about this? I don't understand. It's a key. Do I get a car or something?" she teases.

"Rain. This one is special. This is the key I lost a long time ago. I don't know where it's been all this time. All I know is you found it that day at the bar. It's the key to my heart, my home, my life. The key to a door I didn't know existed until I met you."

"Nik."

"Rain. I'm not ready to open that door, but I know you are the only woman who can. You found the key, so I'm giving it to you—it's yours. Clearly, it was meant to be found by you. I need you to take it and protect it because honestly, Rain, I never met anyone like you, and I'm sure I never will again. Maybe one day, when I'm ready for it, it will find its way back to me—when I'm ready to open that door, we could do it together. But now is not the time. I made you a promise that day over eggs Benedict and coffee. I agreed I wouldn't come to claim you like I'm your man." She smiles when I use her words. "I'm giving it away because I don't know anyone more deserving to have it than you. Remember how much I miss you every time you look at it. How much I wanted to be that man for you." I stand and bring her with me. I bend and press my lips to hers, pry hers open, taking possession of what's mine for the moment.

We stand like that awhile, holding each other, breathing each other in. Outside, the sky is dark, the wind is whirling, and it's raining. Inside, it's warm, and tucked in my arms is the most beautiful woman in the world. Rain in Seattle never felt so good, and all I have to say is, let it rain.

CHAPTER 29

The Man I Know

Raven

THIRSTY. THAT'S THE BEST WAY I CAN DESCRIBE HOW I FELT WHEN Nik emerged from the closet this evening dressed in his dark blue silk suit, white shirt, and lavender tie. He's so fine that I had to psych myself out to avoid jumping his bones. On the drive to dinner, my sex was pulsing the entire time, thinking about what I wanted him to do to me. His revelation tonight at the Space Needle that he was giving me the key to his heart to protect was too much for my heart to handle, and I almost passed out when he kissed me. Of course, we never ate dessert and had to bring it back home with us because we were just too hungry for each other, which is why Nik is unzipping my dress.

"Finally," he says as it falls to the floor, pooling around my feet. I step out of it and quickly remove my underwear while Nik's clothes fly piece by piece to a chair nearby. He pulls me to him when all his clothes are off, and I feel his length thick against my stomach. He dips his head, kisses my neck and cheek, and then captures my mouth. His kiss is wet, needy, powerful, and I can't breathe. He wraps his hand beneath me, cradling me while I hold onto him as he lowers me to the bed and then pulls me to the edge. He nudges my legs apart, lifts one over his shoulder, pulls my mound toward his mouth, and eats me out. He's biting, licking, sucking my clit, and the sensation sends me over the edge. My back arches off the bed, meeting the rhythm of his tongue licking into me as he eats me through the first wave of my orgasm.

"Nik," I scream, not recognizing the pleasure in my voice. He lifts his head and smirks at his work, then gets on his knees above me and pulls me further up the bed. Then he reaches for a condom, sheaths himself, leans down, and kisses me, giving me a taste of myself mixed with his sweetness. I reach for him, my sex still throbbing, desperate to have him in me, to be connected in a way only his body can provide.

"Rain, I need you like the earth needs the sun," he says. He positions himself between my legs and pushes in slowly, inch by inch, until I'm finally full of him. Then he begins to move in and out of me, gradually picking up the pace, and I begin to feel another orgasm pushing its way out of me. "Let it go," he pants in my ear. He continues his rhythm. My body explodes, coming again as he continues pumping while my walls clench around him, milking his body as he pulls my orgasm from me. And when the pulsing subsides, he kisses me. It's lovely, gentle, wanting.

"Nik," I call to him as his rhythm increases, and he chases his release, pumping and grinding.

"Come with me," he says, moving in and out with forceful, messy thrusts. And I know he's about to lose himself in me, and I feel my sex clench down on him again. "That's it, beautiful. Oh god, Rain." Our bodies are sweaty, and I taste the salt on his skin as he kisses me before burying his face in my neck, grunting sounds of pleasure. Our bodies clash over and over. We're both growling and calling to each other until we collide at the height of our climax, and I swear I can feel forever in his arms.

"Oh, god, Nik."

"Rain."

When we finally come down from our high, and our breaths settle, we get in the shower, where I can't help but have Nik again. We know this is our last night together, and we don't try to restrain ourselves.

"I'm ready for some cake," I tell Nik as we dry each other. He helps me moisturize my skin, then he hands me a robe, slips on a pair of boxers, and leads me out of the bathroom.

"It's almost midnight. We should toast to our seventh day," he says, leading me to the kitchen.

While I plate our cake, Nik gets glasses and pours the champagne. I bring everything to the other side of the counter.

"Wait, I didn't give you your anniversary gift," I announce and rush to the foyer to retrieve it. When I return to the kitchen, I find Nik sitting at the counter waiting. I go to sit next to him, but he pulls me on his lap, facing him.

"You didn't have to get me anything. You're all I want tonight." He dips his head to my neck, which I've come to realize is one of his favorite spots.

"Open this." I hand him a card and a box.

Nik takes the card and opens it first. It's a handmade watercolor painting of the Space Needle. He opens the card and reads my words.

"To the man I've come to know, Nik, without a C. The day I met you, you bore the scars of a façade you wore for more years than I know. Yet something deep inside you found its way past the façade to me. I believe it's the real you, because the smile that radiates from you when you look at me tells me everything. That Nik, without a C, is more than he pretends to be. Your word is gold. Everything you committed to, you did. You are a protector, and I never have to count to three for backup. You are generous. In the time we've been together, I've wanted for nothing. You are honorable. I've never felt disappointed or disrespected. You are beautiful, and your good looks are unmatched except by your brothers. Smiley face. You are insatiable, and I can't get enough of you. All these things are you, and you can't hide that fact. Not from me. Not from yourself. And I thank you for walking into a bar on a Tuesday afternoon to find me. Rain."

When he finishes, he stares at me, and I look away because I see him fighting the two halves of himself.

"Look at me, Rain," he commands. I look up, trying to rein in my emotions. Reaching up, he cups my face and kisses me. It's soft and loving, but it doesn't last long. "Thank you." He puts the card on the counter and retrieves his gift. He opens the box to reveal the bracelet I bought him. It's a mix of large round gold beads, onyx, and one large black diamond. In the center opposite the diamond is a small gold rectangle.

I take it from him and point out the inscription. "Look here. This side says Rain, and this side says Nik. On one side is the day we met; the other has tomorrow's date. Well—it's today now. Our anniversary is forever commemorated here." I take the bracelet and slide it on his wrist.

What I don't share is that a week ago, at this very moment, I was wrapped in Parker's arms, or that on this date when I was five, my dad was pretending to be the tooth fairy, leaving ten dollars under my pillow in exchange for my tooth. I won't cite any of the hundreds of memories at my disposal that mark this day. Instead, I look at him and watch how he rolls his fingers across the precious spheres, the smile on his face, the warmth of his body against mine. In the future, when I remember this date, I'll remember this moment with him. I'll remember how for one week I belonged to a man who made me feel like I could spend forever in his arms. I'll remember Nik.

"This is beautiful, Rain. I'll wear it every day from now on." He kisses me again, and I let him ravish me until I can't breathe before I break the kiss. "We need to go back to bed," he pants.

"First, I want some cake."

He shakes his head, reaches past me, and holds one of the plates between us while he feeds me cake. "Anything for you." He feeds me a few more bites of cake, returns the plate to the counter, and gets our champagne flutes. "Toast. To all my days with Rain lived and imagined."

"To the man I've come to know. Cheers." I look at my watch, and its past midnight. "Take me to bed, Nik," I tell him, and he does because we have a lifetime of living to fit into a few hours, and neither of us wants the day to begin or end.

Nik takes me repeatedly, making good use of every surface: the wall, the bed, the shower, until we fall asleep, content, consumed, and clinging to one another like fresh clothes from the dryer.

When it's all over, I open my eyes and crawl out of bed. I put my clothes on, gather my things, and look around the house to see if I missed anything. This is the part where I usually evoke my first experience in detachment, letting decades-old memories wash over me until I can't take it anymore. Instead, I go back into the bedroom.

Nik looks so peaceful, lying on his back, one arm resting on the pillow above his head. The past week with this man has been amazing, and I don't want it to end, but it has to. Even though it hurts. Not only am I leaving him, but the brothers I never had, a loving family I so desperately desire. A family I can begin again with my sister.

Reaching in my purse, I remove the phone that ties me to them. I walk over to the bed and place it on the nightstand beside his head. I need to say goodbye. Bending, I sit on the side of the bed. When it dips, Nik stirs, and his arm instinctively reaches out and wraps around my waist.

"Hey," I whisper.

"Hey." His eyes open and lock on mine. "You're dressed."

"Yeah. I gotta go get ready for work. I wanted to say goodbye."

"Let me get the driver."

"My car should be here by now."

He sits up, moves to get out of bed, and I give him room. He puts on his robe and reaches a hand to me. I stand and take it, and he pulls me into him.

He holds me and inhales. "Rain, you're so beautiful." He pushes my messy hair over my shoulders. "You made me remember there are things more rewarding than power and status. Thank you." He dips his head and kisses me. It's soft and quick.

"I need to go before your sexy accent talks me out of my clothes." We both laugh.

"Okay." He breathes against my lips.

He takes my hand and leads me to the door. The driver takes my things, and I turn to Nik before I leave.

"Thank you for being the man I knew you could be."

I turn, get in the car, and go.

The Most Beautiful Girl

Noah

THE CITY TAKES ON A BLUISH-GRAY HUE AS THE CLOUDS ROLL ACROSS the sky, blocking out the sun. Standing at the wall of windows in my office, looking out over the city, I grab my wrist, rolling my fingers along the bracelet Rain gave me, wondering where she is. Is she thinking about how good it was between us? How we spent our time tangled together until we became one? How our breaths and heartbeats were so in sync, I don't know where I started and she ended? I'm reminded of the song "The Most Beautiful Girl in the World" that I sang to Rain the first time she walked out on me. The words still ring so true. If only I could have one more minute with you, Rain.

"Here's the man of the hour." I turn around when I hear Mak's voice as my brothers file into my office. I sit behind my desk and Rok hands me his phone. "You may want to take a look at this," he commands.

"Don't tell me this deal is going sideways again."

"Just read," he presses.

I scroll through a press release. *"Blake Wallace, nephew to billionaire developer Wade Wallace, steps down as VP of Cost Associates, the media company where he's worked for the past five years. Wallace cites personal reasons for his exit. He has not stated what his next move will be."*

"Did you have anything to do with this, Nik?" Concern laces Rok's voice. I hand him back his phone.

"No. He called Rain the other day."

"What did he say?" Mak probes.

"I didn't ask. Rain said he would never bother her again."

"She did this?"

"No. Someone else did."

"Seems your girl has some powerful friends," Rok chimes in. He's right. It would have taken some influence to make this happen on short notice. It leads me to question everything I could have learned about Rain had we been more to each other.

"She's not my girl. It's over." My heart clenches as I say the words aloud.

"Nik, man, what are you doing?" Rok asks.

"Taking care of business. In ten minutes, we're negotiating our second largest deal."

"I told you, we got this. Our attorney reviewed everything. Today's meeting is a formality to hash out any last-minute questions. You did great work on this," Mak reinforces.

"We still have the Wade deal brewing, which is in its infancy. There's a long road ahead on that one."

Mak stands and goes to look out the window, then turns to me. "Jude told you you're in the lead."

"I know that," I interject.

"I had Jewel book your follow-up meeting with Wade. You have two weeks to prepare. This is business—things will continue moving forward. Don't let this stand between you and the woman you want."

"I'm not the man for her. KDC is all I know. It's all I can focus on right now. When these two deals are done, I'll feel better about our position in the market." Then I can reset and focus on life outside work—just not now. But I don't say any of that. I don't tell my brothers that Rain has me rethinking my priorities and that maybe if I push past my fear of losing something, anything—then having the one I want by my side would be worth the risk. That maybe after all of this…I'll go find her and claim her as mine.

"Rain could be gone by then. Are you willing to risk it all? To lose her?" Rok asks. It's a legitimate question, and I already know the answer. I don't *want* to lose her. But I can't claim her…not yet.

"Listen, I still need to identify the mystery bidder in the Wade deal. I talked to Jude. He wasn't aware there was anyone besides those of us who attended the meeting in San Francisco. The Wade deal is still on the line until I have that person's identity. Nothing is settled until we have an agreement in place."

"Nik. Go get our Sis."

I take a deep breath. I need to shut down this conversation about Rain because I can't hear her name without my soul aching. Letting her go was the hardest thing I've done, but the right thing in the moment. Holding her in my arms before she left was suffocating because I had to resign myself to the fact that it would be my final time seeing her. Rain. I imagine dipping my head into her neck, inhaling her essence. Even now, traces of jasmine and honey linger in the air, reminding me of the woman who was mine for seven days.

"Let it go, Rok. She's gone. We have a meeting to run. Let's lock down this deal. You guys ready?"

I look between my brothers, wait for their response, and reflect on my life. Long ago, my father relocated our family from London to Seattle. At the time, London was all I knew. My family, friends, culture, the…

rain. That was my life, everything I loved. Then, in an instant, it was all snatched away. It took some time for me to pull myself together from what I thought was a devastating loss. My father pulled me out of my dejected state by making me focus on my studies, which helped me get grounded. It helped prepare me to run our family business, to acquire something that no one can take from me, and to gain power. Now my ability to structure a deal surpasses my father's. In school, I regained confidence, and by my final years in high school, there was no stopping me. I was on the path to being like him. Then, a girl caught my eye. I saw her at school during my senior year.

I was immediately drawn to her laugh. Like Rain, she caught my gaze with her brown eyes, and I knew I had to talk to her. I went across the cafeteria and introduced myself. Our connection was instant. We made plans to talk after class, and we did that for a week while I got to know her. Then I asked her out on a date. That Saturday was going to be great, but it never came. That Thursday, some drunk driver took what was mine on a slick rainy day. That was the day I turned in on myself, buckled down, and focused on the things I could control: my destiny, my legacy. Women became something fleeting for pleasure, and I became the man I am. I became Noah Ignatius Knight, my father's son. So, even though Rain's the one woman I'd be willing to take a chance on, it's too late. She's gone. And now, I have a deal to make, a business to run.

"Yes. We're ready," my brothers say in unison.

"Then let's go."

CHAPTER 31

A Woman Named Rain

Raven

THE SOUND OF MY ALARM BLARING JERKS ME OUT OF MY SLEEP. STILL groggy, I reach my hand to the nightstand and tap my phone's screen to turn it off. It's later than I usually get up, and I'm surprised to find myself still lying in bed. I can't remember when I fell asleep, but I must have kept my mind from reliving the past week with Nik.

After celebrating our last night together, Nik and I were tangled in each other long past our expiration date well into this morning. We agreed to a limited time together. Leaving him was hard, but it was the right thing to do. Despite my initial hesitation with our arrangement, the seven days we spent together flew one by one until there were none.

Finding my way back to a life without Nik seems simple on the surface. Concluding my meeting today, my driver will be waiting with the car. Then, I'll board a plane, and within two hours and fifteen minutes, I'll return to San Francisco. When I arrive, Parker, will welcome me with open arms. But thoughts of Nik, his scent, his taste, his touch, will last long after I leave.

I drag myself out of bed and head to the bathroom, going through the motions to get ready. Looking at myself in the mirror, I try not to get emotional even though it feels like my heart is about to burst. I fell for Nik. I fell for a powerful man who is thoughtful, generous, and protective, even though he doesn't realize he's all those things. But I have to keep reminding myself it was only an affair. He's not mine.

I take my time in the shower, allowing the water to wash over me. It's the first time in days I've been in a shower without him. As I lather the washcloth and slide it down my neck, I remember the trail of kisses he left. Every movement reminds me of him. My body is sore in ways that still thirst for him, even though we were together only hours before. I remember the weight of his body on mine and wonder if he's awake. I can almost feel his hair's short, textured waves brushing against my thigh. An hour from now is when he usually wakes up and greets the day inside me. Even now, I feel echoes of him between my thighs.

My phone rings, pulling me through the thick fog in my head. It's Parker on FaceTime. I swipe a tear and exhale, releasing the breath I'm desperately holding.

"Rain. I'm calling to wish you good luck on your meeting today."

Whenever I see him, I can't help but smile. However, deep down, other emotions fight to the surface. I try to suppress them. I focus on finding solace in my best friend while fighting back the tears. "Thanks, Parker. I can't wait to get back to you. I see you have my favorite suit on."

"Rain, ah, what's that look? I miss you too, but I need you to pull it together. Hold on, it's almost over," he says knowingly, because Parker and I are inextricably linked whether I like it or not, and I can't hide the pain.

"I can't help it. I miss you, and uhm, I'm trying to be strong. I...I feel a lot of pressure trying to land this deal. And uh—What I'm doing is so unhealthy. Ugh, I'm sorry, Parker. You're right. I need to pull myself together." I cover my face with my hand to hide the tears, but the ache is too unbearable.

"Rain, don't do this. Look at me. Look at me, please. I know it hurts. Trust me to help you through it. Things will be fine. We'll be together in a few hours. I promise. Open your eyes and look at me, Rain." His voice is stern, and rightfully so. I uncover my eyes. I need to pull my shit together. I can do this. My breaths come deep as I tighten my lips and force a smile, then focus on his face, taking in the shape of his lips, the definition of his jaw, and the brilliance in his eyes. I let his image consume my thoughts, pushing everything else aside. He watches me, concern clouding his eyes until my breath becomes normal, and I'm so glad he's in my life. Parker.

"There she is. There's my Rain. You can do this. You good?"

"I'm good." At least, I wish I was. I'm a mess, but he knows. I inhale, trying to get it together.

"I promise I got you."

"I know you do, Parker."

"You need to get ready. It's a big day for you. Remember our plan. Focus on your meeting. Everything else can wait. Now tell me you'll kick ass and take names at the meeting."

I laugh to keep the tears at bay. "I got my iPad, and I'm taking names."

"That's my Rain. I'll be waiting for you when it's all over. You got this. Now go, so you can hurry home. I love you."

"I promise I'm going to crush this meeting, then I'm coming back home to you. Love you too," I say, ending the call and letting the last drops of water fall down my cheeks.

I hate this part. The constant games I play with myself to mask memories. The crippling reel that runs like groundhogs' day every morning in my mind. The ability to use this curse to disassociate from what I want most, to cut my heart out and walk away, repeatedly. It's too much. I agree with Parker—this has to end. Once, he suggested a potential solution to help me. I'm going to take him up on his offer. I type out a message on my phone:

Me: Remember the investigation you offered to help me with?

Parker: Yes. But you need to get to your meeting.

Me: Do it.

Parker: Consider it done. Now, please focus on your meeting. See you soon.

I ENTER THE BUILDING, AND TAKE THE ELEVATOR STRAIGHT TO THE executive floor. I close my eyes and try to allow the last few vestiges of the week to run out like celluloid from a movie reel. This is the part that sucks about having perfect recall. The constant mind games. The things I want to forget but can't. How do you forget a feeling? In vain, I remind myself that it was just one week of sex. That none of it was real. That there is no us. That I need to move on with the rest of my life. That I need to go home.

Home…to fix the things I've been running from. To take back control of my life. My need to be seen and heard stems from the day my father walked out. I realize that now. I've been pushing people out of my life, protecting my heart from men who have the power to break me like the loss of my father's love did. That day, he took my love, my confidence, my power.

Today, I'm taking that back. I will stand on my own and be

acknowledged for who I am and what I bring to the table without the shadow of a powerful male figure validating me. That's what Parker was all those years ago, what Nik has been these past seven days. People had to take notice, do what I said, step in line; otherwise, there were consequences to pay at the hands of the man at my side. Not today. Alejandro has moved aside so I can fly on my own to navigate this deal, solve the problems, and rise to the occasion. His absence proves that I have what it takes to be seen and heard and that I am powerful in my own right. He could have been here, but he's not. June could have sent in the big gun from her corporate legal counsel team, but she didn't. Because all this time, it was me. I am the one who will get this deal done.

I open my eyes when I hear the elevator ding, announcing my arrival on the executive floor. Goodbye, I say aloud to no one right before the doors open. I resign myself to the fact that it's over. As soon as I step beyond the elevator doors, I'll be Miss Raven Rain Nichols, Esquire.

As I exit the elevator, every step forward, each click of my heels, connotes the closing of a symbolic door of my time in Seattle—one step, one day, one door closed, cleansing my palate of his taste, scouring his scent from my skin, purging my mind of memories of him. Memories of a woman named Rain who met a guy named Nik, without a C, at a bar on a Tuesday afternoon in Seattle. With my last step, I erase all memories of…Nik.

"Right, this way, Miss Nichols. Your colleagues are waiting for you in the conference room." The executive assistant I've been conversing with gestures to the open conference door. I step in, and my clients greet me.

There is nothing unusual about the conference room. Two sides are bordered by a wall of windows overlooking the Seattle skyline.

A narrow wall is clad in horizontal wood slats where a large monitor hangs. Around the long wooden conference table in the center of the room are twelve chairs, but only six places set, three on either side of the table, with water glasses strategically placed on the table in front of each chair. I walk to where my clients stand near the wall of windows.

"Miss Ross. It's good to see you again." I extend my hand to June Ross, the new COO of Ross Enterprises. She greets me and then hugs me like we're old friends. And standing next to her with one hand held out to me and the other in his pocket is her handsome brother Jake Ross, the CFO.

"Mister Ross. It's a pleasure to meet you, sir." I place my hand in his.

"Good to have you on the team, Miss Nichols. Alejandro and my sister sing your praises." I nod and smile. "The development team should be here in a minute. Have a seat," he says, then gestures for me to sit beside him. I take a seat. "We're excited to get started," he adds.

Reaching into my bag, I take out my iPad, open the case, and hear the secretary say, "They're ready for you in the conference room," followed by footsteps.

Briefly, I glance at my watch. It's nine on the dot. Good, they're on time. Looking up, I lock eyes with the man standing at the threshold….

Nik?

THE END?

BLURB

———

Seven Days in Seattle

One week. No strings. No names. No feelings. What could go wrong?

Rain

This Seattle meeting will change my life…just not the way I expected.

Instead of focusing on my presentation, I'm dealing with a cheating boyfriend and sister who bailed on me. The only good thing to happen is when a stranger at a bar offers a pretty distraction: a one-night stand, no strings attached, no questions asked. A distraction from my mess of a life is exactly what I need….

But our one-night stand turns into a week-long affair. He only wanted sex, no feelings, no last names, no talk about business, nothing personal. And I was fine with that. Until I wasn't.

Nik

I don't have time for relationships. I have a company to run, a legacy to uphold, a reputation to protect. I only care about power and success. I don't do dates and I don't do tomorrows. I only do one-night stands with women who know the rules and don't ask for more.

But then I met Rain at a bar. She's beautiful, smart, and sassy. And suddenly, I want more. The more time we spend together, the more I want from her. Her name. Her story. Her dreams. And I was fine with that. Until I wasn't.

Fate is about to punish us for staying anonymous…by throwing us into each other's lives in the worst possible way.

Seven Days in Seattle, a contemporary romance, is Book 1 of the *Let it Rain* series.

The Days with Rain

Book 2 of the *Let it Rain* series.
PROLOGUE
Heaven

Parker Page

TWO WEEKS AGO.

It's hard to focus with her around. Traces of jasmine and honey linger in the air like lust long after she leaves my arms. Although I informed her during dinner that I needed to retire to my study to prepare for tomorrow's brief, I anticipated her following me here. And despite the fact she has her own home and even though there are fifteen other rooms in my house, she's here. In a city the size of San Francisco, she should be somewhere else. She should be resting somewhere soft, not splayed sideways, sleeping on a sofa in my study. Still, somehow, she's here…with me.

I've resigned myself to the fact that this is how we are with each other, forever bound by a single thread, sending signals between us. This has been the soundtrack to our relationship for as long as I can remember. We've been apart, hanging by a thread on the fringes of each other's lives, separated by distance, and at other times together tangled and messy, but always connected.

Now, I sit behind my desk and study her across the room, watching silently as she slumbers on the sofa. I sigh. She's beautiful. Her brown hair spills wildly across the pillow and falls in waves over the side of the couch. Light from the lamp casts a soft hue on her honey-colored skin. Her slender fingers curl and tug at the fur throw that covers her long, lean body. She won't sleep soundly until I put her to bed. I know that from experience. Because after twelve years of living and breathing in a world where she exists, there's not much I haven't learned about the woman who's become my best friend.

The click on my Rolex signifies it's midnight. Monday is here all too soon, and in a few hours, I must put her on a plane, and she'll be gone. I close my laptop, stand, and go to where she's lying on the sofa. I kneel before her, brush a curl from her face, and tuck it behind her ear.

"Hey," I say softly.

She stirs slightly, but her eyes stay closed. And like I've done a thousand times before, I scoop her into my arms. I carry her upstairs, through the house, down the hall, and place her in my bed. I step into my closet, remove my clothes, drop them in a basket, and then pull on a pair of silk pajama pants she got me. When I walk back to the bed, I slide in beside her, wrap my arms around her, and pull her into me. She could be anywhere in the world now, but she's not. She's here with me. And at this moment, holding her in my arms, inhaling her essence, *this* feels like heaven.

The Days With Rain
Copyright © 2024 Rita. A. Gordon

———

30 DAYS IN BELFAST

***Publishers Weekly* Indie Spotlight February 2023 (Romance & Relationships)**

"An addictive, rollicking tale of friendship, love, and lust."

— Kirkus Reviews

"Gordon's debut offers readers a winning combination of intrigue and romance, revealed slowly through the lens of opulent travel and luxurious living."

— BookLife Review

"I loved the relationships between the characters, the storyline was heartwarming and after a while, I couldn't put it down. Would definitely recommend!"

— LoveReading, Indie Books We Love, starred review

"A easy, beautiful, knowledgeable read!"

— Goodreads Reviewer, five star review

---

30 Days In Belfast

PROLOGUE

We Have Time

"If you love somebody, let them go, for if they return,
they were always yours. If they don't, they never were."
– KAHLIL GIBRAN, *A Tear and a Smile*

"I'LL RACE YA," SHANNON CALLED AS SHE RAN PAST ROSE TOWARD THE foam remnants of a forgotten wave on the shoreline.

Rose stopped scribing her initials in the sand heart drawing, a covert confession of love to her celebrity crush. She jumped up and headed toward the water. "Wait for me," she shouted to Shannon, who didn't see her. The glare from the sun dancing on the waves mimicking a million miniature mirrors distorted her view. Rose chased a wave and jumped in the water, pushing through the powerful current. When it subsided slightly, she popped up. "Shannon!" she called over the waves, but didn't see her friend. Rose continued to push through the currents, shoving the waves back with her arms that were growing sore by the minute. With each breath she took, she became more panicked, still unable to spot her friend.

Rose looked toward the shore to see if Shannon had made it back. "Shannon, where—" Rose called out before being sucked under by the current. Before it all became a faded memory.

Fifteen years later, the aftermath was fuzzy in her head. She remembered eventually getting herself to shore. The shock and overwhelming sense of loss she felt when she realized Shannon was not by her side finally came into focus as people crowded around her in the sand. An endless stream of questions rushed through her. The sudden end of a forever friendship stolen by sun, sand, and sneaker waves. Rose felt her face grow warm as memories of Shannon flooded her mind. Her heart started to race. Panic washed over her as she relived the day her friend died. All she wanted to do now was run.

"Rose, talk to me. I know it feels like it came out of left field. Tell me what you're thinking." The sound of Alejandro's voice sitting across the table pulled her out of her head. He was staring at her with a mix of concern and longing in his eyes. Shelved was the swoon-worthy smile that usually greeted her. The smile that made her melt after spending weeks away from her man. He reached his hand across the table.

Rose averted Alejandro's gaze and looked around his London flat, where they had just spent the last three evenings wrapped in each other's arms. Where they had made love for hours until they were both sore, satiated, and spent. Where they had shared rare stolen moments between their busy schedules. She was the one who convinced him to get the flat since he spent so much time traveling between New York and London. He was busy building his career as an international attorney, and Rose was recently promoted to COO. A reward for endless hours helping her father build his business and developing new technologies to innovate the company. Living on the west coast, paired with the busy travel schedule that came with her new position, meant they spent more time on video calls than in person.

Rose focused her attention on the modern, muted earth tones of the room. Her eyes were drawn to a painting she commissioned: A Black woman with a crown of flowers blooming from her head and partially covering her face. Rose remembered posing for the portrait with her chin turned toward her bare shoulder. "Think about your man," the artist had instructed her.

Now, she was sitting across the table from the man she thought she could build a life with. His words washed across her, pulling her down like the sneaker wave that snatched her childhood friend from her life forever. Stirring within her was the same sense of shock and sudden loss.

Rose sucked in a breath. "You sure about this?" she said, sounding as if negotiating a business deal—placing a wall around her heart and tamping the need to reach across the table to take his hand.

"No. But I do know we're both committed to our work. The time in between when we finally get together keeps growing. I'm torn between you and the job, and I don't want to ask you to bend for me. I respect that you're building your career, too. I want to make it work but can't see a way. You just got promoted and want to make a name for yourself away from your father's shadow. That's a tall order, and I'll use all my resources to support you in that effort. But trying to build something more between us is no small feat. Think about it. How many things did you and I have to shift to get these three nights together?"

"Quite a bit," she answered, hesitant to strengthen his argument.

"That's exactly the point. You and I know that you had to rearrange twice as much as me. I won't continue asking you to do that. Your father is my largest client. I know the demand he puts on me. I can only imagine how exponentially higher that is on you. I care about you, but I won't be the one to stifle your success. Let's take a step back and focus.

Let's give ourselves a year." Alejandro leaned back in his chair and ran his hands through his hair.

Rose knew he was rethinking his words. But they were out, weighing heavy between them.

Was he right? Should they take a break, allowing time to establish themselves? Could they walk away and get back when the time was right? Would it ever be right?

The idea of them not being a couple made Rose feel like she did when she lost her best friend. The same emotions flowed through her all over again. She paused to think, unaware of what was keeping her from ending the conversation, putting her foot down, and refusing his suggestion.

Rose closed her eyes, inhaled, and opened them. Alejandro's gaze was still locked on her. "This isn't about something else. Or is it? You—" she started.

Alejandro stood, rounded the table, and pulled Rose to her feet and into a tight embrace. He planted kisses all over her face before touching his forehead to hers.

"Oh, Rose. Don't ever think that. I…I'd be hard-pressed to believe I could be with anyone other than you. You are the center of my universe, but I know I'm not yours. This is me setting you free—giving you time to do what you need to do. To be you without me interfering."

Rose listened intently, her breath becoming synchronized with his.

"I'm not saying it's just about you," he continued. "I also need to figure out why I haven't moved heaven and earth to be by your side. And for that, I'm at fault." Alejandro swallowed, then turned to look out the window. Rose held onto his hand, walked up behind him, and pressed her chin to his back.

"Okay." Rose paused. "We'll give it some time."

CHAPTER I

A Rose is Still a Rose

"What's in a name? That which we call a rose
By any other name would smell as sweet."
— WILLIAM SHAKESPEARE

"I'VE GOT EYES ON THE PICASSO," TROY, ROSE'S CHIEF OF SECURITY, said into his headset.

Troy surveyed the airport tarmac before opening the car door for Rose. Picasso was the security handle Rose chose because of her love for art. A love that led her to establish an art foundation in her name, and to open an art gallery filled with art she had curated. As far as Troy was concerned, Rose could refer to herself as whatever she wanted, granted she followed his endless list of security protocols.

Rose Ross was the thirty-two-year-old chief operations officer for Rick Ross Enterprises, and the daughter of Rick Ross, CEO of the company bearing his name. But unlike her father, who possessed a string of monikers—the country's richest Black man, Black billionaire, father, and husband—Rose had just one: daughter of Rick Ross, or Rick Ross' daughter, depending on who was talking. She winced inside every time someone referred to her outside her name. Rose loved her dad, but she wanted to be known as more than just the daughter of Rick

Ross. To not be swallowed in the shadow of the wealthiest man in the country. To pave a path that hadn't already been walked. That was why she was about to board a plane and fly over five thousand miles from San Francisco to Ireland to do a favor for a sick friend and host the annual patron of the art exhibition in Belfast.

"I'm about to board now, Mia," Rose said in her earpiece as she stepped out of the vehicle. "I'll check my rough draft as soon as I board. We'll make the timing work. Even if you're there for an hour. Anyway, who's to say that I can even pull something like this off in less than thirty days. It's never been done before." Rose put her hand in Troy's as he helped her from the car.

"Thank you," Rose mouthed to Troy. She touched his shoulder as she passed him and headed to the plane.

Once onboard, Rose greeted all the staff, sat at one of the tables, took off her earbuds, and put her phone on speaker. "Okay, I'm pulling up the schedule now," Rose announced, opening her laptop.

"I'm telling you I'll be cutting it close," Mia said over the speaker.

"You're right. It's close, but it's doable. You can fit in about an hour— maybe more at the exhibition before your flight. Looking at the photos, the main gallery has a domed glass ceiling. I need to account for the long days and push the event time out to take advantage of the night sky. I'm not sure how it'll play into the final plan, but that's why it starts so late," Rose said, pointing to her draft art exhibition outline on her screen as if her friend could see it over the phone.

"Don't worry. I'll be there. I'm so glad you're doing this." Mia's voice was cheery.

Rose looked up as Troy entered the plane and watched while he gave the crew instructions. When the door closed, Troy went to sit across the aisle from Rose in one of the leather seats near the window. She observed as he set up his laptop.

"Hey, if you hadn't introduced me to Brianna, I wouldn't be on my way to Belfast. The least I can do is ensure you're there to see it. Anyway, I have a lot to think about while I'm there." Rose scrolled through her screen.

"Please tell me you're not pulling double duty," Mia urged.

"A team member is filling in for me while I'm traveling, but I'll still attend key meetings via video, of course," Rose answered, glossing over the weight of her work as a major world provider of sophisticated machine learning platforms for artificial intelligence. Additionally, she was spearheading work on legislation to propose uniform standards related to data access, data sharing, and data protection. She shifted in her seat. "But that's not the issue. Dad's pressuring me on some things."

"I suppose stuff you can't talk about."

"Nothing you need to worry about," Rose said matter of factly. But in reality, anything related to her dad was a big deal.

"And I suppose there's a timeline associated with whatever it is?"

"I—" Rose stopped when one of the attendants approached her.

"Ms. Ross, we'll be taking off shortly. We have a flight time of ten hours and twenty-five minutes. The weather should be about sixty-five degrees when we arrive. Would you like anything to drink?"

"Nothing. Thank you," Rose replied. The attendant nodded her head and went to address Troy before heading back to her station.

"Rose?" Mia piped up over the phone.

"We're about to—" Mia cut Rose off before she could finish.

"Wheels up. I heard. What are you not telling me, Rose?" Mia asked, her voice filled with concern.

Rose thought about her call with her dad earlier that morning. The proud tone in his voice was etched in her brain when he told her he wanted her to succeed him as CEO. She hadn't thought about what was next for her at Rick Ross Enterprises. She had been hyper-focused on work and had given up everything—including her man—to focus on the business. Now, she felt she was finally in a place where she was firing on all cylinders, allowing her to pursue her passion in art on the side. Although it was inevitable that her dad would eventually decide to hand the reins over to someone, the timing felt odd. Did he accelerate his plans because of her—because of what she was doing in Belfast? She wanted to make a name for herself, not get lost behind his. She needed time to think.

Rose sighed. "I have three weeks to get back to Dad with a decision on something."

"Whatever it is, I know you got this. Just stay focused. Don't get distracted, and call me if you need *anything*," Mia said.

"Thanks, Mia. And if a distraction is your code word for men, don't worry. I'll be focused on the event. Anyway, I gotta go. I'll see you at the end of the month."

"I sent you a brief to review before we land," Troy said while tapping his screen, just as Rose ended her call. She had gotten used to his all-business-all-the-time communication style.

Rose pulled the documents he sent her up on her screen. "Give me the Cliff Notes, Troy."

"You need to read through what I sent. The folder labeled *staff* is the people who work in the house as house staff. The one labeled *trade* is the contract resources you requested. I included a layout of the grounds for the property and all the building schematics."

"And? I know you sent more than just what I requested. What's this?" Rose asked, clicking into a folder on the screen. "The one labeled *king*."

"Biographies. It seems your host, Brianna, has two brothers visiting her."

Rose scrolled through a list of articles and files detailing their backgrounds, and settled on a link to the King Enterprise company website. She clicked through to the founder section. "Are these her brothers?" Rose turned her screen toward Troy, displaying two well-suited gentlemen that could pass for billionaire book boyfriend male models.

"Yes. Those are the brothers."

&

30 Days In Belfast

Copyright © 2023 Rita. A. Gordon

ACKNOWLEDGEMENTS

Wow, this is my second time around the sun with this writing thing. Thank you to my readers for joining me on my writing journey. Your support is the encouragement I need to continue publishing these stories. To everyone who purchased my book and took the time to write a review—bless you. Thank you, Cassandra, for your editing skills and constant support on my writing journey. Thank you, DeAnn, for opening your home to me. This story exists because of our connection. Thank you to the authors who answered my call for help while attempting something new. Evelyn Sola, your advice helped me unlock a new way of storytelling. Kenya Goree-Bell, your guidance taught me the importance of consistency in writing. Thank you, Jacqueline Luckett, for inspiring me throughout my writing journey. Our talks nourish my soul. Thank you to my beta reading team for ensuring I stay true to the main characters. Thank you to my sister Bess for listening to endless random thoughts on character development. Thank you, Deborah, for continuing to be in my corner through this journey. And to all those sitting silently in the wings…thank you.

Thank you all,
Rita

THIS BOOK IS A WORK OF FICTION AND WRITTEN PURELY FOR ENTER-tainment. It is not meant as a historical guide to Seattle. If you want to learn more about Seattle's history and the African diaspora, there are plenty of reference materials online or in your local library.

You can also find places to support the work to sustain the African-American community and culture in the greater Seattle, Washington, area. Here are a few organizations making a difference in support of the African diaspora in Seattle:

Seattle Equitable Development Initiative

Learn more here: https://www.seattle.gov/opcd/ongoing-initiatives/equitable-development-initiative

Africatown Land Trust

To learn more about Seattle's Africatown Land Trust and how to support its community-building efforts, visit https://www.africatownlandtrust.org/.

Black Community Impact Alliance

Learn more at http://www.bcia-intl.org/.

Community Roots Housing

Learn more at https://communityrootshousing.org/.

Byrd Barr Place

Learn more at https://byrdbarrplace.org/.

Northwest African American Museum

Learn more at https://www.naamnw.org/.

August Wilson

To learn more about August Wilson or ways to support his legacy, visit the following:

August Wilson Archive: https://augustwilson.library.pitt.edu/index.html

August Wilson Society: https://www.augustwilsonsociety.org/

August Wilson House: https://augustwilsonhouse.org/

Photographed by Abigail Huller

Rita Gordon is a California native living in the Bay Area and is a San Francisco State University graduate. As an emerging voice in the contemporary romance genre, Rita brings a fresh perspective to storytelling. Inspired by the power of love and the beauty of cultural exploration, her writing captures the essence of human emotions, leaving readers spellbound with each page turn. In addition to writing, Rita is an avid reader who's amassed an extensive collection of books that fills the rooms of her home. When not reading and writing, she travels, draws flower designs for her coloring books, and volunteers in her community.

To learn more about the author, visit **ritaagordon.com**.

Standalone Novel
30 Days in Belfast

Let It Rain Series
Seven Days in Seattle
The Days with Rain (coming 2024)

Coloring Books
Little Flower Garden
The Big Flower

Journals
On A Positive Note
Grateful

www.ingramcontent.com/pod-product-compliance
Lightning Source LLC
Chambersburg PA
CBHW061236310726
48971CB00007B/2089